P9-API-655

He could feel her full-length against him

Karan's every curve was familiar as Charles wrapped his arms around her and held her. And suddenly, he knew this was right. On some level, he'd known—had always known—that if he touched her, he could never convince himself he was content without her.

He'd known.

"Charles." Her voice filtered through him, the activity around them fading away. For this moment there was only the two of them. The way she fit completely against him until he was aware of only her.

So right.

No history. No complications. Just them and a simple, unavoidable truth.

It didn't matter whether they were married or divorced, whether he was avoiding her or she was demanding the impossible of him— their bodies knew each other.

He didn't want to let go.

Dear Reader,

Life is a matter of perspective. Half-empty? Half-full? Karan thinks her luck is all bad. I think her luck is all good—she simply doesn't realize that yet. When Karan is forced out of her comfortable world, she experiences an entirely new side of life. Of course, this blessing feels like a curse at first, but as she opens her eyes to the people around her and their circumstances and needs, she discovers purpose and meaning that redefines her own place in the world. She discovers ways she can help and the fulfillment that comes from giving.

This journey brings her back to the man she never stopped loving. Charles has already discovered the secret of helping others, but when he sees his ex-wife through his own evolving perspective, he finds a woman with the honesty and courage to face her issues. And he finds the courage to face his own so they can be together again.

Ordinary women. Extraordinary romance. That's Harlequin Superromance! I hope you enjoy Karan and Charles's love story. Let me know at www.jeanielondon.com.

Peace and blessings,

Jeanie London

The Husband Lesson
Lesson
Jeanie London

TORONTO NEW YORK LONDON
AMSTERDAM PARIS SYDNEY HAMBURG
STOCKHOLM ATHENS TOKYO MILAN MADRID
PRAGUE WARSAW BUDAPEST AUCKLAND

Recycling programs
for this product may
not exist in your area.

ISBN-13: 978-0-373-71716-3

THE HUSBAND LESSON

ABOUT THE AUTHOR

Jeanie London writes romance because she believes in happily-ever-afters. Not the "love conquers all" kind, but the "we love each other so we can conquer anything" kind. It's precisely why she loves Harlequin Superromance—stories about real women tackling life to find love. The kind of love she understands because she's a real woman tackling life in sunny Florida with her own romance-hero husband, their two beautiful and talented daughters, a loving and slightly crazy extended family and a menagerie of sweet strays.

Books by Jeanie London

HARLEQUIN SUPERROMANCE
1616—FRANKIE'S BACK IN TOWN
1635—HER HUSBAND'S PARTNER
1699—THEN THERE WERE THREE

**HARLEQUIN SIGNATURE
SELECT SPOTLIGHT**
IN THE COLD

HARLEQUIN BLAZE
153—HOT SHEETS*
157—RUN FOR COVERS*
161—PILLOW CHASE*
181—UNDER HIS SKIN
213—RED LETTER NIGHTS
    "Signed, Sealed, Seduced"
231—GOING ALL OUT
248—INTO TEMPTATION
271—IF YOU COULD READ MY MIND...

*Falling Inn Bed...

For all those who volunteer their
time and talents to help others.
Real-life heroes and heroines.
May you all live happily ever after;-)

CHAPTER ONE

"I DON'T HAVE A DRINKING problem, Your Honor. I have a problem drinking," Karan Kowalski Steinberg-Reece explained, though it positively hurt to justify herself to *this* woman.

"I'm listening, Ms. Kowalski Steinberg-Reece." The judge gazed down from her superior height on the courtroom bench. She emphasized the *Ms.* and dragged out each syllable as though implying the marriages hadn't lasted as long as the names.

"I have low blood sugar." That was all Karan would say. The toxicology results would speak for themselves.

Her attorney, a close friend of her second husband, had coached her at length about behavior during the sentencing since she and the judge had a history.

Honorable Jennifer Sharpe-Malone had once been known as Jenny, a wannabe cheerleader who hadn't made the cut in four years at Ashokan High. Of course, Karan had made cheer captain all four years, so she'd been a judge at tryouts. It had been hard enough finding positions for her inner circle of friends.

Wannabe Jenny hadn't been in her inner circle.

Just Karan's luck that with all the judges in New York's Catskill Mountains she'd wind up in court before this one.

"I'm well aware of your medical condition," Wannabe Jenny informed her. "I've reviewed the deputy's report. The deputy also stated you appeared more impaired than the results of the field sobriety test and the toxicology report revealed."

More luck. Karan had gambled by cooperating with the deputies because she hadn't wanted her license automatically revoked for refusing the test. One glass of champagne. One *stupid* glass and her blood alcohol content had been .05. A fraction of a percent lower and she wouldn't be in this courtroom at all.

"State law doesn't require my client to consent to a field sobriety test, Your Honor." Her attorney seized the opportunity. "Only the chemical test, yet Ms. Kowalski Steinberg-Reece cooperated with law enforcement and consented to both."

"Noted, Mr. James, and for the record I'm aware of the law." Wannabe Jenny turned a peeved gaze to Karan. "Did it ever occur to you to call a taxi?"

"Yes, Your Honor."

"Keep things simple and straightforward," her attorney had said. *"Don't offer explanations unless the judge asks."*

"Why didn't you?" the judge asked.

"Leaving my car at the resort presented a problem."

"Oh?"

"I didn't have anyone to drive it home for me."

"You were at the Inn at Laurel Lake, isn't that right?" Wannabe Jenny glanced down at the documents before her.

"Yes, Your Honor."

"The Inn does have a parking garage. For a reasonable fee, they would have attended your vehicle until you were able to safely retrieve it."

No question. But retrieving her car hadn't exactly been the issue. Drawing attention to the fact that she hadn't driven her car home was. But Wannabe Jenny wouldn't want to hear that. She was already mentally filling in the blanks. Karan could see it all over her crab-apple expression.

"If you weren't happy with the idea of taking a taxi back to the Inn to rescue your car the next day, you might have refrained from drinking."

She made it sound as if Karan was a lush. "I didn't drink per se, Your Honor. I only toasted the senator when he announced his bid for reelection."

Her attorney shot her a withering glance. Entirely unnecessary. Karan knew the instant the words were out of her mouth that defending herself was a mistake and dropping the senator's name a wasted effort.

Wannabe Jenny was out for blood.

"If one obligatory toast impaired you to this degree, then you might have considered waiting for your liver to process the alcohol before you left the party, Ms. Kowalski Steinberg-Reece. Or booking a room for the night since you were at a hotel." Her tone dripped with a sarcasm that couldn't possibly be considered professional courtroom behavior. "If that didn't suit, you might have asked the senator to drive you home."

It took every ounce of Karan's considerable willpower to keep her mouth shut.

"Since you obviously don't have any friends in this town who could have taken you." Wannabe Jenny seemed to be talking simply to hear herself. "Whatever the excuse, your decision to drive while alcohol impaired wasn't a good one. You should be thankful you didn't hurt yourself or, God forbid, someone else. Tragedies happen all too often on the roads."

A tingle started behind Karan's left eye, a familiar tingle that signaled an oncoming headache. She was very grateful she hadn't caused any accidents, in fact, but wasn't about to admit that to Wannabe Jenny. Another explanation wouldn't pass her lips.

The tables had turned in the decade and a half since high school, and Karan wasn't the judge anymore. Wannabe Jenny would assess the offense during this hearing and consider the mitigating factors before sentencing. The long-ago past aside, Karan was an upstanding member of this community.

She hoped that would count for something.

A fine would be best-case scenario. But even if she was ordered to attend a substance-abuse education class, she would smile graciously, thank Wannabe Jenny and hope the class was available online like other traffic violation programs.

This situation was humiliating enough without sitting in a windowless room with drug addicts and real alcoholics for hours on end. She already had a mug shot on the sheriff's website. One that anyone could pull up to view. Fortunately she'd been dressed for the senator's event. If not for the identification number around her neck, she might have been posing for any head shot.

"Ms. Kowalski Steinberg-Reece," Wannabe Jenny addressed Karan in that I'm-so-enjoying-the-upper-hand tone. "Are you aware that one-third of the traffic fatalities in New York State involve impaired or intoxicated drivers?"

"Yes, Your Honor."

"And that New York State has a STOP-DWI law?"

"Yes, Your Honor."

"Do you understand the difference between driving while ability is impaired and driving while intoxicated?"

"Yes, Your Honor."

"What is it exactly?"

"DWAI is a traffic infraction. DWI is a criminal misdemeanor."

The smile suddenly playing around Wannabe Jenny's mouth, a mouth tinted with a shade of red that drew attention to the fine lines that could have benefitted from a good cosmetic surgeon, made Karan swallow hard.

"Very well then. Ms. Kowalski Steinberg-Reece, the State of New York finds you guilty of driving while ability impaired. It is the judgment of this court that your driving privileges be suspended for ninety days. You'll pay a five-hundred dollar fine to the clerk when you are remanded into custody to serve fifteen days in the county jail."

Karan's best friend gasped behind her. Her attorney cursed under his breath, but she could only stare. Had Wannabe Jenny just said *jail?*

"Your Honor." Her attorney didn't bother to hide his annoyance. "That's the maximum sentence allowable."

"Again, I am aware of the law, Mr. James."

"This is Ms. Kowalski Steinberg-Reece's first offense."

"It's not her first offense with low blood sugar," Wannabe Jenny replied. "She seems well aware of the potential effects of alcohol on her condition."

So was Wannabe Jenny. Not even the shroudlike black robe could hide the effects of *sitting on the bench.* Once upon a time Wannabe Jenny had been petite and fit. Not so much anymore.

On the other hand, Karan's condition forced her to eat small meals every few hours to steady her sugar, which had the added benefit of running her metabolism at full tilt. No complaints there.

"Yet even knowing the potential effects," Wannabe Jenny continued, "your client chose to toast the senator then get behind the wheel of her car before her body had adequately processed the alcohol. By serving the full sentence, I hope her first offense will also be her last."

Karan waited for her attorney to earn his astronomical fee—a fee she'd insisted on paying even though she'd hosted him in her homes many times throughout her three years of marriage to his close friend.

"May I approach the bench, Your Honor?" Her attorney waited until Wannabe Jenny nodded and then he crossed the courtroom.

Karan waited, too, barely daring to breathe, not allowing herself to react in any visible way. She reminded herself that her attorney was more than competent. The only thing she could do was trust him to do his job.

This situation was a nightmare. Of course she should never have gotten in her car tipsy. Not even to drive the few miles of lonely highway to her house. If she could relive the night over, she would make a different decision. Because Wannabe Jenny was right about one thing—Karan knew the limitations of her condition. She didn't go near alcohol for that very reason. She drank club soda with lime to keep the servers busy at functions, but the only alcohol that ever passed her lips was the odd glass of champagne for toasts. And then only the very best champagne.

Sometimes she toasted with no trouble whatsoever and barely felt the effects of a glass, but when her sugar was low, even a few sips could hit her like a truck. So she always sipped cautiously until she knew what the effect would be.

That night Karan had broken all her usual rules and now paid the price. Resisting the urge to turn around, she sensed Susanna's presence behind her, a good friend who'd taken time off work to be moral support. At the rate they were going today, Karan might need Susanna to post her bail.

But she refused to react, refused to give Wannabe Jenny the satisfaction. So Karan stood her ground and watched silently as judge and attorney spoke in hushed tones, discussing her actions and punishment without any input from her. The minutes were marked only by the sounds in the courtroom.

A whisper of polyester from the bailiff's pants as he shifted restlessly from side to side.

The mechanical hiss of a vent when the air-conditioning cycled on, barely keeping the summer heat outside.

The creak of a hinge from the rear of the courtroom as a door opened and shut again.

The muted patter of footsteps as someone strode confidently between the rows of seats, nearer and nearer.

The sound of Susanna's urgent whispering was the final straw, and Karan glanced over her shoulder to find her best friend talking to Jack Sloan, who looked as handsome as ever in his official blue-and-brass uniform.

Well, well, well. Bluestone Mountain's police chief had decided to grace her with his presence.

Back in the cheerleading captain/Wannabe Jenny days, Karan had envisioned a brilliant future with this man. They'd dated through to the end of high school and well into college. Then Jack had switched his career from law to *law enforcement*. Karan had no intention of becoming a cop's wife when she'd been born to be a society bride to a high-powered husband.

Such a shame, too, as Jack had only grown more handsome in the years since college. And if his defection hadn't been criminal enough, he'd recently married the very woman who'd been a source of major irritation to Karan all through high school.

As far as Karan was concerned, Jack owed her big, and she'd told him as much at the station during booking. Of course, he'd promised to help but hadn't done a thing as far as she could tell. In all fairness, Karan knew he couldn't simply make her situation vanish as easily as he might have a parking ticket. Still, she'd hoped for something more than the busy, newly married police chief's appearance in the courtroom. Men. Not a damned one of them ever delivered.

Wannabe Jenny glanced up and noticed the new arrival. "Chief Sloan. Nice of you to join our little reunion."

Only Wannabe Jenny would point that out. What were the chances that her thirst for blood would be quenched after this nightmare was finally over?

Jack only inclined his head and said, "Judge Malone."

"Your ears must have been ringing because we were just talking about you. Thought for sure you'd decided to skip today." She motioned him forward. "Please approach the bench."

Jack came through the gate the bailiff held open. "Didn't want to miss the fun."

Fun? Karan positively hated this small town, hated the gossip mill and everyone knowing everyone else's business. *Having everyone know hers.* She had a gorgeous apartment in Manhattan and a bungalow on the Connecticut shore, so why did she even bother keeping a house here again?

A good question that she didn't have an answer for. But as she watched the Ashokan High reunion, Karan vowed to call a real estate agent as soon as she walked out of this courtroom. She'd had enough of this nonsense. Quite enough.

She waited for her invitation to the bench, but one never came. Obviously, she was expected to stand by while everyone else made decisions about her life. She tried to squelch her annoyance, knowing there was no one to blame but herself. But knowing didn't take the edge off. Not her anger at herself for this mess. Not her fear that Wannabe Jenny wanted blood for long-ago wounds to her pride. Not Karan's annoyance that the years hadn't turned Jack from high school football star into a balding cop with a doughnut belly.

Then Susanna's fingers slid against Karan's and gave a light squeeze. She wasn't much for overt signs of emotion, and her best friend since middle school knew it. But Susanna also knew Karan better than anyone in the world. She knew how much Karan hated feeling out of control because they'd been weathering life together—boyfriends, graduations, weddings, divorces and funerals. Susanna didn't mind sharing how she felt. She actually liked overt signs of emotion. Unexpected hugs. Reassuring touches.

She seemed to like them even more since her husband had died. Karan wished she could be as open as Susanna. Always there. Always caring for the people she loved. Even when life threw devastating curves.

Of course all that emotion came with a dark side, and Susanna could worry like no one Karan had ever met. She got positively insane sometimes, but life wouldn't be life without Susanna. They were as close as sisters—or what Karan imagined a sister would be like given she was an only child.

"Ms. Kowalski Steinberg-Reece," Wannabe Jenny announced in her I'm-the-shark-in-the-fishbowl voice. "With Chief Sloan's help, I think we've worked out an arrangement that may be more to your liking."

Susanna gave another squeeze then her hand slipped away. Karan faced the firing squad stoically. Her attorney narrowed his gaze, warning her to stay quiet. He didn't have to because Karan had a gift for reading people. She kept her mouth shut.

"Since you're a low-risk offender, there is an alternative sentence that, if you agree, will take the place of your jail time."

Karan didn't dare to breathe. So far so good. The thought of living behind bars for more than two weeks made her faint. She looked dreadful in orange. *So* not her color.

"In lieu of incarceration," Wannabe Jenny continued, dragging out the suspense. "you'll be required to complete three hundred and sixty hours of community service."

Karan mentally calculated. Three hundred and sixty hours translated into fifteen days. Okay, still good.

"Chief Sloan has been working with Mayor Trant and a number of community leaders to launch New Hope, Bluestone Mountain's first domestic violence shelter. You can assist their efforts by completing your service hours under the supervision of one of the program directors. You can complete the hours at your convenience, Ms. Kowalski Steinberg-Reece, but be aware you're also required to attend weekly group and private treatment sessions for the duration and your driving privileges will remain suspended until you complete the mandated hours and appear back in court before me.

"At that time I'll review your case and reinstate your privileges if you've satisfactorily met the terms of this ruling. If you do choose this alternative sentencing, I'll waive the three-hour substance-abuse education class you're otherwise required to take by law. Would you like a few moments to speak with counsel?"

Waive the three-hour class? How generous. But visions of windowless rooms filled with drug addicts danced in her head, so she managed to say politely, "Yes, Your Honor."

Her attorney returned to the table, and Karan sank to the chair for a powwow.

"Paris Hilton only got two hundred hours of community service and she's gone way past her first offense," Karan hissed in his ear.

"Don't forget she got a year's probation." He shot a glance at the bench as if worried they might be overheard. Jack and Wannabe Jenny were too busy chitchatting to pay attention. "Japan wouldn't even let her enter the country."

Like Karan wanted to go to Japan. "Is this honestly the best you can do?"

He scowled. "I don't know what you did to this woman, but I promise you won't get a better offer. Jail or alternative sentence. Your call."

Visions of Lindsay Lohan's latest trip to the pokey replaced images of windowless rooms. The local press would have a field day if Karan went to jail since the woman who ran the *Bluestone Mountain Gazette* was another Ashokan High alumnus who hadn't had any use for Karan and her circle of friends.

At least she could spin community service in a domestic violence shelter into something not as humiliating as jail. "Alternative sentence."

"Good choice." Her attorney popped to his feet. "Your Honor, my client would like to accept the alternative sentence in lieu of jail time and thanks you for your consideration."

Wannabe Jenny looked smug. "Good luck then, Ms. Kowalski Steinberg-Reece. I'll look forward to reviewing updates about your progress."

No doubt. Probably didn't have anything else to do while eating her microwave-frozen dinners at night.

"Thank you, Your Honor." That was as polite as Karan could manage. Wannabe Jenny might have the gavel in her hand right now, but the accompanying black robe washed out her sallow skin. She needed to either invest in decent makeup primer or have a conversation with whomever had chosen black as the color of choice in the courtroom.

Karan jumped when the gavel cracked with aggressive finality and Wannabe Jenny said, "Court adjourned."

For today, anyway, because Karan would be back.

Unfortunately.

CHAPTER TWO

CHARLES STEINBERG WHEELED HIS Jeep Wrangler into the parking lot behind the three-story Victorian where he'd spent more time during the past eight months than he had anywhere but in the operating room. Releasing the clutch, he pulled up the emergency brake, noticing how the sun sparkled on the newly installed windows, as bright and promising as the place itself.

He felt a satisfaction as if he'd personally installed those windows rather than cutting the check that released funds to the contractor who'd done the job.

Charles's contribution had been in the coordination and decision making, in determining essential need to balance the budget, in the long-range planning and development of outreach programs. He'd done his fair share.

And though he hadn't originally chosen to become one of the directors of this project, Charles prided himself on living by his grandmother's oft-spoken saying: *"Bloom where you're planted."*

He had. With the help of other dedicated volunteers, New Hope of Bluestone Mountain, Inc. had been born. The town's first certified domestic violence prevention and emergency shelter.

The front porch light now shone 24/7, a welcome to families in crisis and the promise of help. Behind freshly painted gingerbread trim, every room had been transformed to become a multiservice facility with offices, counseling rooms and two complete floors of suites that served as temporary shelter for women and children in need.

For such a noble endeavor, the neighborhood wasn't all that much to look at. In the years since Charles had come to town, the large property lots in this area had attracted enough businesses to be zoned commercial. Still, there were a few residences like this one tucked away on forested acreage between auto repair shops and convenience stores. The out-of-the-way location was what made the house perfect as a shelter.

Charles got out, noticing the sleek gray Jaguar that looked out of place in a parking lot separated only by a security wall and evergreens from the loading docks of Bluestone Mountain's only Walmart Supercenter.

He didn't bother pulling on the Jeep's cover. There wasn't a hint of uncertain weather in the summer sky. Besides, he wouldn't be here that long, and only had to touch base with his codirector about some volunteer scheduling decisions that couldn't wait until Monday.

He'd already had a long day in surgery, having arrived at the hospital way before the sun had come up this morning. Five surgeries later then rounds and he'd earned the right to this weekend's fishing trip.

Charles had made it to the flagstone path when the security gate ground open again. A familiar white Toyota Camry appeared, slipping into the space on the opposite side of the Jaguar and coming to a sharp stop.

Rhonda Camden, Ph.D., New Hope's codirector and his partner in crime. Running late as usual.

The door swung open and she hopped out, dragging a briefcase that overflowed with papers. She looked as windblown and hurried as she always did, and after eight months of working together, Charles knew why—she juggled more balls in the air than most people between her job as director of the town's crisis center and her private practice. Add volunteer endeavors such as New Hope...

Smiling broadly, Rhonda gestured to the house and all they'd accomplished together in the past eight months.

"Matthew impressed yet?" she asked, referring to the chief at St. Joseph's Hospital where Charles was on staff.

"You'd think. I'm either in surgery or I'm here. But the man is a hard sell. Maybe you should put in a good word for me."

Not that he thought anything would impress St. Joseph's chief. Matthew West was going to make Charles sweat out an invitation to join the Catskill Center for Cardiothoracic Surgery, the most professional and highly regarded team in the area, and projects like New Hope were a part of the process. He'd already reconciled himself to running the gauntlet until the chief was satisfied. Or until he found another candidate to join the coveted team. Whichever came first.

She rolled her eyes. "Right. Your boss has even less of a regard for my field than you do if that's possible."

Charles thought it might be, and he couldn't deny her claim, either. He hadn't known much about, or had much use for, clinical psychology before seeing Rhonda in action. He was a surgeon. His interest was all about *what* was happening inside the body, not speculation about *why*.

"I told you I've revised my opinion of your field."

She passed him and headed up the steps. "You mentioned it. I'm not convinced I should believe you."

"You read minds for a living. You should know if I'm lying."

She didn't take the bait, only laughed, and he launched himself up two steps at a time to reach the entrance before she did. After inputting his security code, he held the door for her.

"Thank you, Dr. Steinberg."

"My pleasure, Dr. Camden." He stepped inside. "So what's this new program that needs immediate attention?"

Turning around, she peered pointedly over the rim of her glasses. "See that showy Jag parked between our cars?"

"I do."

"I suspect that belongs to our court-ordered volunteer."

Charles came to a stop with the door still half-open. "Court ordered? I don't like the sound of that."

"Some folks need a little help recognizing the merits of helping others."

"You're killing me with suspense." Actually, the suspense wasn't killing him, but the need to get home, pack a bag and get the hell out of Dodge was.

This was Rhonda's expertise, and after working beside her, Charles had the utmost of confidence in her decisions. If she said they should take on a court-ordered volunteer program, then Charles accepted her word.

"No felons or pedophiles, I promise," she assured him.

"Never even crossed my mind." He pulled the door shut until the lock clicked tight. Another thing about Rhonda— she was crazy invested in helping women. So much so that he'd wondered more than once whom she knew or what might have happened in her life to make her such a passionate advocate.

"Hey, Deputy Doug," she greeted the sheriff as they passed the room that had been transformed into the on-site Sheriff's Department substation.

The deputy, spit-polished in a uniform that lent an air of authority and safety to New Hope, glanced up from the desk where he monitored video surveillance of the property with the phone cradled against his ear. He waved.

Charles inclined his head as he passed. "Our resident deputy is okay with you inviting criminals onto the property?"

"*Not* criminals." Rhonda huffed over her shoulder and headed down the hallway toward the administrative offices. "They're women the court feels have something to offer and deserve a chance to get back on more productive paths."

"That's very…politically correct."

"I couldn't say no, Charles. It's a worthy cause and we need the help. Our volunteer base is a third of what it needs to be, and with the screenings, orientations and training, that won't change for some time."

Charles was personally acquainted with the duties around here and wondered what these formerly upstanding women might have to offer. He didn't bother asking since they had arrived in the office and the administrative volunteer sitting at the desk said, "Your appointment is here, Dr. Camden."

"Thanks." She motioned Charles into their shared office. "Close the door."

He did as she asked, surprised when she dropped her things on the desk and went straight for the observation panel on the wall. Sliding the shutter open, she peered through the viewing glass into the reception area.

"Nicely dressed felon," Rhonda said drily.

The observation panel had been established as a security measure in a place filled with them. They'd modeled New Hope after other domestic violence programs around the country. The unfortunate truth was that domestic violence could erupt anywhere and often followed its victims.

Precisely why New Hope's security measures were

top-notch. Not only was there a fully-staffed sheriff sub-station, but the facility was hardwired to the Bluestone Mountain Police. A silent alarm would dispatch officer backup and SWAT resources within minutes. From state-of-the-art internet security to detailed precautionary procedures that involved other domestic violence agencies around the state, New Hope, for its remote location in Bluestone Mountain, was a cutting-edge facility.

Rhonda motioned him over. Charles honestly could not have cared less, but the path of the least resistance was the fastest way to get out the door and up to the river. Crossing the room, he peered through the glass at the woman standing in the reception area, idly thumbing through a magazine.

A tall, slim woman with sleek blond hair and delicate features that would be right at home on the cover of the magazine she held. Nicely dressed was an understatement. This woman's wardrobe could feed a developing nation.

"Jesus." He staggered back, nearly tripping over Rhonda.

She jumped out of his way, steadying herself on the desk. "What's wrong?"

For a moment he could only stare. The words were in his head but wouldn't come out. He blinked. He took a deep breath. He tried again. "You invited my ex-wife to volunteer *here?*"

"Excuse me. What are you talking about?" Rhonda was clearly confused.

Charles wasn't talking about anything because he was still too busy trying to reason through why one all too familiar and very unwelcome blonde was standing inside this facility.

Court-ordered community service?

Rhonda stepped around the desk and thumbed through

the folders that had slid half out of her jam-packed brief-case. "Here it is. Her name is Reece."

Sure enough, the folder tab had *Reece* printed in bold black letters.

"Karan Kowalski *Steinberg*-Reece."

Rhonda's frown melted and she glanced at the folder again. "Guess that will teach me to read what's inside. Gosh, I'm really sorry, Charles. The program sounded like such a great deal when Chief Sloan mentioned it."

"Chief Sloan?"

She nodded.

A freaking setup if ever there was one. "He obviously suggested it because he didn't want to deal with her himself."

Rhonda sank onto the edge of the desk with the closed folder neatly in her lap. She looked at him with an invit-ing, psychoanalyzing expression on her face. "Chief Sloan knows your ex-wife, too?"

It took Charles another speechless moment to reason that through. Rhonda wasn't from Bluestone Mountain. Like himself, she'd come to the area to attend Van Cort-landt College, an elite private university in the valley. She'd wound up settling here after completing grad school. Unlike him, or Chief Sloan for that matter, she'd managed to avoid running into Karan.

"They have a history," he said.

"I see. And you think Chief Sloan sent her our way because he'd rather we dealt with her?"

"Jack sits on the board of directors. He was involved with this project long before I was, and he didn't ask me to let her volunteer here because he knew I'd say no damn way."

Rhonda conceded the point with a nod then flipped open the folder and scanned the documents inside. "Okay,

I'm reading. Not seeing what the big deal is about her. I also don't see… What does she do for a living?"

"Professional social climber."

Rhonda frowned. "Come on, Charles, you married her. How bad can she possibly be?"

He had no words. Just a knot in his stomach.

Rhonda tossed the folder onto the desk and returned to the security panel. "Hmm. I'd say she's getting impatient because I'm running late. But she is very beautiful. I guess you must have been blinded by her beauty."

He had been. No question. Charles could still remember the first time he'd ever set eyes on Karan. He was in med school in the midst of a particularly brutal stretch. *He hadn't slept in over forty-eight hours. The autumn sun seared his eyeballs after being holed up in the medical library for he couldn't even remember how long. The quad was packed with booths and students, and he wished like hell he was headed home for a few hours of shut-eye. No such luck.*

The Feminization of Poverty event beckoned.

Dr. Nan Bryson was a popular anthropology professor from Harvard who toured the country speaking on an alarming trend gaining speed in academic circles. The fact that she was coming to Van Cortlandt was a big deal, particularly as one of the undergrads had managed to do what the deans of the anthropology and sociology departments combined hadn't been able to do—get Dr. Bryson to speak while traveling through the Catskills. To honor this visiting professor, the faculty had pulled out all the stops to ensure the talk was well attended.

Charles had zero interest in sociology, anthropology or women's issues but after bombing an exam, he'd appealed to the professor for mercy. Charles hadn't had time to study because he'd been invited to observe surgeries at St. Joseph's Hospital—no way could he pass up the opportunity. The professor had offered an opportunity for some extra credit.

Charles wouldn't have missed the event if he'd had to be carried here on a gurney. He needed every dime of his scholarship money so he didn't have to spend the rest of his life paying off student loans. That meant keeping up his GPA.

He was assigned to work the book booth and did nothing but try to keep his foggy brain functioning. While using hands that were learning to perform delicate maneuvers on organs and arteries to count out ones, fives and tens, he saw her.

Hot. The hottest. Details didn't register. The punch to his gut did. Suddenly, all the tired vanished and his pulse pumped at warp speed. Blurry vision instantly saw with clarity as if he'd sharpened his sight on the edge of a scalpel. Only after he could breathe again did he notice details.

Blonde. Lean. Tall. She barely looked real with that pale silky hair blowing around her face. A face as exquisitely feminine as the rest of her. He couldn't see the color of her eyes, but they were lighter. Blue or gray, maybe.

Then she smiled.

That full pink mouth made him think about kissing.

He had no idea who she was but even sleep deprived, he knew she was someone important. She walked with the college president, several of the deans and a woman he recognized from the jacket of the book he was selling—Dr. Nan Bryson. Then she disappeared backstage with her group and was gone.

But not from Charles's thoughts.

He couldn't get the image of her out of his head. He sold books, made change, but his brain replayed every detail he could remember, ached with trying to remember more. And the most important detail of all: who was she?

He intended to find out.

Once Dr. Bryson's talk started, the book booth would quiet down and he could slip away to grab coffee. No one would miss him for ten minutes and he'd make a few calls on the way.

When the president took the stage and announced the beginning of the program, the noise level on the quad dropped. Charles tucked the cash box under his arm and timed his exit. While listening to the president welcome their guest to Van Cortlandt, he slipped the cell phone from his pocket. Then the president introduced the person responsible for Dr. Bryson's visit, the person privileged with introducing their speaker.

The blonde walked onto the stage.

She wore a blinding smile, seemed completely at ease in front of the crowd as she began the introduction in a honeyed voice that matched up with every sleek inch of her.

Charles set the cash box on the table. He slipped the phone into his pocket.

Karan Kowalski.

Now, here she was again, two husbands later. Standing in New Hope's reception area, which was exactly the last place on the planet she should be.

And he had that same knot in his stomach. Only the years had turned anticipation into dread.

"Charles?" Rhonda's voice penetrated his brain. "Charles, are you all right?"

Was she joking?

He dragged his gaze from the observation panel, and found Rhonda watching him, seeing way too much with her trained psychotherapist gaze.

"Are you going to be able to handle this?" she asked.

"Do I have a choice?"

"You always have a choice."

"One that doesn't involve abandoning my post and losing my shot to join the Catskill Center?"

She shrugged, and he could tell she was fighting a smile. "We'll have to figure that part out. I'm curious, though. Does your ex-wife know you're affiliated with this program?"

"I have no idea. I never see her." He stopped short. "Correct that. I run into her at the hospital on occasion."

"Hmm. I just wondered. From what I understood from Chief Sloan, she had to agree to the alternative sentencing. I'm interested to know if she knew you'd be here."

Interested? There was only thing Charles wanted to know. "What are you planning to do with her?"

"I have no idea until we talk and figure out what she can do."

"Good luck with that. We didn't install a tanning bed, so I can't imagine—"

Rhonda stopped him with a raised hand. "No opinions please. I'm intrigued enough. I'd rather form my own impressions without yours coloring my professionalism. Your ex-wife has been ordered into counseling. I thought it made sense for me to treat her since she's our trial run with alternative sentencing."

He nodded, still struggling to pull the pieces together to decide what he was going to do with this. Running into Karan each and every time he walked through the door wasn't going to work. That much he did know.

"Why is she in court-ordered community service and counseling?" he asked. "What in hell did she do?"

"DUI? DWAI? One of them." Rhonda twisted around

and flipped open the folder on her desk. "Driving while ability impaired."

"Drugs?"

She shook her head. "Alcohol."

"That's about the last thing I would have expected."

Rhonda waved him off again. "Shh."

Karan didn't drink. Never had. When other college students had been getting plowed during rush week, she'd made it her life's quest to find other ways of unwinding and having fun. Picnics. Boating. Trips into the city for gallery showings.

He remembered how much he'd once liked that about her.

Karan's dislike of alcohol was deep-rooted, physical and psychological, the result of a low blood sugar condition and an alcoholic mother. Throughout their marriage, she wouldn't pick up the phone at night without screening the call. She'd never said why, but Charles had known she was avoiding her mother, who normally started drinking after the sun set.

DWAI. That didn't make sense for the woman he'd known. Then again, he hadn't known Karan in a long time. He had heard she'd gotten divorced again, which was probably why she was back in Bluestone Mountain. Maybe the divorce had driven her to drink.

Had she cared that much for husband number two?

Charles couldn't reconcile that with the woman he'd known. Karan didn't care about anyone but herself. She used men then jettisoned them. Charles had come home from the hospital one day to find a key in an envelope and a storage facility filled with everything he owned. Jack Sloan hadn't fared much better—only he'd been smart enough not to marry her, so he hadn't had to retain an attorney and sign papers.

But DWAI? Was it possible, by some miracle, Karan had actually cared for husband number two?

The way she hadn't cared for him.

"So how does this work in your field, Rhonda?" He did not want to be thinking about Karan, feelings he didn't know he still had being dredged up without permission. So what if she cared for her second husband? "Do we have conflict of interest?"

With any luck they could get out of this whole alternative sentence thing. Let Jack handle Karan and her grief instead of dumping the problem onto New Hope. Charles had done his time. He'd earned a break from Karan and her drama. For the rest of his life.

"I don't see conflict, but there's only one ethical thing to do." Depressing a button on the intercom, Rhonda said, "Lori, you can show my appointment in now."

"Damn it." He couldn't get away without running into Karan in the outer office.

Rhonda shrugged. "Nothing left to do but deal with her."

Deal with *Karan*...wasn't he supposed to be fishing?

CHAPTER THREE

KARAN FLIPPED PAGE AFTER PAGE of the celebrity magazine, trying to interest herself in the current state of high-profile marriages and who had or hadn't been invited to the latest A-list playgroup outing. But she couldn't seem to get past the fact that she was inside the childhood home of the woman who'd managed to get Jack down the aisle.

Frankie Cesarini. Ugh. The very thought of her was enough to make Karan twitch. Fortunately, they'd had only limited contact since Frankie had come back to town.

Of course, Karan could have gotten Jack down the aisle years ago, *if* she'd wanted to be a cop's wife. No, thank you. Still, to her knowledge, Jack hadn't even come close to marriage in all the years since Karan had dumped him. The man obviously had never gotten over losing her. Who could blame him? They'd been so good together. With her by his side, he could have been running for senate himself by now.

What admittedly surprised her was *who* had finally gotten a ring on his finger—a woman who'd once been the antithesis of everything Karan considered relevant. No family. No money. No friends. No chic whatsoever.

Nowadays Susanna worked for Jack's new wife and swore the woman resembled nothing of the girl who'd once been nothing more than bad hair and a smart mouth. Karan had trouble believing that and would have dismissed the possibility as nonsense from any other source. But she couldn't dismiss the reality of this house. Or the fact that she was inside it and would be for another three hundred and fifty-nine hours and forty-six minutes.

From what she understood, the entire structure had been extensively renovated, which meant she couldn't blame the generic furnishings on Jack's new wife. The outside wasn't bad. The house itself was a three-story Victorian with lots of windows and gingerbread trim. Fresh paint, new windows and proper landscaping had only brought out the character. Karan did wonder if there had been conflict involved with the hamlet of Bluestone Mountain purchasing the police chief's wife's childhood home.

Wouldn't surprise her in the least. Also wouldn't surprise her to learn there hadn't been a cop in town willing to drag the police chief before a judge. As if that would have done any good with a judge like Wannabe Jenny. She, like the rest of the girls at Ashokan High, had thought the sun rose and set on the former football star.

How could Karan have forgotten how much she hated this town?

A door cracked open and a woman close to her age appeared. "Dr. Camden will see you now if you'll follow me."

Only fifteen minutes late. Any other doctor and Karan would have waited closer to an hour, so no complaints here. She cautioned herself to start finding reasons to smile through this nightmare, no matter how small. Guaranteed there would be precious few in the weeks ahead.

Tossing the magazine onto a table, she started her trek into hell bravely, glancing at the woman's name badge.

"You're a volunteer," she said. "Is your job greeting the visitors?" Playing hostess for the duration of her sentence might not be too terrible. She could deal with people.

The woman smiled. "That among other things. Switchboard detail and lots of administrative duties for the counselors."

"I see." Karan wasn't interested.

They entered a smaller reception area and the woman went straight to the door marked *Director,* tapped lightly and pushed it open. "Here you go."

"Thanks." Karan smiled. Then, taking a deep breath, she moved past the woman and into the office, ready to deal with this situation head-on.

The sooner she started the sooner she'd finish.

Karan noticed the blonde woman standing behind the desk, but it was the man in front of the desk who stopped her cold.

"Charles?"

He looked the way he always did. *So* handsome that the very sight of him startled her. There was just something about his chiseled features, the way his dark eyes contrasted with his lighter hair. Not blond, but not quite brown, either. A sandy in between. His closely trimmed beard and mustache only emphasized the maleness of his face.

His expression was the same, too. *So* arrogant that she crashed right back to reality.

Dr. Disdain, she'd once called him. At least that had been his attitude toward her.

"Karan." He didn't even have the grace to utter any social niceties. No *"Pleased to see you."* No *"You look well."*

Of course not. The man stood there looking as if he was above everyone and everything and wished he was anywhere in the world rather than facing her.

Karan's feelings might have been hurt had she not been so surprised to see him. And had she cared what he thought about her. She didn't.

Of course, she wasn't rude. "I'm surprised to see you. What are you doing here?"

"I'm Dr. Camden, Karan. Please call me Rhonda." The blonde behind the desk extended her hand. "Turns out we have an unexpected situation."

She shook the doctor's hand. Rhonda wasn't a natural blonde like Karan herself, but Karan did approve of the highlighting job. Skillfully done to look natural. Not like so many of the streaky chicken-yellow horrors on the streets nowadays.

"I'm bracing myself." Karan meant it. Bracing herself for the shock of yet another *unexpected situation.* Bracing herself to be standing two feet away from this man.

And darned if her heartbeat hadn't already kicked up a few notches. He'd always had that effect on her. He was too attractive. Tall with that baseball player's body. A perfect blend of athletic and muscular. And darned, too, if she didn't remember exactly what the terrain beneath his lightweight black sweater and gray pants looked like.

Far too attractive for her good.

Rhonda's mouth quirked. "I wasn't aware of your history with our director when I agreed to participate in the alternative sentencing program."

"You're the director?" she asked Charles, surprised. "Not spending every waking moment in surgery anymore?"

Where he'd spent the majority of their marriage.

"Codirector, actually," he replied in that deep voice she remembered so well. He inclined his head at Rhonda. "We're partners in crime around here."

Karan bristled, unsure exactly what he meant by *that.* Was he taking a jab at her legal trouble? Or referring to something personal between him and his codirector?

"So you didn't know Charles was involved with New Hope, either?" Rhonda asked.

As if Karan would want him to witness her humiliation. The woman must be as crazy as her patients. Karan managed to say politely, "No. I'm afraid I didn't."

Charles and Rhonda exchanged a glance.

Personal, *definitely.*

"Okay then," Rhonda said. "We need to decide how to proceed."

"Conflict of interest," Charles offered, pointedly ignoring Karan.

Rude man.

Rhonda ignored him, which pleased Karan to no end. "Karan, how do you feel about all this? What are your thoughts about volunteering at New Hope now you know Charles is on staff?"

Any possibility of getting a gun? She wasn't sure yet whether she'd shoot herself or him. "I can't answer that until I know how he might impact my...*work.*"

As good a way as any to phrase it, she supposed.

Rhonda folded her arms over her chest. "I'm in charge of the program, so you'll report to me. But Charles is often around. There's no question about whether you'll run into him."

"Any idea how often?" Karan pointedly avoided looking at him. Two could play this game.

"I'm not sure how we can put your skills to use yet, so I can't say if you'll run into each other a lot or a little. Depends on where you'll be. He's kind of everywhere."

"Conflict of interest," Charles repeated.

Rhonda scribbled something on the outside of a file folder with Karan's name. "I still don't think so. Not if all parties are aware of the situation and are consenting. But I can always check with the police chief to be sure."

"The police chief is the one who suggested the alternative sentence, remember?" Charles was positively scowling. The man obviously didn't care if he hurt her feelings.

Rhonda only shrugged. "The judge then."

"I'd rather not if you don't mind." The last thing Karan needed was Wannabe Jenny taking another stab at her. She'd already had to beg permission to drive her car to New Hope.

Rhonda shifted her gaze between Karan and Charles. "Then what's it going to be, people? We need all hands on deck. Are we up to working together for the benefit of families in crisis or would we rather cut our losses now?"

If nothing else, Karan appreciated the woman's frankness. And the fact that she'd hadn't mentioned the mandated therapy sessions. Karan's sentence wasn't governed by state privacy acts or confidentiality. Anyone could visit the sheriff's website and get a good chuckle at her expense.

Charles didn't reply.

Neither did Karan. The therapy part of the alternative sentence was contingent upon a facility offering the services, which was precisely why Wannabe Jenny had waived the three-hour substance abuse class. She didn't have too many choices that didn't involve wearing orange.

"So, Charles and Karan," Rhonda said brightly. "Does silence mean we all agree to play nice?"

Karan almost smiled. She wasn't sure why. The playground metaphor, maybe. With every fiber of her being she knew Charles wanted her to agree there was a conflict of interest to save him from forcing the issue. He'd been here first.

Unfortunately for him, she wouldn't give him the satisfaction. If he wanted her off his turf so badly he could help her get time off for good behavior.

"I'd like this nightmare over with," she told them. "If

that means dealing with Charles Steinberg for three hundred and fifty-nine hours and—" she glanced at her watch "—thirty-one minutes then so be it."

Rhonda inclined her head in approval. "Charles?"

He nodded, *still* refusing to look at her. Honestly. How juvenile could a grown man be?

"You're done with me, Dr. Camden?" he asked.

"I am, Dr. Steinberg. Thanks for making the time."

"No problem at all."

Charles meant what he said. Karan could tell he liked Rhonda. The sentiment appeared to be mutual, which made Karan wonder again if these two were involved in more than work. Wouldn't that be the icing on the cake?

But she didn't care about Charles's love life. No way could she have possibly kept up with him. Not according to the Bluestone grapevine. Apparently, he dated anything that moved, and Karan couldn't exactly say she was surprised. He'd have to look far and wide to replace the wife he'd thrown away.

Why should she care what the man did with his life? She didn't. She also couldn't help but notice how tired he looked with dark smudges beneath his eyes. The way he used to look when he was operating on little or no sleep for too many days running.

"I'm out of here," he said. "Ciao."

Rhonda smiled. "Enjoy your trip. I love rainbow trout."

"Noted." Charles finally met Karan's gaze, and his smile faded fast. "Welcome to the New Hope and good luck."

He headed out the door without another word. Karan watched him go, all contained energy that shouldn't have been so familiar this many years after the fact. Funny the things that stuck in her brain.

And who knew the man did volunteer work? That bit of

news hadn't made it around the grapevine the way news of his many conquests had. Did Wannabe Jenny know Karan had once been married to a codirector of this program? *That* would have her cackling over her microwave frozen dinners.

Jack had known, no question.

Add one more no-good ex to the growing list. Maybe Karan should address how she'd become such a loser magnet since she was forced into therapy anyway.

"Okay. Now that's settled." Rhonda shoveled folders into an open briefcase then deposited the whole thing on the floor. "Let's get to business. Please have a seat and make yourself comfortable."

Karan glanced at her choices—two upholstered chairs in front of the desk or a leather sofa that looked like the perfect place for New Hope's overworked codirectors to catch some shut-eye. Or enjoy a few stolen moments together.

Karan knew doctors so well.

Sinking onto a wing chair, she watched Rhonda continue to clear space on the desk. The blue blazer fit the therapist nicely and complemented her highlighted hair, but she'd obviously purchased the white blouse beneath it off some rack in a department store.

"That's much better." Rhonda sat and peered across the now clean surface. "So what's been going on?"

The casual question came as a surprise. But only for a moment. The question was only deceptively casual, Karan knew, a trick to gain a patient's confidence.

"I'm in a bit of legal trouble."

Rhonda upped the smile a notch. "So I hear. Let's talk about that."

The moment of truth. "I'm not sure what to say. I've been ordered by the court to explain my actions to a stranger, and I resent the intrusion in my life. But, that said, I also acknowledge how my actions invited the intrusion. I made a bad decision one night and I've been paying for it in spades. Starting with a judge who's still mad she didn't make the cut on the high school cheerleading team. She's suspended my driving privileges with the sole exception of coming here. And I had to beg for that concession. If this isn't bad enough, I walk through the door to find my ex-husband, who can't stand the sight of me, and a therapist who I'm not sure isn't involved with said ex."

"Great, we've got a place to begin." Rhonda didn't miss a beat. Leaning forward, she propped her elbows on the desk. "First of all, I'm not involved with your ex-husband in any way but professionally. Everything said in any session between us is bound by confidentiality. However, if you're not comfortable, we can ask the judge to reassign you. There are several good therapists on staff here. I only took the job because you're our first foray into using community service hours. But having met you, and given your connection to Charles, I'm good with turning you over to someone else if you want. The choice is yours."

Karan was inclined to take Rhonda at her word, even though she wasn't wearing a wedding band. The only ring she wore was a rather attractive topaz set in silver on an index finger.

"Thank you, but that's not any choice at all. As you said, we'd have to ask the judge for permission and I'd rather not subject myself to that until I absolutely have to."

"You feel as if the past has influenced the judge?"

"She threw the book at me for a first offense."

Rhonda flipped through some papers. "Well, no denying that. What role did you have in her not making the cheerleading team?"

"I was the captain."

"I see. And how do you feel you might have been sentenced with a different judge?"

"I don't think I warranted the maximum allowable sentence." Karan tried not to sound petulant. "The judge thought that because I'm aware of the effects of alcohol on me given my condition that I should have erred on the side of caution, which I usually do."

"So what was different about that night?"

Karan supposed she should have expected the question and had a ready answer. This woman was a therapist, after all, digging deep to root out problems—or to be convinced there weren't any brewing in Karan's psyche.

There weren't any, thank you.

"I drank too quickly. It's that simple. Those first few sips usually tell me whether or not I'm going to have a problem. If my blood sugar is steady then I can enjoy a glass of champagne. Never more than one. And my friend, the senator, had announced his bid for reelection, so I wanted to share a toast." She shrugged. "By the time I realized I was feeling tipsy it was too late."

"How soon afterward did you leave the function?"

"Too soon," Karan said drily.

"Okay, so something was different that night. I'd be curious to know what it was." Rhonda glanced at the wall clock. "Well, we don't have a lot of time left today. Largely my fault, so my apologies. I was already running late from my day job when I discovered your connection to Dr. Steinberg. So, let's shift gears now."

Fine by Karan. She took a deep breath and settled in the chair, willing herself to relax.

"I'd like to know a little more about you, Karan. About where you feel you might fit in around here."

"That's a very good question."

Rhonda seemed to understand the significance. "We have all sorts of things going on around New Hope. Lots of services for our families and outreach programs, which translates into the need for a lot of volunteers. We'll find something suited to your particular skills, I promise. So, what kind of work do you do?"

"Well, I don't really have time for a conventional job. My days are too full and require too much flexibility to make rigid commitments like that."

Rhonda was too professional to openly show emotion, but the surprise was there. "With what exactly?"

That question was a little more difficult to answer. "Social engagements. Projects. Sometimes I feel like all I do is run around putting out fires. You know how it is—something's always up with one of the houses, or the finances need attention, or I'm asked to coordinate some event."

Rhonda was silent for a moment, clearly considering. "Okay then. Let's start with what you think you'd like to do around here. Any ideas?"

"I'm gifted with interior design. My last husband's Manhattan offices were featured in an international medical magazine." The generic interior of this place could certainly use some help to make it look welcoming and homey, which Karan thought should have been the whole point of an emergency shelter. She kept that opinion to herself.

"I'll certainly keep that in mind as we work around here. We are hoping to build another structure on the property for offices, so we can devote more of this house to sheltering families. But that's still down the road. We just finished renovating everything and have tapped out our resources. Only temporarily, I hope. How about administrative tasks?" Rhonda asked hopefully. "We've got wonderful people in place but they could use a hand."

"I don't think I'm your person," Karan admitted. "I have a personal assistant who handles my administrative tasks at home."

Rhonda wasn't deterred. "Medical experience?"

"I've married two doctors."

That got a chuckle. "Any hobbies? Gardening perhaps?"

Honestly. In her Louis Vuitton ballerina flats from the summer collection, did she really look like someone who enjoyed playing in dirt? "I hire lawn crews for all my properties."

"Do you like children?"

They were getting warmer. "My best friend has two. I've taken her daughter into the city for shows and her son to see the Yankees play."

"Okay, great." Rhonda flipped through the folder again, this time scanning more closely. "I see here that you have a Masters in public relations from Van Cortlandt College. I did my graduate work there."

Karan nodded. Not such a surprise. The Ivy League school was a popular draw to the area.

Well over a century ago, people had surged to Bluestone Mountain when miners had discovered feldspathic greywacke, the rare, dark blue sandstone that made her hometown a unique location, and a wealthy one. Now the area appealed to an elite and eclectic crowd because it lacked the commerciality of the nearby hamlets of Woodstock and Bearsville.

When most of the Catskill region had been earmarked as part of New York's Forest Preserve, not all of that land was publicly owned. Private colleges like Van Cortlandt owned property along with people of means who wanted a fast escape from Manhattan. Precisely why she kept a home here.

Until she could talk to a real estate agent, that is.

Add another project to her list.

Rhonda closed the folder. "All right, Karan, let me mull on this a bit. I'm sure we can come up with the perfect something."

"I hope so. We need exactly three-hundred and fifty-nine hours' worth of perfect."

"Trust me. You'll be an asset to our program. I can feel it, and I'm big on trusting my feelings."

It was hard not to like this woman. Even though that was the last thing Karan wanted to do with her court-appointed therapist. Especially a woman who worked closely with Charles.

"So let's wrap this up for today," Rhonda said. "I'd like you to keep a journal for your homework."

"Keep a journal, as in writing?"

Rhonda nodded "You don't have to share what you write. The journal will help you reflect on our discussions and give you a place to refer to when we talk again. Sound good?"

Not what Karan had expected, but it didn't sound difficult. "Not a problem."

"Great," Rhonda said. "Please bring it with you. It doesn't have to be anything fancy. A spiral notebook will do the trick. I'll give you a question after we talk. You'll be in charge of remembering it." She glanced at her desk with a wry smile. "I'll write it down. I won't be able to find it again."

Karan did smile then. Rhonda must have gotten to be codirector of New Hope on sheer personality because she was clearly an organizational nightmare. Maybe Karan should refer her personal assistant, who was a positive genius at organizing.

She didn't get a chance because Rhonda said, "I'd like you to reflect on what was different about that night. Okay?"

"Okay." Karan would have plenty of time to reflect since she wouldn't be driving anywhere until her next visit to New Hope.

CHAPTER FOUR

Karan's Journal
What was different about that night?

THAT NIGHT WAS NOTHING SPECIAL from what I remember.
No different than the thousand other parties I've attended.
Great food. Even better conversation. I can always count
on Brent to host a decent party, which is one of the reasons why he's such a successful politician. I never even
blinked while writing my check for five thousand dollars
to *his campaign*. I'm sure most of his supporters don't.
Two terms in office, work on the Banking and Finance
Committees—he's more than proven his good sense and
character.

And he has been a good friend. He ran interference
when that busybody Ginger Downey commented on my
solo arrival. Brent grabbed my hand and twirled me and
announced how delighted he was that he'd get a chance
to dance more with me. When he wasn't dancing with
Annette, of course.

Annette was so sweet when she caught me in the
powder room to ask if I was okay. I wouldn't have missed
this party for the world. Only the most influential names
were on the guest list. Mine, of course, had been one of
the first.

Certainly well above Ginger Downey's.

Now that I think about it, I was also excited about

getting out. The past few months…well, I haven't felt settled anywhere. When I'm in the city, I'm out-of-sorts because I miss my routine with Patrick. But I'm not settled in Connecticut, either. Being at the beach makes me feel as if I'm on vacation. I need to be rebuilding my life, establishing new routines.

That leaves Bluestone Mountain.

On the upside, I'm close to Susanna.

On the downside, I'm close to Mom, which is always a mixed bag. But she hasn't been too difficult lately, so no complaints. I thought she might be going to Brent's party because she likes the Inn at Laurel Lake—one of the few places around Bluestone she cares for—but she was in the city for another event.

I remember being excited. I made a special trip into the city to shop for evening wear and completely lucked out when I found the most darling Akris appliqué dress. I spent the better part of the day at Mill Hill Resort and Spa preparing for the night with the usual workout, massage, mani, pedi and facial.

I put my hair in a ponytail to show off the gorgeous tulle inset shoulders of the dress. I was excited, no question. More excited than I can remember being in quite some time. Since before Patrick left.

I can't remember when things started to change, but somewhere between the Russian caviar, the Wagyu rib eye and the conversations with an A-list of local, state and federal officials, the sparkle of the night dulled. All the laughter and discussions about the cigarette tax and small business loans, all the reconnecting suddenly lost its appeal.

Maybe that was my first clue. After all the preparation, all the careful attention to detail, I wanted to leave long before the party had ended. I remember thinking that all the preparation felt like an enormous waste of time. I was bored at best, distracted at worst, and after asking Congressman Bruij to repeat his question not once but an appalling *twice,* I was more than ready to say my goodbyes and head home.

Yes, now that I think about it that definitely should have been my first sign of trouble.

But how could I leave until Brent made his announcement? I couldn't. Ginger would have certainly drawn attention to my early departure and started up talk about how I was rebounding after my *latest* divorce—nosy woman. Now there's someone who needs a hobby. Crocheting maybe, so she stays home and I won't run into her as often at social events. But I absolutely refused to give her ammunition to use against me. Not to mention that leaving before the announcement would have been rude considering how Brent and Annette had gone out of their way to be nice.

No, even upon reflection, I really had no choice but to tough it out and pretend to be interested.

I suppose the Dom Perignon Rosé helped me do that.

One sip and I managed to nod in all the appropriate places whenever Judge Townsend stopped his soliloquy about the unique responsibilities of probate, adoptions and guardianships long enough to draw air.

Another sip and I directed leading questions to State Assemblywoman Whaley, who argued emphatically for the property tax cap and against an increase of income and excise taxes as an alternative to educational cuts.

I seem to have kept right on sipping, raising an almost-empty flute when Brent *finally* made his announcement. Then I kissed him and Annette and headed for the door.

My small misstep at the entrance was another sign of trouble. The doorman saved me from disaster, unceremoniously hauling me upright when the heel of my slingback caught on the runner. I slipped entirely out of my shoe and was forced to cling to him to stay upright.

Of course he asked if he could call me a taxi. I recognized the code for: *should you get behind the wheel?*

It was one stupid glass of champagne. Besides, leaving my car wasn't an option, not when Jessica's husband was the general manager of the Inn. If he saw my Jaguar in his parking lot overnight, he'd tell Jessica, who would tell Marietta, who would tell Becca...and so on until every cheerleader who'd once been on my team would start the Bluestone gossip mill grinding.

Everyone would speculate about who I'd spent the night with. Or assume I'd had too much to drink. Then word would make its way back to my mother, who never missed anything that happened in this town. I did not want to get *that* phone call.

I produced my claim ticket and told the doorman I was fine to drive. He looked doubtful, but I just flashed him my most reassuring smile and told him the truth—only one glass of champagne.

I headed outside to wait, so the night air would help clear my head.

Why had I been looking forward to seeing all these people again? I couldn't remember. I should have probably just sent Brent the check.

The valet took forever with my car, and I wondered if he'd gone to confirm how much I'd had to drink. With liability being what it is nowadays I couldn't fault a business for being cautious. Even though I was left outside shivering. That had been my choice. I could have waited indoors.

Or better yet, I could have stayed in Manhattan. Then

leaving my car wouldn't even have been an issue. I'd have simply tipped the valet and let the doorman call a taxi.

I wasn't sure what I'd have done if the doorman gave me trouble. What could I do? Call Susanna? Still would have meant leaving my car. Unless Susanna brought along Brooke, who's now driving even though Susanna is awfully tight-fisted with the car keys considering Brooke's heading off to college in a few weeks. But that's just my opinion. And Brooke's, of course.

I didn't want to be used as a nonexample for my beautiful, impressionable goddaughter. And Susanna wouldn't be able to contain herself and resist the chance to drive home a life lesson. She couldn't resist mothering on a good day let alone when I drop a perfect opportunity in her lap.

Being between husbands at the moment, I had no one else to call and my mother wasn't an option. All I wanted to do was get home. And home was only a few miles down a long, very lonely stretch of highway late at night.

CHAPTER FIVE

OKAY, SO KARAN HAD GOTTEN HER initial therapy session and her first homework assignment behind her in less than twenty-four hours. That left the rest of her alternative sentence looming before her like an endurance test. With any luck, Rhonda had come up with a brilliant job for Karan and when she arrived at New Hope today, she'd be able to clock some hours to speed this process along. Today would be the perfect day for it—since Charles *wouldn't* be there based on the conversation she'd overheard between him and Rhonda yesterday.

Karan decided to pop into her mother's on her way into town. Technically, she would be on her way to New Hope as her mother lived on the same lake. Couldn't get to New Hope without passing the house where Karan had grown up so she wouldn't be violating any sentencing conditions. And there really was no point in dodging the visit. Not when her mother had made it a point to call to find out how the interview had gone yesterday.

Karan drove toward the main road that led down the mountain, maneuvered up her mother's driveway and parked in front of the house. The place dominated a hill-top with a steep-pitched driveway her father used to joke was better left iced in the winter so they could slide their cars to the road. Of course driving back up had required chains.

But he'd chosen this property because it boasted a

spectacular view of Mohawk Lake, which nestled in the forested mountainside north of Bluestone proper. He had his own boat dock, lots of room to snowmobile and several acres on all sides padding him from the nearest neighbors, which had pleased him enormously. The house was her mother's creation, a showcase as majestic as her father's view.

Karan's own house was situated on a modest half acre on the eastern shore. Close, but not too close. And her house didn't remotely resemble her childhood home. Not in size. Not in design. Not in any way except the view.

"Abigail, hello," Karan called as she stepped in the foyer.

Her mother's housekeeper appeared quickly from the direction of the kitchen. "Karan, I thought I heard your voice. Had the radio too loud. I'm getting as deaf as a rock." Her good-natured laughter echoed in the cavernous foyer. "But don't mention that to your mama."

There would be no need, Karan knew, since her mother probably already knew. She didn't miss much. But Karan didn't point that out as she leaned over and hugged the soft, round little housekeeper. With her apple cheeks and twinkling blue eyes, Abigail looked like Mrs. Santa Claus.

But looks could be so deceiving. This sweet-faced lady might wear her white hair in a bun, but she called things exactly the way she saw them. And anyone who dared to give her a hard time would get beat with the rolling pin. She had to have a spine of steel to care for Karan's mother.

"Mum's the word," Karan agreed.

"Beautiful, and gracious, too. Are you okay?" That bright blue gaze could have sculpted ice. No question about whether or not Abigail had been brought up-to-date on Karan's troubles.

"No worries. You've got your hands full enough here."

"Pshaw. Nothing I can't handle. It's practically still the crack of dawn. Would you like coffee? What about breakfast? Now's the time if you do. *Before* you head up to see your mama."

That was code for: *your mother is in a mood.*

She would want to be briefed on Karan's situation, give her only daughter advice and be motherly. Of course Karan had timed the visit so she could stay only a limited number of minutes.

"Thanks, but I've stalled long enough. I'll head up." And with any luck get this over with quickly.

Abigail inclined her head stoically. "The sitting room."

Karan heard the unspoken *"Good luck."*

Making her way up the stairs, she headed toward the room where her mother enjoyed coffee in the mornings while reading the paper, handling correspondence and otherwise preparing herself to join the living.

Karan tapped on the door then pushed it open.

Years ago, when Karan and Susanna had been in high school, they'd read Jane Austen's *Pride and Prejudice* for a lit class. Thus began a love affair with Mr. Darcy that had weathered decades. No matter where they were, no matter what was happening in their lives, they'd drop everything and get together to watch whatever new version hit the television or theaters.

Their absolute favorite to date was a television miniseries that had run on the Arts and Entertainment channel. They would submerge themselves in Regency England and watch all five hours straight through.

It had become such a tradition that Susanna's kids had joined the party, and even her late husband, Skip, had been known to walk through the family room, catch a bit of dialogue and sit to finish the episodes with them.

Mr. Darcy's venerable aunt, Lady Katherine, was the

epitome of a regal lady, no matter what version of the story. Karan always thought of her mother as Lady Katherine incarnate.

"Hi, Mom."

Georgia Madden-Kowalski sat at a Rococo-style table, the china coffee set neatly within reach, four newspapers before her, keeping her current on events from local to global so she could converse easily about any topic at social functions.

She gazed over the rims of reading glasses, face fully made up, even though she still wore her lounging robe, preferring to ease into the day.

When Karan had been young, she'd thought her mother was the most beautiful woman in the world with her spun-silk hair, porcelain skin and striking light eyes. Adulthood hadn't changed that opinion. Her mother was still one of the most beautiful women Karan knew.

"Good morning, dear." Her mother smiled in welcome. "You look very lovely this morning."

"Thanks, Mom, you look well, too."

"Come sit. Tell me how everything went yesterday. Would you like coffee? I'll have Abigail bring more."

"Thanks, but no. I've had some." Setting her purse on a side table, she sat across from her mother, who folded a paper and set it aside to give Karan her undivided attention.

"How did everything go?"

Karan met her gaze across the expanse of the table and gave a casual shrug, determined to do her part to keep this conversation light. "Well, I'm happy to say the people were welcoming. I'm not exactly sure yet what I'll be doing there, but the program director seemed eager for me to start."

One of them, anyway.

Karan weighed the merit of mentioning Charles. Did she roll the dice and chance that her mother didn't find out?

"So it's a big place then? I haven't seen much about it in the papers. Only public budgetary reports and minutes from the town council meetings. And that exposé, of course. They must have run a full week of stories about women, and men surprisingly, who'd broken away from abusive relationships. Apparently, domestic violence is epidemic."

Her mother was clearly interested, so the odds of her *not* discovering Charles's involvement at some point weren't looking good. If she did find out and Karan hadn't mentioned it…

"I did get a surprise while I was there."

"Really?"

"Turns out Charles is one of the program directors."

Her mother stopped with the cup poised at her lips. "Your Charles?"

Karan nodded.

She took a small sip, considering, then said, "Well, that is news. Why is a cardiothoracic surgeon involved with a domestic violence program?"

"I have no idea. But from what I've been told few people are actually paid employees. The majority are volunteers. Charles shares managerial responsibilities with a psychotherapist who has a local practice."

"Is this the psychotherapist you're seeing for your… treatment?"

"It is. A lovely woman. I wasn't entirely sure what to expect."

"No. I imagine not," her mother said slowly. "Not as a *patient,* at any rate. Socially, I've met several and have had positive interactions."

"True, true," she said lightly, leaning over to brush some invisible dust from her Prada loafers.

"And what does Charles think of you being a patient in a facility he manages?"

Karan groaned inwardly and braced herself. "He welcomed me, didn't say much more. I'm not sure he knows specifically what I'm doing there."

The cup settled in the saucer with an audible sound, and her mother said derisively, "Karan, everyone knows you've been court-ordered into treatment."

"Thank you, Mother. That's helpful to know."

Georgia frowned thoughtfully. "You don't think everyone will assume you divorced Charles because he was abusive?"

"Why would anyone assume that?"

"Why wouldn't anyone assume that? You're in treatment in a domestic violence facility. Ordered by the court. Charles is there volunteering his time. Seems rather obvious."

"Mother, he's an upstanding surgeon who's been a part of this community for years."

"But you were ordered there by the court rather than go to jail, dear. Not so upstanding, I'm sorry to say. Your life has become quite the sordid affair."

Not a mention of the champagne that had gotten her in this mess. Of course not. Her mother had nothing to say about that. Not when the pot would be calling the kettle black.

But Karan had no intention of engaging, so she didn't say anything. There could be no right response with her mother looking for a reason to argue.

"I have no way of knowing what people might think," her mother continued. "I do know I've received many condolences from friends and acquaintances because you're reflecting poorly on this family."

God, Karan *hated* this small town where there was nothing better to do than gossip. "I'm sorry for that."

"Add your latest divorce, and I look as if I didn't do my job properly as a mother."

Except at this stage of the game, Karan was an adult who was entirely responsible for her own behavior.

She didn't point that out.

"Drinking and driving, Karan. Honestly. You really should have had more sense."

This from the woman who spent half her days working out and sweating in a sauna to reverse the effects of the alcohol from the night before.

But, in all fairness, her mother kept social drinking social. The rest of her drinking she did in the privacy of her own home so she didn't get behind the wheel.

"No argument there, Mom," Karan said carefully, trying to project sincerity. Too flip and her mother would go off all over her. But she couldn't seem too eager to commiserate with the inconvenience her mother was enduring as a result of Karan's mistake. She was, after all, the cause of the inconvenience, and her mother was nowhere close to stupid.

No, Karan's only course of action right now was not to engage, weather the storm and flee as soon as she could.

Her chance came only blessed moments later when Abigail knocked at the door and slipped into the room, holding up a rolled linen napkin.

Blessed woman! This was a staged visit if ever Karan saw one. She seized the opportunity with both hands.

"Got to run, Mom." Popping up from the chair, she hurriedly gave her mother a kiss on the cheek. "I'm taking a chance even being here with my restricted driving privileges."

Seriously restricted.

Karan caught Abigail's gaze on her way out and that one winked cheerily.

Then Karan was skimming down the staircase and out the front door. She had reached her car when her cell phone vibrated. She was almost afraid to look, fearing that her getaway wasn't a clean one after all, but the display revealed a welcomed caller.

"Good morning, Susanna." Karan cradled the phone against her ear and slid into her car.

There was a relieved sigh on the other end. "You sound completely awake for the crack of dawn on a Saturday. I would never have called you at this hour, but your message said—"

"No worries. I wanted this day off to an early start."

"Really? Does this have to do with your first visit to New Hope? Tell me what happened."

"It's official, Suze. I'm in hell."

A beat of silence. "Things didn't go well yesterday?"

Karan turned at the end of the drive. "Whew, I'm back on the road and I wasn't caught. Made a quick pit stop at my mother's—"

"Are you *crazy?*"

Karan was about to reply that her mother had that affect on her as Susanna well knew, but Susanna didn't give her a chance.

"I was in that courtroom, Karan. I saw Judge Jenny in action. Why would you give her a reason to send you to lock-up and throw away the key? Do you want to be incarcerated?"

"Actually might be the lesser of two evils at this stage of the game."

"Things didn't go well yesterday." Not a question anymore.

Karan braked to slow her descent and maneuver a switchback curve, enjoying the way the sun dappled the road through the overhead trees. She had a flash of memory of how much this road had once felt like coming home. It had been one of the reasons she and Charles had decided to buy a place so close to Karan's parents. She liked the welcoming feeling, and he'd liked the idea of being close to family.

Of course, her father had been alive then.

And she and Charles had been in love then.

"Let's just say things didn't go as expected," Karan said. "You will never guess who's a director at New Hope."

"Not someone else who has it in for you, I hope."

"Charles."

"Your Charles?"

Karan chuckled. "That's exactly what my mother said. Yes, I'm afraid. My ex—Charles."

"Oh, you really are in hell."

"Officially. Jack set me up, Suze. I know it. That rat. Mr. Police Chief probably felt the need to pound his chest and entertain his new wife by torturing her high school nemesis. Honestly. Don't you think there should be some sort of statute of limitations on retribution?"

"That's silly. Jack was trying to help you out. Are you sure he knew about Charles's affiliation?"

"Quite sure."

"Then he probably thought you were better off with Charles than Judge Jenny. That's all."

Karan gave a harrumph, unwilling to concede the point yet unwilling to argue. While she had dated Jack, her involvement with the man had ended in college. Susanna, on the other hand, had married her high school sweetheart,

Skip, who had happened to be Jack's best friend. That friendship had lasted right until Skip had died from non-Hodgkins lymphoma barely three years ago.

"Let's move past Jack," Susanna coaxed. "I want to hear everything about Charles."

Karan knew exactly what Susanna was trying to do. She was too firmly entrenched with Bluestone Mountain society nowadays to be comfortable with this little trip down memory lane. She worked for Jack's wife. Maybe not technically, but they both worked for the same management company, so they inhabited the same workspace forty-plus hours a week. Susanna didn't want to discuss anything to do with Frankie Cesarini. And as Karan was on a time frame, she conceded with a sigh and let her best friend win this round.

CHAPTER SIX

"MAN, IT'S A DIFFERENT WORLD out here," Charles whispered into the morning calm, his voice the embodiment of contentment.

The words were out of his mouth before he could catch them, inviting a reply and intruding on this alternate reality, where the only sounds were from nature. The forest buffered civilization, and though Charles knew Route 42 was out there somewhere, all he could hear was the current splashing over rocks and lapping the hull of the boat as this mountain tributary rushed toward the river.

The sun had been steadily rising. The light filtered through the trees on the riverbank and shone off the water, making him peel away a layer of clothing as the early-morning chill yielded to a perfect summer day.

Charles supposed he had Karan to thank since she'd introduced him to hiking on Devil's Path so long ago.

Karan?

The thought of her came at him sideways. His fingers froze on the grip of his fishing rod.

How the hell had *she* intruded on his perfect day?

Okay, so maybe she'd been the first one to lead him on an expedition through the craggy trails of this mountain range. The high peaks and deep gaps themselves had spawned in him a love of the Catskills that didn't look like it would be wearing off anytime soon.

Charles could also argue that growing up on the flat

terrain of Florida had primed him for a change of scenery. That was, after all, exactly why he'd chosen Van Cortlandt College. To finally live somewhere with real seasons, although his mother always swore after a few winters up here, he'd come home again appreciating Florida's temperate climate.

He hadn't proven her right yet, and Karan had absolutely no place in his quarterly weekend trip with fellow anglers during the middle of trout season.

Or anywhere else in his life, for that matter.

He was relieved for the distraction of the inevitable reply when it finally came.

"Damned straight it's another world," Jay said. "Personally, I vote for not returning to the real one."

Matthew gave a snort—laughter maybe.

That's the way it always went on these fishing trips. Quiet reverence for the dawn eventually accelerated into excitement as they woke up, or whenever one of them hooked and landed a catch. And, of course, as the day heated they were forced to break open the beer cooler.

The guys were always the same, too. Matthew West, chief of staff at St. Joseph's Hospital, had been hosting these seasonal trips for half a dozen years now. He owned the cabin. Jay Reiber, Internal Medicine, owned the boat. Henry Hyatt, ob-gyn, had the wonderful wife who always spent a week cooking so they wouldn't starve while they were away. Summer. Autumn. Winter. Spring.

Charles wasn't sure what his contribution was beyond filling the coolers with beer, but he wasn't complaining.

"I thought that was always the plan?" Henry was still half-bent over the tackle box, spending more time knotting his fly than actually fishing because he insisted the lighter line would give him an edge.

Another unproven theory.

"Can't swing it for a few more years," Jay admitted. "Not unless Matthew puts me up in the cabin rent-free."

Another snort from Matthew. Laughter definitely.

"You really think you can pay off those student loans in a few more years, Jay?" Charles reeled in for another cast.

"Shouldn't be a problem. I'm good with budgeting, and I don't live beyond my means like others I won't mention."

"You general docs must not run up loans like we specialists do." Henry laughed. "But I don't think you're going anywhere soon. You'd miss us too much."

"I wouldn't be too sure about that," Charles said. "Jay can always watch the videos if he gets lonely. Or did you miss that he brought the camcorder *again?*"

Henry glanced up from his line and followed Charles's gaze to the photographic equipment in question, packed in pricey waterproof gear for the boat ride. Jay and his camcorder were also becoming a tradition.

"He didn't notice because he never gives Jay anything to record and put on YouTube," Matthew weighed in, earning a scowl from Henry.

"I am a man with a plan." Jay dragged his line. "*Angling Amateurs* is getting quite the following on the internet, thank you very much. And when it grows up, I'm changing the name to *Accomplished Anglers* and spending my early retirement charging clowns like you big bucks to be taken to the best spots on every river and stream in the Catskills."

"You go, Captain Jay." Charles didn't doubt the man would eventually accomplish mission objective. "But you might need a bigger boat."

"I'll have one. Or two. Or a whole damned fleet."

"If you want footage to show your fan base, then you'd better grab your camcorder," Matthew said. "I got one."

It would be Matthew who scored first today, and with a quiet precision not unlike they used at the hospital when ambulances pulled into the E.R. and lives were on the line, they moved into action.

Jay grabbed the camcorder. Henry grabbed the net. Charles headed toward the gear as Matthew waged an exquisite battle with what appeared to be a sizeable catch.

"Brown," Henry said, the first to spot the struggling fish on the end of the line.

"Henry called it," Jay said. "Got a big brown here." He was recording everything while narrating with educational, amusing declarations as he mocked Henry for his efforts while trying to net the twisting fish before it broke away.

Matthew cursed, and Jay howled with laughter as Henry fought to net the trout—a dozen pounder if an ounce.

"Watch closely, fellow anglers," Jay's radio-personality voice continued. "And see the amazing Henry net without netting. Looks like he's tangling that fish. There you go—*tangling*. A brand-new technique and you saw it first on *Angling Amateurs*."

He kept up the steady chatter while zooming in to watch Matthew work the brown free. Charles stepped in with the pliers and the gloves to assist.

Then came the display footage. They all knew the drill by now and Matthew stood in the official pose and held up the brown, who gasped obligingly for future viewers.

"A keeper," Jay said.

Matthew agreed. "A worthy adversary."

Since they were only allowed five catches a day by law, anything less worthy got tossed back to survive another day.

"Tangling." Jay laughed after he stopped recording. "*Tangling*. Do you get it? Angling means fishing with a line and tangling means Henry got the whole thing tangled up in the net. Damn, I'm good. Any more questions about early retirement?"

Jay was talking to hear himself because no one else cared. Charles broke into the beer cooler to start the celebration.

"All hail Captain Jay." Jay caught the icy beer Charles tossed his way and raised it high. "Another reminder of why I continue to sacrifice the comforts of a good woman and a home filled with little mouths to feed."

"Sacrifice?" Charles winced. "That picket-fence lifestyle will drain you worse than the loans, dude."

"And your ass would be eating beanie wienie from a can if not for my wife, I should remind you." Henry pointed out before drawing deeply from the bottle of Bass Ale.

"Don't waste your breath." Matthew leaned against the bench seat and slanted an approving glance Henry's way. "Playboy Charles here has commitment issues. He won't hear a word you say. Trust me on this."

"Like I even have time for a life anymore." Not everyone was cut out to be a married man, and Charles had already learned the hard way that he wasn't one of them. He wasn't about to make apologies. Especially not to Matthew, who'd fared no better in the marriage arena with an ugly divorce behind him.

"Where you been, chief?" Charles said. "Just so happens I've finished my eighth month at New Hope, and if you haven't heard, we're launched and hosting families already."

Matthew tipped the neck of the beer bottle in acknowledgement. "I've heard."

"Impressed yet?"

"That you're still at St. Joseph's all these years later."

Charles laughed. "And you doubt my ability to commit."

Any less commitment and he would have run out the back door when he'd spotted Karan at New Hope. Now there was a real sacrifice—being forced to put up with his ex-wife for the term of her community service.

But St. Joseph's chief of staff didn't need any reminders about Charles's commitments gone bad. Neither did Charles for that matter, because he resented that Karan was inside his head again, turning up like a bad penny as his grandmother always said—whatever the hell *that* meant—and disrupting his peaceful weekend.

Setting aside the bottle with a clatter, he reached for his fishing rod. He wanted his fifteen seconds of fame on YouTube. He wanted to commune with nature the way the Native Americans had when they'd used these streams and rivers to travel. This was his time to take a break from reality, to step away from the constant demands of the O.R., from New Hope, from the pressure of Matthew dangling the appointment in front of his nose like a worm on a hook.

He cast the line and projected the same focus he used in surgery onto the sound of the stream, on the wildlife in the trees and the shore, on the absence of demands on his time. Today was his. To relax.

And he did. Charles cleared his head into restful emptiness. The beer cooled his throat. He shed another layer of clothing as the sun rose, glinting off the gunwale as the boat rode with the current.

Then a phone vibrated.

All gazes swiveled toward the gear, toward the insistent tremor of sound that intruded on the quiet.

"Henry, you have any babies coming?" Matthew asked.

Henry shook his head. "Lawrence is on call. I'm not expecting anything he can't handle."

"It's mine." Charles reached for his BlackBerry and

glanced at the display. New Hope's main switchboard. With a sinking feeling, he depressed the talk button, knowing he wouldn't be getting this call unless there was trouble. "Steinberg."

"It's Deputy Doug, Dr. Steinberg. Sorry to bother you, but we need a director."

Charles could practically feel the gazes on him. He covered the receiver and whispered, "New Hope."

Matthew nodded. Jay cast his fly. Henry went back to making knots.

Charles asked, "What's up?"

"Smoke detection system went off. Security company called the fire department."

"Is there a fire?"

More curious gazes. Jay mumbled something under his breath that sounded like: "To hell with real."

"No, no fire."

Charles exhaled a breath he hadn't realized he'd been holding. "Then what triggered the system?"

Deputy Doug hesitated long enough that Charles knew he wasn't going to like the answer. "Burned popcorn."

"Come again?"

"Burned popcorn. One of the volunteers didn't know microwaves have popcorn buttons. She set the timer and got distracted. Place smells godawful."

The adrenaline began to ebb like the boat's wake behind them. "Any damage?"

That would be about the last thing New Hope needed.

"Microwave took a hit, and the place is going to smell for a while unless you've got money in the budget to call one of those disaster recovery services to air out the drapes and carpets. But maybe we can keep the windows open long enough."

Which was good considering they'd almost broken the bank getting the place up and running, and he hadn't budgeted much for maintenance repairs on a newly renovated house.

Instead, Charles had sunk the bulk of their assets into handling the monthly expenses until they reached out to the community to secure more funding. It had been a sound plan, but obviously he should have budgeted for stupidity.

"Who puts a bag of popcorn in the microwave and walks off?" he asked. But the instant the words were out of his mouth, Charles knew.

"The new volunteer with the Jag." Deputy Doug didn't sound amused. "One of the kids wanted a snack."

Charles stared at the river ahead, an entirely different world, one where ex-wives weren't lurking beneath trees that dipped leafy boughs into the water. "What do you need from me?"

"The fire chief is conducting an inspection now, but we've got everyone outside. The fire escape procedures all worked like a charm, too, so you know. Got everyone out safely and quickly, but the fire chief won't let everyone inside until a director signs off on the incident report."

"For burned popcorn?"

"It's the emergency status of the shelter, fire chief says. Standard procedure."

"Have you tried Dr. Camden?" Charles asked.

"Called her first, but she's in the middle of some crisis at the center. Can't get through, but I'll keep trying."

As director of the crisis center, Rhonda could very well be talking someone off a roof. Unfortunately, by the time Charles got ashore and to the cabin where his Jeep was parked… "I'm going to be an hour no matter how I cut it."

"Then I'd get a move on. Got a bunch of little kids here who are going to start asking for drinks and bathrooms soon."

Charles scowled.

CHAPTER SEVEN

KARAN WATCHED THE FIRE CHIEF vanish inside the building again, leaving her in the parking lot, baking in the rising summer sun, surrounded by a group of equally inconvenienced people.

An annoyed fire chief. Several amused volunteer firefighters, one of whom had carried out the smoking remains of the popcorn bag and pronounced a time of death. He'd earned a round of laughter at Karan's expense.

Two Bluestone Mountain police officers. Add the staff and volunteers from New Hope, who'd all dutifully banded around the residents. Three one-parent families. All mothers with children ranging in all ages from unborn up. Each and every one of them understood the fire chief couldn't let them back inside the house until a director arrived to sign off on the incident report.

Not a one of them had been unkind although this situation had been entirely Karan's fault.

Deputy Doug slipped the cell phone into a case on his utility belt and directed the nurse. "Let's move everyone over to the gazebo where there's shade. The kids can run around and entertain themselves in the play yard."

"It's going to be a while," the nurse said. Not a question.

"Afraid so, but he's on his way."

He. Charles.

Wasn't the man supposed to be on a fishing trip?

Charles didn't want her at New Hope. He'd made that

apparent, loud and clear. Karan didn't want to be here, either, or around him for that matter.

Common ground. Imagine that.

But why the man would be so nasty...*he'd* been the one who couldn't be bothered to show up to live their life together. She'd tried everything she could think of to get him to address the problem—because until they knew what the trouble was they couldn't resolve it. There had even been that horrible time when she'd been convinced he'd met someone new. He swore that wasn't the case, and everyone she'd known who worked at the hospital had corroborated his story.

So he'd continued to withdraw further and further from her until he barely came home from the hospital anymore. When he did, he felt like a stranger. She'd talked to her married friends, read every book she could find on the subject. All to no avail. She couldn't make him address the issue. Eventually, she'd finally been forced to accept that their marriage was irretrievably broken. The worst part was that she had no idea why he'd gone into full-fledged retreat mode. She still didn't.

So why he would behave as if *he* was the wronged party made no sense whatsoever.

And now he was on his way here.

She should have gone home the minute she'd logged onto the duty roster to find that Rhonda hadn't yet assigned her a duty. Trying to fit in on her own had turned out to be a bad, *bad* idea.

"Why don't we start a game of kickball?" Elizabeth the shift therapist suggested. "There's sports gear in the shed. Keep the kids engaged for as long as we can."

The nurse nodded. "Great idea. The exercise will do us good. Except you, LaShanna. You can keep score."

LaShanna, a mother of two, was so pregnant she looked as if she might pop at any second. "Fine by me."

Elizabeth withdrew keys from her belt and headed toward the shed. "Be right back."

Kickball? Karan wanted to know when her life had degenerated into a bad sitcom.

"I'm so sorry," Amy whispered.

It took Karan a second to register that the woman, one of the shelter residents, was speaking to her. "For what?"

"For this…mess." She waved a hand around, looked genuinely distressed.

Amy had to be close to Karan's age. Well spoken. A few pounds wouldn't have hurt, but otherwise pretty in a natural, earthy way. Her boys weren't little. Not teenagers yet but not that far away. Middle school, maybe. She didn't know kids.

"This *mess* isn't your fault, Amy."

"If Cody hadn't been bothering you for a snack—"

"I was hungry, Mom." Cody looked at Karan with unhappy eyes. "Thanks for trying though."

If the kid had been hungry before, he must be starving by now. "Accidents happen. Next time you can show me how to make the popcorn," she said to lighten the mood.

It worked. The boy smiled. "Okay. It's not hard if you know what button to push."

Which presupposed the microwave still functioned. With all the smoke that had been billowing out of it, Karan wouldn't be surprised if the firefighter called another time of death.

"I'll look forward to the lesson."

Balls and plastic bases appeared and Cody took off toward the action, leaving Karan to walk over with his mother.

"Kickball is a good idea," Amy commented. "Get the

kids to interact. I don't know about the others here, but mine miss their friends a lot."

Karan supposed kickball could be viewed as a bit of a silver lining in this storm cloud. "That must be hard."

"This whole situation is a nightmare. They haven't seen their friends or any of my family. With all the moaning and complaining they did about school and homework, they never had a clue they would actually miss it."

"Aren't they on summer break?"

A ghost of a smile crossed Amy's face. "They wish. They're taking a few virtual classes to keep in practice, since we've dropped out of our life completely. New Hope is affiliated with a great online school, so no complaints there. But I'm a teacher. They couldn't get out of school if they tried."

"I guess not. So you're out of work then, too?"

Amy nodded. "I was teaching at the elementary school they attended, but I don't think I'll be going back. I keep telling myself it's a good time to make a change. Cody starts middle school in September and Bryce is only a year behind him. I'm just hoping we can get everything settled by then."

"I hope it all works out." What else could she say?

They caught up with the rest of the group, so the conversation ended. But Karan couldn't deny her surprise. Not only by Amy's frankness, but her occupation. A teacher. She seemed like a perfectly normal soccer mom, no different than Susanna, who spent half her life driving her kids from school and sports practices to friends' houses and the mall.

Yet here was Amy in an emergency shelter. Karan had no clue about the details of the woman's situation, but it wasn't much of a stretch to guess it must have been bad for her to uproot her kids and drop out of her life completely, as she'd said.

Karan didn't know much about domestic violence, but for some reason she hadn't expected to run into a mother who reminded her of Susanna. Karan made a mental note to glance at the paperwork Wannabe Jenny had loaded her down with during sentencing. She'd tossed it into a pile in her office, but her assistant wouldn't have thrown it away.

Elizabeth appointed Cody and LaShanna's oldest son, D'Marcus, as team captains, which clearly thrilled them to no end. She also directed them to choose a mix of kids and adults for each of their teams so the adults wouldn't feel left out.

That got a smile from Amy.

Not Karan, though. She was mentally preparing a reason why she should assist LaShanna with the score-keeping when Cody pointed to her as his first pick. His younger brother looked crushed. Karan was, too, truth be told, but she couldn't toss that little boy's effort back at him. So, forcing a smile, she went to stand beside him. Hopefully, he wouldn't live to regret his kindness, since she'd never actually played kickball before. But she'd been watching sports all her life. Her father had been a fan of anything, college and professional, that could get him on the sidelines to watch games.

"Might be good to run down on the rules," she suggested after the teams were chosen.

Cody, who had chosen his brother as a third round pick, looked a bit crushed himself now, but she winked reassuringly.

The rules were simple enough. Kick the ball. Run to base. When her turn did finally come, she nailed the ball and took off for first base to cheers of encouragement.

More kicking. More running. More cheering. She

performed admirably, and everyone seemed willing to forgive that she was the very reason they were outside melting in the growing heat. Karan was on third base when she sensed *him*.

Why she would even be aware of him was a mystery. The man was a memory from a long-ago, painful past, one she'd rather not dwell on in her present. But she was so aware. No point denying it. She could practically sense him the second his Jeep pulled into the parking lot, felt as if she was on display as he walked around the building. He was not happy. It was all over him, from the long, no-nonsense strides to the stony expression on his face.

No surprises there.

He was still dressed for fishing, wearing worn jeans and dirty deck shoes that looked damp. And stank, no doubt. Unfortunately for her, he might look unsavory, but the jeans still rode low on his hips and the T-shirt didn't do much to conceal the impressively muscled chest and rock-hard abs below. No need to ask if he still worked out regularly.

His gaze skimmed across her, and for some reason Karan couldn't possibly explain, her breath caught in her throat, a physical reaction despite the scowl on his face.

Her saving grace came when the game came to an abrupt halt as several of the key players recognized Charles. Both the therapist and the nurse left their posts to greet him.

Karan detected the faint odor of fish as he passed, not acknowledging her at all. Rude man. They'd been married for over four years. The least he could do was acknowledge her presence.

But there was also a tiny part of her, deep down inside, that was so relieved he didn't. She hated responding to him against her will. This man had proven to be heartache underneath the shiny wrapping, and he seemed to enjoy breaking hearts if the way he lived his life was any indication.

Besides, she wasn't fit to interact with him on equal grounds right now when every inch of her felt sticky and her summery pantsuit was a wrinkled mess. The sun might be making her bra cling uncomfortably to her skin but it hadn't managed to dry the dew on the grass. No, she would *not* look at her shoes.

Charles powwowed with Elizabeth, the nurse and Deputy Doug before heading inside with the deputy. Karan suspected they were inspecting the place because the firefighters disappeared inside again and no one returned for a good ten minutes.

The moms made a valiant effort to keep the game going, but once the firefighters reappeared, the kids were more interested in seeing the fire trucks drive off.

Finally. Air-conditioning beckoned, and Karan went to stand on the gallery in the shade while awaiting official word they could go inside before she wound up smelling worse than Charles. Fingers crossed he wouldn't hang around long. No doubt the fish were eagerly awaiting his return.

Luck wasn't on her side. Really. The fire chief thanked everyone for their cooperation and took off himself. Everyone eagerly filed inside, but Charles chose then to address her.

"A moment of your time, please," he said.

Cody swept past, looking mildly regretful, as if she'd been called into the principal's office. He might feel bad for her, but he had no intention of joining her.

Cody's eyes widened when he stepped inside and he made an exaggerated gagging sound. "You sure it's okay to be in here? I feel brain cells dying."

"Ugh," Bryce chimed in. "I won't ever eat popcorn again."

Amy narrowed her gaze and shut them both down with a look.

Karan didn't say a word. She only tried not to gag on the charred air. But horrible though it smelled, it was blessedly cool. The uncomfortable feeling of cotton clinging to clammy skin quickly abated.

She accompanied Charles, resisting the urge to talk for no reason other than to hear something other than this silence between them, a silence that left her all too aware of how the past was scrambling into the present. She had nothing to say to him yet the simple act of walking together felt familiar and natural as though years hadn't passed since they'd stood in front of a judge in a divorce court.

And that awareness.

She hoped he felt it, too. A lot more than she did. Would serve him right.

Karan's hopes for a private discussion were dashed when he led her toward the scene of the crime.

One look at the microwave, door hanging wide to reveal the blackened interior of what had been a new piece of equipment, made her wince.

"I'm sorry." There, she got that out of the way. It was only fair. However rude this man might choose to be, the simple fact was he—along with everyone else around here—had been inconvenienced because of her error.

Even the neatly trimmed beard couldn't hide the way his mouth tightened. He came to a stop in the middle of the large, industrial-like kitchen and looked down at her. There was no missing the way he seemed to brace himself, as if needing to prepare even for such a simple act.

Honestly, what had she done to earn such hostility from him?

"This is the second time you've been on this property and you're already taking it apart. What were you doing?"

"I was microwaving a bag of popcorn." That much should have been obvious.

"Since when do *you* cook?"

She didn't dignify that with a response.

He turned and glanced inside the scorched interior.

"We need to replace that." Elizabeth appeared in the doorway. "Margaret doesn't cook in it, per se, but the residents heat up what she doesn't serve hot on the table. You want us to use petty cash?"

"Is there enough money to cover it?" There was no missing the concern in Charles's voice. "Didn't see this coming so I never wrote a replacement in the budget."

Elizabeth shrugged. "We don't need anything fancy."

"Make sure it has a popcorn button," he added.

That did it. Karan felt bad enough without Charles adding insult to injury. Honestly, what had she ever seen in this man? Something must be wrong with her. Had he always been so unpleasant?

"I'll replace it," Karan said.

He scowled down at her. "Unnecessary."

"*Not* unnecessary."

Elizabeth tiptoed out the door and vanished.

"Karan, don't be—"

"For the record—" Karan wasn't interested in hearing anything else he had to say "—if I'd have had any idea you would be part of this alternative sentencing, I'd have let the judge throw me in jail."

She spun on her heels and strode across the kitchen to a staff locker area that might have once been a mud room. Heading straight to her locker, she retrieved her purse and car keys and left by the back door. Since she didn't officially have a job, she wasn't abandoning her post.

Breathing deeply of the hot, but blessedly fresh air, she clicked her key fob to start her car. She slipped into it, then remembered.

From home to New Hope.

From New Hope to home.

Between the hours of 8:00 a.m. and 10:00 p.m.

Wannabe Jenny had been quite explicit.

Karan could practically hear Susanna asking, *"Do you want be incarcerated?"*

"I'm in hell," she whispered to no one in particular and rested her forehead on the steering wheel.

The air-conditioning blasted her as she indulged in a moment of absolute nothingness for as long as it took to cool off from the temperatures and the heat of her reaction to the rude man who ran this program. She was going to banish every remnant of *him* and only think about how refreshing it felt to be out of the sun. How each breath wasn't tinged with the horrible stench of burned popcorn and charred electronics.

How Charles was inside New Hope, so close but so far away.

She remembered this feeling, too.

No, no, no! She was not thinking about him. For one blessed moment, she was going to pretend she was driving to her beach house in Connecticut, where she could enjoy the summer sun, which was exactly where she might be if she could drive.

When she finally lifted her head, she glanced in the rear-view mirror, beyond the parking lot, beyond the heavily wooded patch of pine and the security wall concealed therein. The next stop was Walmart. So close yet so far away.

Technically, this was New Hope business. But Wannabe

Jenny hadn't said she could drive for New Hope business. She'd said: *From home to New Hope. From New Hope to home. Between the hours of 8:00 a.m. and 10:00 p.m.*

Susanna was absolutely right. Was Karan willing to risk another visit to court if she got caught driving? With the way her luck was running lately, she'd get caught.

So what could she do—ask Charles for a lift? She'd rather scale the wall herself. Grabbing her purse and keys, she shut off the car and headed out into the heat.

The Supercenter might have backed up to New Hope's property line, but in reality skirting the perimeter involved several long city blocks to access the parking lot.

By the time she arrived inside the air-conditioned store, she wasn't nearly as enamored with her Prada loafers. For what she'd paid, she would have thought they would be somewhat comfortable for walking. *Not.*

She found the display of microwaves, chose the most expensive model, which should have all the bells and whistles, then checked out the listing of features on the back of the box.

Yes, a popcorn button.

She hoisted it into a cart.

Making one last trip into the grocery aisles this time, Karan grabbed several industrial-size boxes of microwaveable popcorn. One swipe of her debit card and she was done making amends.

It didn't occur to her until she got outside that she didn't have her car.

She stared out at the parking lot with its veritable sea of cars. Luxury cars. Economical cars. Beaters.

"Hell is a never-ending stretch of highway where I get to walk for all eternity and watch everyone else drive."

No one heard. No one responded. No one cared.

There was nothing to do but keep pushing the cart.

Karan had the receipt for her purchase, so she wasn't worried about being stopped as she shoved the cart out of the parking lot. But the right front wheel had some glitch that made it hard to push over the escalations in the old sidewalk.

But she was determined.

She didn't want the memory of Charles's whining about money to follow her home. Not for an appliance that cost a piddling hundred dollars and change. Please. She'd give away a house or two not be subjected to Charles Steinberg and his moods. She wanted this project done and over with so she could go home and pretend this day had never happened.

Of course, this neighborhood wasn't the greatest. Tree roots had long ago upended much of the sidewalk and the hamlet of Bluestone Mountain obviously hadn't seen to the repairs. Pushing the cart felt like an uphill trek, particularly when she had to use her body weight to bump the cart over the big breaks in the concrete. And it was hot, hot, *hot*. She glanced at her watch. Almost noon. Naturally.

A car turned the corner ahead, bass pounding obscenely through the open windows as it cruised down the street toward her. She endured catcalls with a stoic expression, never slowing her pace, mentally cautioning the kids in that car not to mess with her. They would truly be sorry, and she'd wind up in front of Wannabe Jenny again. This time for beating a random kid to a bloody pulp with a boxed microwave.

She kept pushing. The pulse-pounding beat faded, but she was sweating so much her toes slid around in her loafers, making the leverage she needed to keep the cart moving difficult.

What had possessed her to buy these shoes anyway?

They were cute. They were Prada. That's about all she

could come with as she maneuvered around the last corner. She could see the driveway to New Hope beyond the auto repair shop.

"Howdy, ma'am," some kid at the repair shop said when he caught her eye.

She ignored him, focused on her goal. And she made it, finally turning off the sidewalk onto the driveway…a sharp upward slope that took the very last of her strength. The security guard at the gate eyed her skeptically and let her through.

Deputy Doug happened to be on the gallery and, gentleman that he was, saved her from having to wheel the cart up the handicap ramp by carrying the box to the door.

"Kitchen?" he asked.

She nodded, too winded to waste breath unnecessarily.

Balancing the box against his chest, he swiped his security card one-handed then stepped aside to let her grab the door.

"We can place the old one in this box and dispose of it," she suggested. "Unless you can think of any reason they'd want to keep it."

"None at all."

Setting the microwave on the counter, he plugged it in. Karan glanced at the manual and tested a few functions to ensure everything worked properly. Perfect. They were back in action.

While Deputy Doug was packing the old microwave away, Elizabeth arrived.

"Think this will do?" Karan asked. "It has a popcorn button."

The woman chuckled and came close to inspect the new addition. "Wow, this is even fancier than the one we had. Look at this defrost function. Margaret will be thrilled."

Karan was glad someone would be, assuming Margaret was the cook.

"That wasn't necessary, Karan." She felt Charles's voice more than heard it, a sound that poured through her until every part of her was hyper-alert.

He was the only man who'd ever made her feel this way.

It took every ounce of her will to turn around. Another deep breath before she found him standing in the doorway. "Never let it be said that I burdened your budget. Again, my apologies for the inconvenience."

She sounded so much more together than she felt. That in itself was impressive.

"I saw the cart outside," he said. "You walked?"

What was with this man's inane questions today? Couldn't he see her standing here sweating so much she must smell like a goat? She inclined her head, refusing to indulge his stupidity.

And he responded by staring at her with his too-handsome face, making her wonder if deep down inside somewhere, he didn't feel the tiniest bit bad for being so mean.

Of course that would presume he had a heart beating in that broad chest.

Karan was sure he didn't.

So why did she even care what he thought?

She didn't, she reminded herself. "If you all are through with me, I think I'll sign out for the day."

Charles shrugged. "Fine by me."

No doubt!

Karan left. She was not going to subject herself to any more of this abuse today. She would get into her nicely air-conditioned car and head home. Then she was going to pay her housekeeper to chauffeur her to Mill Hill Resort and

Spa, where she would convince her masseuse to squeeze her in between appointments. On a Saturday, no less.

She'd almost made it out the door when Deputy Doug caught up with her. "You know it's illegal to take a shopping cart off store property, don't you?"

Karan stared.

He gave her a goofy half grin. "Well, I know you only *borrowed* it to deliver the new microwave and were planning to return it right away."

Argh.

CHAPTER EIGHT

RUSH HOUR TRAFFIC WAS LONG gone by the time Charles pulled into New Hope and, as anticipated, the property had settled down. The staff hanging around after the close of the business day was not only skeletal but specifically prepared to deal with anything that may come up during the night.

According to Rhonda, the goal was to give the families who sheltered here a sense of normalcy. Quiet nights created routine, a sense of winding down after busy days, a semblance of privacy in a place where families had been forced by need to sacrifice even that simple dignity.

Rhonda's car had been in the lot, so after making a pit stop into the kitchen, Charles went to the office.

"What are you doing here?" he asked. "It's Monday."

"I could ask the same about you."

"Figured things would have quieted down by now."

She peered up over the rim of her reading glasses. "Really? Did the fact that the volunteers usually clear out by now have anything to do with that decision?"

"What makes you think that?"

"Because your ex-wife used the exact same logic. She'll be here soon."

"Oh, come on." He rapped a fist into the palm of his hand. "She's coming when she thinks I won't be here?"

"Well, you usually aren't."

No, he wasn't. He was in surgery all day on Mondays

and found his weeks ran smoother when he took time to get organized in his home office before things degenerated into craziness. "I put a package in the refrigerator for you. Think I'm going to give it to Margaret instead."

That perked her right up. "Fresh rainbow trout?"

He feigned a threatening expression. It wasn't Rhonda's fault that his plan to avoid Karan backfired.

"You are a class act, Dr. Steinberg."

"And you are here unexpectedly, Dr. Camden. I thought you had patients in your practice on Mondays."

"My six o'clock had to reschedule until later in the week, so it's not a big deal to swing by before my next one."

A lie. There was no *swinging by*. Rhonda's crisis center was in the heart of downtown Bluestone Mountain while her private practice was in an office close to the hospital. New Hope was on the outskirts of town in another direction entirely. She was trying to keep him and Karan apart.

He didn't get a chance to decide if he appreciated the effort when she said, "But I am glad I caught you before Karan shows up. I wanted to apologize about Saturday. I'm glad you could salvage some of your weekend. If there had been any way for me to be here, I would have."

"No apology necessary. It happens. Thought you might be talking someone off a roof."

"Thankfully not. Just running interference with the county and the police. An incident with a patient."

Admittedly, Charles was sketchy on what constituted an incident in Rhonda's field. "Doesn't sound good."

"Never is." She shrugged, and he saw resignation in that one small gesture, got the sense she needed to talk. "John."

He went the Socratic route. "The patient?"

"He ticks along great until something rocks his boat."

"Something rocked his boat."

"It did. Sometimes it's his meds, and his dosage needs to be adjusted. More often than not something upsets him then he stops taking his meds entirely. The police know the situation. They only call me when it's particularly ugly."

"It was ugly."

She nodded. "His apartment manager threatened to evict him. That set him off even more."

"Is he violent?"

"No. Just disruptive. Obviously mentally unbalanced, so he can make people really uncomfortable when he goes off."

Rhonda looked troubled, and Charles understood. He cared about his patients as far as helping them to the best of his ability. But there were some patients who managed to sidestep the boundaries he'd erected around his personal feelings. Sometimes, for whatever reason, they slipped inside.

A hazard of the trade, one that kept those in his profession compassionate, he liked to think. He hadn't realized the phenomena extended into Rhonda's field, though he supposed he should have. Live and learn. New Hope, and the people affiliated with it, had been altering his perspectives since he'd gotten here. Had that been Matthew's plan all along?

"So what happens to John now?" he asked.

"They'll keep him in lockup until his medication reaches a therapeutic level again then release him. I talked the manager out of evicting him. This time. I'll bump him back to daily visits to the center and keep my eyes on him for a while."

Charles sank onto the couch, stretched out his legs. Had he not waited to come here in an effort to avoid Karan, he'd have been at the gym by now and home and a quiet night in his office wouldn't be far behind it.

"Doesn't sound like much of a solution," he admitted.

"It isn't. But it's the only one he has."

"Bouncing between jail and the crisis center? Why's that?"

"When he's on his meds, he's functional yet outreach services aren't quite enough. You know as well as I do that state funding can only accomplish so much. That's what's holding us back here."

"Sounds like a flawed system to me."

Rhonda considered him, looked thoughtful. "John's exactly the type of person the system was created for, a person who genuinely needs help. He'll always need help. The flaw is when the system expends its resources sustaining people instead of helping them get on their feet. Exactly what we do here. We give people new hope. Whether it's learning employable skills or coping strategies or dealing with self-esteem issues or legal services. We give people a place to live safely until they can start fresh."

He liked that about Rhonda. She didn't hesitate to challenge his perceptions. "John doesn't have anyone?"

"Not anymore. He's well into his fifties. Had an aunt and uncle once who looked out for him, but they passed a few years ago. Their church still helps him out. They found this apartment. His disability check covers the rent and he feels settled there. I'd hate for him to lose it."

"Then he's lucky he has people to run interference."

She gave a lopsided grin.

"So," he said to segue through the awkward silence, "you find something for Karan to do around here?"

A tiny frown creased Rhonda's brow and she slipped

off her reading glasses. "Not exactly. But from what I hear the kitchen isn't the best place."

"Um, no. That much I could have told you. *If* you wanted me to tell you anything about her."

"Which I don't."

"Which you don't."

"I heard she replaced the microwave."

"She did." A classic Karan solution. Writing a check could solve almost any problem. "If you haven't found a place, why does she have you swinging by on a Monday night?"

Suddenly Rhonda was sliding open desk drawers. "Now what did I do with that file? I swear, I am such a scatterbrain."

His turn to frown. Rhonda was dodging his question.

Then there was a rap on the door.

Rhonda glanced up apologetically. "That will be her."

Charles was on his feet before Rhonda called out, "Come on in."

The door opened, and there Karan stood in all her glory, looking as impeccable as usual in a long flowing skirt and silk tank top. Her hair had been swept back from her face in a ponytail that reminded him distinctly of the striking young woman he'd met in college.

Fighting the recognition that felt like a punch to the solar plexus, Charles forced himself to look past the woman who impacted him physically. He forced himself to see her through trained eyes, not the gaze of a man who'd once been in love but the diagnostic gaze of a physician.

She didn't exhibit any signs of a substance abuse problem. Her eyes were clear. Her skin radiated a healthy, fresh-faced glow. She'd been blessed with great skin and the money to maintain it. From where Charles stood, she looked as fit as she always had. And damned if he didn't feel relief. Full-fledged, outright *relief* that he didn't see any outward signs of trouble.

If Karan was surprised to find him here, she didn't show it. She also gave him the option of not engaging, inclining her head and smiling politely as she stepped into the room. But that wasn't good enough. No, idiot that he was, he let his racing thoughts and her smile get the better of him. This woman had always tested his impulse control. Looked like some things didn't change with a signature before a judge.

"Good evening, Karan," he said, inviting a response.

He got one.

"And you, Charles. I was under the impression you don't usually come in on Monday nights."

"I don't. Not usually."

"My luck then."

Obviously not the good kind.

Meeting his gaze levelly, she faced him and, for one blind instant, he was rendered mute, a phenomenon from so long ago he hadn't even remembered. Not until he stared into those clear gray eyes and saw how they sparkled. A full-blown case of the middle-school-horny-boy effect. The disconnect between his thoughts and physical reaction rendered him speechless. Damned hormones.

Only now the effect was amplified by a serious dose of reality because in this case reality lived up to the fantasy. Charles could only stand there, struck by the sight of her, by the memory of how she would feel against him naked. She was sleek toned curves, smooth lightly tanned skin. He might not have thought about this woman in years, but he remembered. Every long lean inch of her. Whatever else had gone south with their marriage, sex had never been an issue.

The thought of sex managed to snap him from his daze.

"This doesn't have to be a problem," he tossed out the first idea that popped into his head. "I can work out a schedule and get it to Dr. Camden."

"Fine. I'll do my level best to accommodate you." Her concession should have appeased him. It didn't. Not when he could barely get past the sound of her voice, a melodious tone that filtered through him in such a visceral way.

The only thing that saved Charles was how she didn't seem impacted at all. Not the way he was. She'd avoid him if that's what he wanted, but she didn't appear to care either way. Her nonchalance aggravated him. Why would he expect her to care?

"Great." He forced his own nonchalance and glanced at Rhonda. "You won't mind running interference."

"That's what I do."

Or tried to, anyway. "Thanks. Good evening, ladies."

He was out of here.

But he couldn't shake the image of Karan, beautiful as ever, so healthy and composed, as if everything was right in her world when everything clearly wasn't. The fact that she'd been court ordered into therapy and community service spoke volumes.

As he drove the familiar route to the gym, questions that hadn't occurred to him before occurred. The first time they'd run into each other, surprise had distracted him. After the popcorn incident, anger.

But right now his impulsive reactions weren't distracting him. He shouldn't be reacting so strongly to her. Not on any level. He shouldn't be wondering if Karan wasn't bouncing back from her latest divorce. He shouldn't be remembering how she'd practically tripped over herself to divorce him.

Of course, Charles wasn't Dr. Big-wig Oncologist. He'd only been starting his medical career while Patrick

Reece, M.D., was already living Karan's kind of lifestyle. She obviously hadn't been able to wait until Charles had worked his way through the ranks to earn a name in his specialty, until internships and residencies yielded to a credible reputation. Or had she simply never loved him the way he'd thought she had?

The way he'd loved her.

Once. *Before* he'd known high-maintenance women and long-term commitments weren't his thing.

He'd come to realize that in the years since their divorce. That part at least wasn't Karan's fault. In fact, if it hadn't been for her, he might not have realized that he had no patience for the constant demands of marriage, the constant drains on his emotions and his time.

Turned out that he didn't like complicated in his personal life at all.

CHAPTER NINE

Karan's Journal
What bothers me so much about making an honest mistake?

I'M NOT EVEN SURE WHY RHONDA sent me home with this question since she already asked it during our session. Maybe she didn't like the answer I gave her. Not entirely sure why I should care since I replied honestly. But I'm determined to cooperate, so… I think it's fairly obvious what bothers me about the popcorn fiasco.

I hate looking stupid. Correction: I hate looking stupid in front of Charles. Although why *he* should factor in is a total mystery. The man has such a low opinion of me already…does it really matter if I give him a little more fuel for his fire?

He knows better than anyone I don't cook much. Or *at all* to be precise. And even if I did, I don't like popcorn. Those kernels wreak havoc on my veneers.

Still, how hard could microwaving a bag of popcorn be? My housekeeper from the Ukraine, who can barely speak let alone read English, can microwave popcorn. I know this because she does whenever Susanna drops by with Brandon. Teenage boys like popcorn. Or at least those of my acquaintance.

But now that I know the secret of the popcorn button, I won't need Marynia the next time Susanna and Brandon visit. I suppose that's one positive to come from this situation.

As long as I'm reflecting here, I also dislike the way one simple mistake erupted into a world-class disaster. And while I was forced to be outside in the heat, waiting until Charles could trouble himself to arrive, I got a front-row seat to the inconvenience my not-so-simple mistake caused everyone.

How could I not feel bad watching Mia, who was apparently recovering from a virus, withering beneath the gazebo with her mother? That little girl was watching all the other kids running around like howling little maniacs, and she couldn't do a thing except sit there feeling bad. The only time she smiled was when one of the firefighters brought her a Gatorade.

Then there was LaShanna, who was forced to chase after her sons in that heat, which was, frankly, a little disturbing to watch. Thank goodness Elizabeth suggested kickball. The game occupied the kids *and* forced LaShanna to sit down. But, of course, that couldn't be the end. No. Charles took so long to arrive that the poor woman resorted to using the bathroom in the maintenance shed because she simply couldn't wait any longer.

A maintenance shed? How sanitary could that possibly be? What if she came down with something? Or her baby was born with some sort of disease or deformity? All because I didn't know the secret of the popcorn button?

Back to obvious again. Does Rhonda really need me to rehash why I felt bad? Especially when no one had blamed me or was remotely unkind.

Except my ex-husband, of course.

If only the fire chief hadn't needed a director to sign off on the walk-through inspection. Not Rhonda's fault. She was working, a completely legitimate reason for being unavailable. But Charles had been *fishing*. Couldn't get much more self-indulgent than that. Not that I'm even remotely surprised. The man had a knack for never being around when he was needed....

"I'm due in surgery." His blanket excuse for everything. Precisely one of the problems leading to the breakdown of our marriage.

We managed to survive the demanding years of his clinical training and an almost impossible year of his internship. All through his med school I wrote cover letters and edited scholarship essays and helped him study so much I could probably be board certified.

I stood beside that man through everything. I kept our lives ticking along smoothly in his absence. I kept his social life primed and ready for him to network with people who would advance his career when he wasn't falling asleep on his feet. I made sure our home was inviting whenever he managed to get there. I brought him warm meals at the hospital when he couldn't. And I was always coming up with creative ways for us to enjoy an active sex life—almost impossible with his schedule—so he wouldn't ever feel the need to look twice at the women who worked with him.

It was my connection that got him an internship in Kingston at a cutting-edge research hospital.

Just when things were finally starting to settle down a little, and I was looking forward to spending more time together all I ever heard was *"I'm due in surgery."*

Even when he wasn't.

As long as I live I will never forget the *night of the last straw*. The memory still makes me twitch. I have never been more humiliated in all my life—current situation included.

Charles had applied for the new combined residency

program at St. Joseph's. We waited for weeks for that reply. It was a huge deal, and when he was finally accepted, I thought we should celebrate. I arranged a surprise party with everything he loved from the people he cared about to his favorite food. I even flew in his parents from Florida because we couldn't celebrate without them.

Everything was perfect.

But when Charles got out of surgery, he was tired, and since he had another one before dawn, he didn't want to drive home and waste time he could have been sleeping.

Waste time.

I can still hear his voice, so emotionless, so uncaring. Seeing me was a waste of time. Of course, I'm far too savvy not to redirect because I had a house filled with people. I had no intention of ruining the night because of his thoughtlessness or because I felt hurt. Not after all the work that had gone into planning his special night.

I abandoned the surprise element and explained we had guests who'd come by to congratulate him. I also reminded him he'd promised to come home.

He never bothered asking who was there. He acted like I was making impossible demands and told me to make his apologies.

That's when I knew it was over.

He didn't care about our guests. He didn't care about our life together. He didn't care about me. I was a waste of his time. I had no idea why or when that had happened, but there was no more denying the truth because I couldn't make him care.

I remember this feeling. I suppose I felt that way after the popcorn fiasco. I was trying to do something good. Back then it had been supporting my husband and letting him know how proud I was of his accomplishments.

The other day I was trying to help Cody, who'd claimed

to be starving when I came across him outside the kitchen, staring at rules posted on the wall.

Children must have adult supervision.

I was an adult. It should have been so simple. Might have been had I not been distracted when Elizabeth called us to the common room to show the DVDs she'd scored for the weekend.

Cody and I took off. If only I'd stayed in the kitchen, I'd have smelled the burning popcorn long before the climate control system did, long before I torched the microwave.

So, I guess another answer to Rhonda's question might be that I not only feel bad about inconveniencing everyone, but I have a teensy problem with feeling inadequate and useless. With Charles in the picture, all I can think about is how he doesn't believe I have anything useful to offer.

Not in a marriage.

Not as a volunteer.

CHAPTER TEN

LIFE WAS LOOKING UP TODAY. Karan had arrived at New Hope to find only one codirector—the one who'd dropped by on her lunch hour with good news.

"Not only do I have the perfect job for you—" Rhonda whipped a sheet of paper from her desk and displayed it proudly "—but I have my colleague's schedule for the upcoming week."

So Charles had followed through. Now they could avoid each other to everyone's satisfaction and New Hope could remain a place for fresh beginnings as opposed to the setting of some black comedy about adversarial exes. Karan should have been grateful, but for some unfathomable reason, she wasn't. Not even close. She felt...she wasn't sure. Deflated, maybe? Perhaps even a little disappointed, which made no sense whatsoever.

She *would* be grateful. Thrilled even. Charles could hear all about her accomplishments through Rhonda and their staff and feel terrible for being convinced she couldn't help. Served him right. Now that there was something suitable for her to do around here. "The perfect job. Let's hear it."

"You mentioned experience with social engagements. Come with me."

Rhonda went to the administrative assistant's desk outside the door. She lifted the top from a stationer's box.

"Here we have social correspondence. Businesses and

community organizations have been hosting events to raise awareness and funding for New Hope since the project began. I had Lori pull everything together so you could see the kinds of events. We need to thank everyone involved and encourage them to continue their efforts on our behalf.

"If you'll take a look at the participants, you can decide exactly who needs to be thanked then draft the letters. And I'm thinking we can edit those drafts into templates to keep on the system. That will save me and the volunteers a ton of time. To date, I've been writing every note personally but there are so many now, I'm not keeping up. And as we start the next stage of community outreach there will be even more." She chuckled. "Well, we're hoping anyway. We want lots and lots of people to become involved in helping around here."

"I'll be the social secretary." This Karan could do. Not only could she do this, she could excel at it. Charles would absolutely feel bad for being so mean. "This is perfect, Rhonda. My assistant drafts my correspondence at home, of course, but I approve absolutely everything that has my name on it."

"There you go." She smiled. "I'm rather pleased with myself, I don't mind saying. I bolted up in bed at two o'clock this morning with the inspiration."

"I'm sorry to have disrupted your sleep. But I am relieved for your inspiration. I don't mind admitting those three hundred and forty-some odd hours still looming in my future have been looking pretty bleak since Saturday."

"Even after our session the other night?"

"Afraid so." Karan would never be so rude as to admit that their latest session—*official* session as their first had been more of a meet and greet to address the Charles situation—had felt more like a chatty interview than some sort of epiphany-inspiring mental health analysis by a professional.

But she liked Rhonda, so Karan had decided to keep her mouth shut and reserve opinion. Therapy might only work if someone needed it, and she really didn't have any frame of reference beyond Susanna's firsthand accounts of visits to a grief counselor after Skip's death.

If nothing else, Karan would go along for the ride, taking the path of least resistance, because she absolutely refused to dig in her heels and waste another minute of her life stewing about how stupidly unnecessary and unfair this part of her alternative sentence was.

She would not give Wannabe Jenny the satisfaction.

Rhonda dug through the box to point out brochures and flyers from the various events that had been held to benefit New Hope along with corresponding lists of the organizers.

"I can't tell you what a relief this will be to get these dealt with," she said. "That's what disrupted my sleep. Had nothing whatsoever to do with you and everything to do with feeling pressured and behind. These letters have been hanging over my head and instead of getting a handle on them, I keep adding to the pile."

Karan didn't bother to ask why she hadn't recruited her codirector for help. Thank-you notes always seemed to fall into the realm of women's work. And, she supposed, that was as it should be. Most men didn't have a clue about the complexities of social niceties, and she happened to know well that Charles was more clueless than most. With New Hope's livelihood dependent upon outside funding…well, Rhonda had certainly come to the right place for help.

"I'll get busy then. What would you like me to do with everything when I'm finished?"

"Just print copies of each and drop them in my box. If I

make it back tonight after my appointments, I'll grab them. If not, tomorrow." Rhonda's smile, a smile that reflected appreciation and confidence for Karan's ability, went a long way to make the thought of the hours ahead bearable.

After Rhonda headed to work, Karan commandeered the administrative assistant's desk and sat down with purpose. She sorted through the contents of the box, scanning brochures and flyers and rosters of volunteer names to familiarize herself with what had been taking place.

The list was fairly comprehensive.

Domestic-violence-awareness walks through town.

Luncheons to rally community volunteers.

Dinners with high-ticket tables and illustrious guests.

The typical buffet of fundraising efforts that Karan was quite familiar with even if they were a variation on the usual theme.

Taking a stand against domestic violence.

She read through a pamphlet from an organization that sponsored a successful women's conference and found the presentation topics more than a little sobering. *Warning signs of an abusive relationship. How to be an effective bystander. How to help families victimized by domestic violence.*

Every shred of literature was branded with *New Hope of Bluestone Mountain, Inc. proudly serving Catskill communities since 2011.*

Okay, the date wasn't so impressive, but the campaign had to start somewhere. She forced herself to move on, to create a document of names, titles and specific functions.

All helpful people who needed to be thanked.

She inputted names, read about the various contributions, all incredibly generous in some not-so-obvious ways. Of course there were those who donated significant sums of money, without whom Karan suspected the events wouldn't have taken place. But there were others who had contributed vast amounts of time. Specific expertise in coordinating an event. Gifts of meeting-room space in buildings. Food from a local grocer. In one instance the linens, tableware and centerpieces that had been used during a catered luncheon.

So many people working to make New Hope possible. Including Charles.

Karan drafted several versions of a recognition letter and saved them as separate files as she mulled the possible reasons why Charles would be so involved with New Hope. She shouldn't be interested, but she was. For a man who spent the bulk of his time at the hospital, serial dating or fishing, the fact that he helped run things around here seemed significant.

She couldn't remember anything that hinted at a nature that championed causes. She wasn't even entirely convinced he'd gotten into the medical field because some streak of compassion made him care about helping people.

Karan let out a huge sigh. Okay, *that* was totally unfair. No matter how hurt and angry she was at the man for a variety of reasons, she couldn't deny how much he cared about his patients. That would be a total lie as she'd witnessed the effect of his caring more times than she could recall. That much hadn't changed about him. Or the fact that he liked to be in control. Give him a scalpel and the ability to influence life and death and Dr. Disdain was in his element. Put the two together, and she supposed directing this place did make some sense.

Not that she'd admit that aloud to *him*.

Her mind drifted from Charles to another puzzle that she had yet to solve—Amy, the schoolteacher who reminded her so much of Susanna as a soccer mom and a career woman. Karan couldn't reconcile that image with what she was reading in these brochures:

> *Domestic violence is a pattern of assaultive and coercive behaviors, including physical, sexual and psychological attacks, as well as economic coercion, that adults or adolescents use against their intimate partner.*

The sort of nightmare stuff the media thrived on feeding the public.

So how did a seemingly normal woman like Amy get involved with a man who acted that way? For that matter, why would *any* woman in her right mind become involved with this sort of man?

Karan couldn't help but wonder because none of these flyers and brochures provided answers about that. She thought about LaShanna so close to giving birth…what kind of man would threaten or abuse the woman who was sacrificing muscle tone to bear his children? She was still mulling the answer when a name caught her eye.

Greywacke Lodge.

Well, well, well. Here was another surprise.

Karan scanned the flyer. Greywacke Lodge had been one of the sponsors for the first annual Return to Peace Brunch. She supposed she shouldn't be surprised to see the place on the list. After all, the woman who ran the retirement community was none other than Frankie Sloan née Cesarini. Who knew, this very room could have been once been the place where fuzzy-haired Frankie had concocted all her crazy schemes and nasty retorts that had earned her such renown in high school.

She'd be getting a generic form letter.

Karan redoubled her efforts, thoroughly annoyed with herself for her wandering thoughts.

By four o'clock, she had a dozen separate files saved with clearly recognizable names, each containing a recognition letter that thanked a recipient for some specific contribution. The grammar was textbook, the wording flawless, the sentiments gracious, New Hope's biographical information exact.

Karan was quite pleased with herself.

Until she attempted to print the drafts.

The action should have been as simple as clicking Print, but she kept receiving *error message 12*—whatever that meant.

She manually checked the equipment, a huge printer/copier combo, half as tall as she was, clearly meant for industrial-size printing jobs. Yes, it was on, and that was the extent of her hardware knowledge. Karan had actually purchased one to place in her former husband's practice after she'd remodeled his office, knew this machine had easily cost five grand if it cost a penny. Definitely not a piece of equipment she wanted to tamper with.

Not after Saturday's incident.

Karan went in search of help. The therapist on duty was in group session with the kids, and though it was the middle of the afternoon on a business day, the only people she could find to help were Margaret the cook in the kitchen, Deputy Doug in the sheriff's substation and Tammy, the registered nurse on duty in the triage center. Unfortunately, no one knew a thing about the printer.

Karan returned to the office and sat at the desk with a frown. She was ready to head home, had been staring at this computer for hours. But Rhonda was expecting these drafts, and Karan didn't want her to make a special trip over only to find they weren't in her box as promised. No,

Karan was going to see this job through to its completion, if for no reason other than to prove she could.

There was another computer station in the office, this one tucked away at a corner desk with a separate printer, scanner, fax combo. She had a similar setup at home.

Would it be possible to print from there? It was only twelve letters, not as if she'd burn up the ink cartridge. Although she wouldn't mind replacing one of those, if necessary. Karan went to take a look and found the system in hibernation mode.

This computer was set up with medical software, but after a little bit of scrolling, she found it still had all the basic office software and internet access. The printer was even on. While she didn't have a flash drive, she could email the letters to herself. At the main desk, she attached the documents to an email and sent them to her online email account.

Once at the other computer, she launched a browser, logged into her email and accessed the files. She opened each one and hit the print button. No problem. While the printer churned out her flawless letters one after the other, she scanned her messages, read one from a sales associate at her favorite high-end department store alerting her that new merchandise had arrived from one of Karan's favorite designers. That was a pleasant little surprise. Maybe she could talk Susanna and Brooke into an outing to the city this weekend.

The last letter ground out from the printer and Karan grabbed the stack of warm paper and delivered it to Rhonda's box that hung on the wall beside the director's door.

Perfect.

CHAPTER ELEVEN

CHARLES SAT IN THE FIRST PEW, leaned forward and closed his eyes. With effort he focused on the silence of the hospital chapel, tried to drown out the frantic beeping of diagnostic equipment, the urgent whispers of his surgical team, the rushing throb of his own pulse as adrenaline kicked in.

He came in here often. Not because he was religious. In fact, the hospital had taken such pains to be nondenominational that the place was rendered fiercely generic. The stained-glass window depicting a woodland scene was at the front of the room where an altar might have been. The glass was lit from within, barely bright enough to chase the shadows into the corners. Yet somehow, the sheer lack of aesthetics lent to the purifying effect of the place.

Not today.

Charles had met the ambulance. A tear in the aortic isthmus. Maybe if the paramedics had detected the trauma earlier…but there had been no specific symptoms and diagnosis had been complicated by the presence of multiple other serious injuries from the accident. It had taken emergency personnel time to discover the partially torn blood vessel.

The adventitia had been intact and, with the nearby structures, had prevented bleed out long enough to get the patient onto the operating table. But not long enough for Charles to repair the damage.

So he'd had to explain to the shocked parents why their eleven-year-old was dead.

"He was riding his bike home from school," the father had said over and over, as if that somehow made a difference.

The boy's mother hadn't been able to speak.

Charles massaged his temples as if he might somehow erase the memory of their shock, his own sense of failure.

If he'd gotten the boy on the table sooner.

If the paramedics hadn't had so much trauma to deal with.

If the driver of the SUV had been paying closer attention.

If the boy hadn't been riding his bike home from school.

Endless recriminations that didn't make one damned bit of difference to parents whose son was on his way to the morgue.

Or to the driver of that SUV, who would live knowing that one split second of distraction had cost a child his future and permanently changed the lives of everyone left behind.

Charles wasn't sure how long he sat there. He only knew that when his cell phone vibrated, he hadn't even come close to making peace with the events of this afternoon.

He glanced at the display, recognized New Hope's number. Connecting the call, he brought the phone to his ear but didn't speak until he'd left the chapel.

"You there, Dr. Steinberg?"

"What's up, Deputy?" Charles wasn't sure why he couldn't talk inside when he was the only one in there. For some reason he didn't feel comfortable.

"Got a situation here you need to know about."

Exactly what he didn't want to deal with right now. Another *situation.* "What's going on?"

The deputy explained about a frozen computer system and a phone call to a service tech, who had networked in and discovered a malicious program. "I called you because I know Dr. Camden is on the way to her office for night appointments and you're on your way out of the hospital. Can you swing by? The tech guy needs someone with administrative access to purge the system otherwise you're going to have a big mess on your hands."

A big mess. As if this day wasn't one already.

Despite the traffic, Charles made it to New Hope in decent time. He was glad he was on emotional autopilot when he pulled into the lot and saw Karan's car.

She was the last thing he wanted to deal with tonight and he couldn't even fault her since he was arriving unscheduled. He headed straight for the substation, where he found Deputy Doug still on the phone with a tech. And Karan.

The instant he saw her standing beside the deputy, looking fresh and stylish and so goddamned poised, he felt that peace he'd been looking for. It washed over him like a wave. Death didn't touch Karan's world. Nothing did. Everything skimmed right across the surface. She didn't deal with death. If she didn't like the headlines in the newspaper, she cancelled the subscription. If she didn't like the tragedy blasting in sound bites, she turned off the television.

Karan didn't deal in real life. Only in indulgence. In the things that didn't make a bit of difference.

She wouldn't have known what the parents of his patient were living today. Wouldn't have had the first clue how powerless Charles felt because he hadn't been able to save a young boy who should have had a full life ahead of him.

Karan didn't let anything get under her skin.

Not even their marriage when it had unraveled. She'd wished him well and moved on to her next husband.

Charles never wanted to live with someone like that, unfeeling, clueless about what she was missing. He didn't want to live like that. And he wasn't. Not with her. Not like her.

Peace.

"Hey, Doc," the deputy said. "Appreciate you coming."

He only nodded. Karan was looking at him strangely, and he didn't have to deal with her. She was Rhonda's problem, and right now he was only tackling one problem at a time. He was glad when she left the room without a word. He hoped she went home.

"What do I need to do?" Charles asked.

The deputy covered the receiver with a hand. "Tech says he'll tell you what he needs but, so you know, we've got a problem."

This one was his to deal with. Taking the portable handset, Charles greeted the tech on the other end and walked to the director's office so he could log on.

With the tech guy's direction, Charles ran through a series of functions on the computer, screen after screen popping open then closing. He focused on the instruction, still unclear about the trouble, but unexpectedly grateful for anything to wrap his brain around, something to give his scattered thoughts an anchor.

"So what's going on?" Charles asked during one of the long silences while he waited for the system to work through some function he didn't understand. "I heard malicious program."

"Spyware," the tech said. "And a worm."

For a moment, Charles could only stare at the computer display, at the bar registering the progress of the program. *Working...working...working.*

"How did this happen? Shouldn't the firewall have caught anything that tried to get through?"

"You've got a secure system, sir. You're safeguarded against pretty much everything and the protection updates automatically twice a day."

"It's functioning properly?"

"Absolutely. That's why the system went down—to prevent the spyware from collecting your data and sending it back to the source. In this case the hacker who wrote the program. Not a real sophisticated one, but it would have done the job."

That sent a rigid chill down Charles's spine. Because New Hope dealt with protected health information, it adhered to all HIPAA compliance requirements and safeguards governing all emergency medical facilities in the State of New York. A violation would cause untold damage.

"What was it trying to collect?" Charles asked.

"Biographical data."

Damn. That would be who was in residence and the exact location of the facility.

Which wasn't made available to the public.

The separate network connections installed here had been a costly safeguard that had been modeled in other emergency shelters. He, Rhonda, the board and the budget committee had all agreed the expense was a basic necessity. Separate networks. One for the residents. One for administrative staff. One to handle sensitive data to protect the residents' identities.

"I didn't think it was possible for a malicious program to access this system," Charles said.

"Only one way it could—it had to be let in."

He sank back in the chair, frowned at the monitor. "I

still don't understand. We set up a station exclusively for medical data and storage. It's supposed to be safe."

"It is. It's a hard setup with only your encrypted medical software and a few necessary basic programs. It's not networked for that exact reason. There's outbound filtering, which is why the system shut down when a rogue program attempted to collect your data." There was a pause on the other end. "The program targeted your system looking for a way in."

Charles heard the concern. "Our system specifically?"

"Yes, sir."

"That spyware program wouldn't have worked on another random system?"

"It was designed to acquire specific data from what I can tell."

Charles shook his head to clear it, understood the significance, and the potential threat to their residents. "How exactly was it *let in?*"

"Looks like through a private email account."

Email? On the med data station? "There isn't an email program on that system. It's only used for the transfer of sensitive and protected data."

And only by trained medical staff contractually employed by New Hope. Volunteers didn't use that computer, and no one else had access.

"Judging by the logs, it seems someone accessed web-based email," the tech explained. "The rogue program was lying in wait, ready to attach itself to a program allowing access on an incoming port. In this case an email from a high-end retailer."

Charles could only stare at the computer, relieved his reactions were still on autopilot. The very last thing he needed was to put them back on manual control. High-end retailer?

No mystery here.

If Karan had had any idea what was good for her, she would have been long gone by the time he wrapped up the call, got the networks running and finished discussing the threat with the deputy.

Obviously not. He found her on the gallery, sitting on the top step, when the best place for her would have been on the other side of the planet.

She glanced up and started right in. "For the record, I was almost out the door when the computer problem started. The deputy asked me to help him check the system in the administrative office so he didn't have to keep running back and forth. Then you came." She eyed him strangely. "Are you okay?"

Concern? Not likely. "Did you use the med data station?"

"Med data station?" She frowned at him. "I'm afraid I don't know what that is."

"It's a computer station in the front office. Not the one on the desk."

Before he finished getting the words out of his mouth, Charles had his answer. Her frown transformed into an expression of horror as she apparently put two and two together.

"Oh, no," she whispered.

"Oh, yes."

Black lashes fluttered shut over clear eyes. "Please tell me I didn't cause…*that*."

"An email from a department store ringing any bells?"

She didn't open her eyes, simply dropped her face into her hands. Shiny hair wisped around her face. He thought she might have shuddered.

Charles wasn't sure what it was about her that suddenly irked him—the remorse, maybe, or the vulnerability from a woman who possessed neither quality. She always landed on her feet because meeting her needs was the only thing important to her.

"To check your email, Karan? Really?"

Definitely a shudder. "I had no idea—"

"What were you even doing on that system?"

She raised her head and looked at him. "Rhonda asked me to draft some letters, but the printer wouldn't print—"

"You broke the printer, too?" This woman was a category five hurricane on two legs. Two long, very shapely legs, and the fact that he noticed angered him to no end.

"No, no." She inhaled deeply. "No, I didn't break the printer. I only used the other computer because I didn't want to start playing with the printer settings and accidentally cause a problem. I was trying to be careful."

"Do us all a favor next time and don't try." The words were out of his mouth before he could think better of them, and once he started, he couldn't seem to stop. "For your information this is an emergency domestic violence shelter—"

"I know—"

"Then think about what that means, Karan. The people who come here need a safe place to go because they're in danger. They're not safe when people compromise security measures by stupidly checking email on the wrong computer."

She paled visibly.

God, he'd blocked out all memory of this feeling, could have lived the rest of his life without ever remembering the heat of sudden anger, as if he couldn't even control what was coming out of his mouth. He hadn't felt this way since being married to this woman.

"Is anyone in danger?" she whispered, as if she was suddenly afraid to breathe.

"I don't have any answers. Deputy Doug is trying to find out who wanted access to that protected data."

"I am so, *so* sorry," she said. "What happens now? You must have procedures in case something like this happens. Please tell me they didn't get any information."

He shook his head, hating himself for not wanting to let her off the hook easily, for wanting to make her understand the importance of what she'd done, for wanting to make her feel *something,* anything at all.

"Why are you bothering to play this game with me?"

"What game?"

"Acting like you care."

She recoiled as if his accusation had been a physical blow. He should have felt remorse. He didn't. That hurt look on her face angered him even more.

"Of course I care. I wouldn't deliberately put anyone at risk. What is wrong with you? Why would you even think that?"

"Because I know you, and you don't care about anyone but yourself."

Her eyes widened. Maybe she was surprised by his bluntness. He certainly was. He felt as if he was standing in the middle of their marriage—the middle of *the end* of their marriage.

"I cared about you." Her admission was no more than a whisper in the night.

"Really? Was that before or after you changed the locks and sent my things to a storage facility?"

Suddenly the hurt in her expression vanished and he saw life signs. The Karan he'd known wasn't going to lie down and take anything for long. She'd come out swinging.

"What choice did I have? You didn't want to fix any-thing. You didn't even want to try to figure out what the problem was. How long did you expect me to wait around until dealing with our marriage was convenient for you?"

"Everything was my fault. Of course it was. Why am I not even surprised to hear that?"

"Not everything, Charles. But at least I tried. You weren't interested. You just ran."

"Of course I ran. You were a bottomless pit. Nothing I did was ever good enough. Every time I walked through the door you were lying in wait with more demands and more of your drama."

"Demands? Drama?" she snapped. "How is wanting to discuss whether I should fix the car or buy a new one *drama?* It's called life where I'm from. Dealing with things as they come up. That's what normal people do."

"No, Karan. Normal people don't turn everyday decisions into theatrical performances. I couldn't even walk through the door without you blasting me with nine thousand things that weren't important. I'd be awake for three days running, making life and death decisions, and you really expect me to care that the dishwasher broke? Everything was urgent to you."

"That's because things usually were by the time you made an appearance. When else was I supposed to address things with you? There were things that needed to be done, decisions that needed to be made. You treated the house like a hotel and me like your assistant. I shouldn't have had to beg you to make time for our life together because you were too busy running."

"I wasn't running. I was working. My residency was demanding, you knew that. You wanted my career as much as I did, so I could keep you in the style you were used to. Dr. and Mrs. Steinberg, remember?"

She waved him off dismissively. "You're ridiculous. I never needed you to keep me. I have a trust fund."

He had no response. She was right. She hadn't needed his income. Or him. His efforts hadn't been good enough, which she'd proven when she'd gone on to marry Dr. Oncology, who was already well established in his career.

He stared at her, struggling to control himself against emotions he shouldn't be feeling. Not so long after the fact. His only consolation was that he wasn't the only one struggling right now, no matter how dismissive she acted.

He could see the stark expression on her face and the way she held herself so rigidly, as if she'd been carved from ivory. The simple fact she hadn't stood told him he'd penetrated, made an impact.

He knew her that well. And, God help him, he didn't care.

He only cared about not feeling this way again, not having to deal with this woman. Ever.

"Here's what we're going to do, Karan. I respect that you're working with Dr. Camden, but I think it's obvious you don't belong in this facility. You want to shop so I'm going to reassign you to work in New Hope's thrift store. That should be more to your liking and still fulfill the conditions of the court. Is your email on file?"

She nodded, still inhaling deeply, looking as if she was having trouble catching her breath.

"I'll make the arrangements and email you the details."

She rose slowly to her feet. "I'm sorry."

He wanted to tell her that he didn't need her apologies. That her words wouldn't keep their residents safe.

But he needed to control this urge to lash out, to win the battle with her regardless of the cost. He wanted to retreat to that peaceful place. "You already apologized."

"I'm not talking about the computer. I'm talking about your patient. Whoever he or she was. I'm sorry you couldn't help."

CHAPTER TWELVE

KARAN CAUGHT THE PHONE ON THE second ring and glanced at the display.

A. Bryan Kowalski. The phone line to the house Karan had grown up in still bore her dad's name. Her mother would be on the other end of the line. Karan didn't even need to glance at the mantel clock to know it was too late to be picking up this call. Not tonight. That scene with Charles had consumed the last bit of energy she had. She simply had nothing left.

"I'll call you in the morning, Mom," she whispered to the handset before returning it to its base. "Hope all is well."

The answering machine clicked on, but her mother didn't leave a message.

Karan knew what that meant.

All was not well.

Sure enough, the ring tone from her cell phone started its jaunty little tune.

Karan stood, momentarily paralyzed until it finally stopped.

The land line rang again. This time when the answering machine clicked on, her mother's voice said, "I don't know what you're doing, Karan, but I've tried your cell and you're not picking up there, either. I didn't think you could drive, so I don't know where you'd be at this hour, but you're obviously too busy for me. Call me when you decide to pick up your messages. I want to talk to you."

Karan still didn't move, didn't have it in her. She couldn't even bring herself to feel anything. Not relief that her mother hadn't had some accident and genuinely needed help. Not guilt that she wasn't willing to pick up the phone. Not even sadness that the loneliness of her mother's life was obviously occurring to her tonight, upsetting her, angering her.

When her mother got angry, she needed someone to blame.

Karan knew it was the alcohol skewing things, but she simply couldn't be that person for her mother tonight. Blaming Karan wouldn't make her mother feel any better. Then she'd get even angrier.

Karan had her fill of dealing with anger tonight.

From the man who'd once claimed to love her.

The cell phone rang again. Her mother would likely leave a message this time, more scathing as her temper escalated, but the cell phone was kinder because Karan couldn't hear what was said since the message rolled into voice mail.

Karan waited for the land line to ring again, questioning her decision, staring into her quiet living room, the sun fading beyond the windows that made up one wall. The mountain slope was shadowed beyond the porch, a magnificent vista in the daytime, a void at night. No need for any kind of window treatments because once the sun set the blackness would be complete.

Wouldn't a good daughter pick up the telephone?

Probably. But Karan wasn't good at anything today. Tomorrow her mother wouldn't remember one bit of this. Not whatever was upsetting her. Not her belief that Karan was ignoring her calls and purposely not picking up the phone.

The phone didn't ring again.

Unfortunately, the damage had already been done. The silence seemed to echo louder than the ringing had. Scooping the phone off its base, Karan depressed the speed dial and speaker function then headed into her bedroom. She flipped on the overhead light, vanquished the shadows then dropped down onto her bed to stretch out. She willed herself to take deep, even breaths like those she applied in her yoga/Pilates classes.

Only skill would help her relax past the effects of this day. Skill and diversion. Life had evolved into one never-ending nightmare. Three hundred and sixty hours hadn't sounded all that bad in the courtroom. It felt like an eternity now.

"Hi, Karan." Susanna's upbeat voice shattered the silence, echoing faintly over the telephone speaker.

"I've been exiled." The very act of talking calmed her.

"You've been what?"

"I've been *exiled*. Charles banned me from New Hope."

"Can he do that?"

"He did do that. He has decided the residents are safer without me on the property. I got confirmation via email on my BlackBerry before I even got home. He's putting me to work in the thrift store because I like to shop. I'm feeling the need to drink a glass of champagne to celebrate my spectacular failure. That can't be good. What do you think?"

There was a snort on the other end. "If memory serves, drinking is what got you into this mess in the first place."

Memory did not serve, but Karan wasn't going to point that out. She simply didn't want to risk alienating anyone else in her life. And especially not Susanna.

"Not drinking. *Driving.* But since I can't drive now there won't be any problem."

There was silence on the other end, and Karan sensed her friend didn't appreciate the attempt at humor. But she also knew better than to ask Karan what she'd done to deserve exile. The very best of friends. All she asked was, "You okay?"

Karan considered that. How was it possible that she could still feel hurt by Charles? Didn't their divorce count for anything? There should be a statute of limitations on hurt. "I will be. Thanks for asking."

"Want to talk about it?"

"Nothing to talk about. Charles Steinberg is an idiot. That's why I divorced him."

"Being alone isn't driving you to drink, is it?" she asked. "Things were…difficult with Patrick."

Difficult was a mild understatement, but leave it to Susanna to get to the heart of matters. Karan loved that about her. Relied upon her ability, too. But she also couldn't deny alternately hating the way Susanna went straight for the jugular when she thought the time was right. With a surgeon's skill and no anesthetic.

Karan wasn't sure how she felt right now.

Divorce was never fun and she was becoming quite the expert. Divorcing Charles had been awful, but she'd been hurt and angry and beyond ready to stop feeling horrible with the constant reminders of how much her husband, who'd vowed to love, honor and cherish her till death, didn't care anymore.

Patrick was…different. She'd liked him. A lot. They enjoyed doing things together. Socially. Leisurely. They were together with career goals and she enjoyed assisting him with his practice. She'd decorated his offices, hired his staff.

But she hadn't loved Patrick. Not the way she'd loved Charles. She'd married Patrick because he would be the perfect husband. And he was. Handsome, successful, ambitious, intelligent, established, companionable. He understood the importance of networking, the nuances of social and political connections and their impact on his career.

Karan had been very content in their marriage.

Patrick, too. Until meeting the British physician who headed the research of some neurological surgical equipment manufacturer. Then their companionable marriage hadn't withstood the test of a woman who could "take his breath away." Karan definitely hadn't seen that coming.

"I love you, Karan," he'd said. *"And I know you love me, but we're not in love with each other. We never were. Life is too short to settle for being comfortable."*

She'd been happy with comfortable and wondered if the attraction he felt for his British physician would ultimately evolve into the kind of lasting love he seemed to think it would. He'd claimed to want to be one of those elderly people hobbling along, still holding hands, still in love because they'd weathered the ups and downs of life together.

Karan had wanted to be angry with him for ruining a perfectly good partnership. She should have been, too, but hadn't quite managed it in the long months since he'd moved out. He'd handled the difficult situation with such integrity that it had been hard to rally much more than hurt that he'd felt he was settling with her. And nurse a bruised ego. No denying that.

"Is it Patrick?" Susanna prompted.

"If he wants to be a little old person holding hands with his soul mate then I hope he finds what he's looking for."

"That sounds noble, but you're out of sorts."

"Don't worry about me, Suze." Karan exhaled a heavy

sigh that didn't take any of her tension with it. "I don't even have alcohol in the house. Well, Marynia might keep something on hand to cook with. I have no clue. I'd have to search the cabinets."

"Don't bother. You could probably get plowed on mouthwash with your sugar issues. Besides, drinking isn't the way to go. You know that better than I do."

"No argument there."

"Then talk to me." Susanna sounded so serious.

Karan closed her eyes, blocked out the sight of her beautiful bedroom. She'd remodeled after deciding to spend some time here after the divorce, had tried to bring the life she'd loved in Manhattan to Bluestone Mountain. Appropriately, she'd gone with an urban contemporary, Italian leather platform bed, tone on tone neutrals and a lovely birch wood. She'd needed a change, she'd told herself, and creating a new environment had kept her busy, for a while at least.

"I'm going to miss this place when I sell it." She tried to summon up some enthusiasm for redecorating another house, couldn't manage even a spark. "Not Bluestone, of course, but this house. I really outdid myself this time."

"You did," Susanna agreed. "But you're not supposed to make life-altering decisions within a year of a traumatic event."

Susanna would know as she'd made a second career out of learning how to deal with traumatic events in a healthy manner.

"With real estate what it is, it might take a while to move this place. It could be over a year by then. You'll let me stay with you when I come to visit, won't you?"

"Of course. You can add on an in-law suite. Or take Brooke's room. To hear her tell it, she won't be back after leaving for college. I'll be lucky if she visits for Christmas."

"She'll come home again. Trust me. She's spreading her wings and discovering who she is, which is exactly what a beautiful young woman should be doing. We were beautiful and young once, too, doing the same thing."

"Well, then, sell the damned house and come stay with me because Brandon's not far behind Brooke. It'll be like we're rooming in college again."

Karan opened her eyes and felt a little better. That was exactly what best friends were for. Susanna knew Karan would never get away with staying in a hotel on visits when her mother still lived in town. But she could get away with staying with her best friend and her mother wouldn't give her too much grief.

"I'm in hell, Susanna. And, for the record, Skip isn't here if you were worried about him."

"You are so not funny. I'm not worried."

"Liar. You worry more than anyone I've ever met."

A pause. "I am worried about you."

"Ha. What did I tell you?"

"Why don't you come over here tonight? We're overdue for a slumber party and I might be able to talk Brooke into watching a movie with us if you're here. I've only got six weeks until she leaves. I want to make the most of every moment."

"I suppose I could walk—"

"Don't be silly. Brooke will leap at the chance to take the car. She's still put out with me that I won't send her off to college with one."

"I understand entirely. *I'm* still put out with you about that. Poor girl."

Susanna gave an exasperated huff on the other end of the line. "Don't start on me or you will walk. She's a freshman. She can't have a car. How is this remotely my fault?"

"You're the one making her live in the dorms, remember?"

"She doesn't need an apartment at eighteen. Please. A few controls in place until she gets the hang of independence is entirely appropriate. Besides, I don't want her missing out on the whole college experience."

"A dozen girls sharing one six-stall, four-shower bathroom is an experience she can live without, I'm sure."

"Four roommates, including her, two bathrooms, and one common area. Dorms have improved since we were in college."

"Thank goodness. Seems like forever ago, doesn't it, Suze? I've unloaded two husbands and you buried one. But at least you have two wonderful kids to show for your effort."

Another sigh. Karan could practically see Susanna, curled up in one of her comfy chairs, abandoning any thoughts of accomplishing anything with what remained of the night. Usually Susanna folded laundry or cleaned the kitchen or engaged in some other domestic-type task to rationalize her time spent on the phone. But tonight she wasn't winded from rushing around multitasking. Tonight she was devoting every speck of her attention to Karan, probably listening to hear what she wasn't saying.

Susanna must *really* be worried.

"Are you ever going to get around to talking about Charles?" she finally asked. "Or are we going to keep touching on everything that pops into your head to avoid discussing him?"

Ah, Suze and the scalpel again.

"Not much to say."

"How's that? The man is back in your life. And not

being particularly civil, it sounds like. I'm rather annoyed, to be honest. I may have to visit the hospital."

That got Karan's attention, and she sat up, tucking her legs beneath her. "Oh, that's exactly what I need. Then he'll exile me from New Hope entirely. Thanks, but no thanks. You know Wannabe Jenny is itching for a reason to send me to jail. *No passing Go. No collecting two hundred dollars.*"

Susanna groaned. "You've left a trail of bodies in your wake. That's the real problem here."

All too true, unfortunately. "It's my gift."

"Spare me."

"It's not as if I try to make people angry."

"It's not as if you *don't* try."

Also too true. But Karan had always been focused on her goals. And to achieve them, she'd had to make choices. Sometimes the choices were easy. As when she'd used her influence to stack the cheerleading team with competent people, trained and capable of bringing the team to the state championship. A team's performance was a direct reflection of its captain, and people like Wannabe Jenny were collateral damage.

Sometimes the choices were much harder. As when she'd finally had to admit her marriage to Charles was over. There had been nothing left for her to do to get him to face the problem.

She'd tried everything, and failed. She'd been left standing in a room filled with people, making excuses, when each and every one of their friends and loved ones knew that Charles didn't care enough to show up when she asked him to. She'd had to make a choice then—to end the misery or let the situation degenerate further and the fallout get more humiliating, more hurtful… But she couldn't admit that. Not even to Susanna.

"Okay, Susanna. I won't deny it. I can be brutal. There, I've said it. Are you appeased?"

"You don't have to appease me," she shot back. "And I don't consider Charles one among the trail of bodies you've left behind. He was responsible for his half of your marriage. Do you have any clue why he's being so horrible?"

"You mean that he obviously hasn't forgiven himself for letting me get away?"

"Karan."

"Or because I seem to be dismantling all his hard work at New Hope piece by piece? And interrupting his fishing trips. Let's not forget that. It might explain the hostility."

"Honestly." Susanna huffed. "Be serious. That's exactly what I'm talking about—the way you two divorced. I know things were difficult with Patrick, but at least you both had closure. You resolved the situation with respect for each other and your marriage. You never had that with Charles."

Another mild understatement. Patrick might have been stupid to give up their perfectly companionable marriage, but at least he'd been responsible for his behavior.

He could have involved himself with his British physician before ending their marriage. But he'd made sure Karan and their joint obligations were cared for. And she couldn't complain since she'd made out very well in the divorce. He'd handled the situation with typical Patrick integrity and thoroughness when he'd decided to take a shot at a life of hand-holding. Poor man had no clue what he was in for. Love hurt.

Wasn't that a song?

By comparison, her divorce from Charles had been Pompeii. "You've got a point," she admitted. "But I'm not entirely sure why the man would be put out with me so long after the fact. He forced me into leaving. You know how long I waited for him to come to his senses before even talking with an attorney."

"I know. But I also know he probably doesn't see things the way you do. Skip could positively stun me with his logic."

"Well, I'm not sure what else I was supposed to do. He wouldn't even discuss the issues. All he did was hide in his residency and blame the long hours he had to spend in the hospital for not being involved in our life. He managed to get the day off to show up in court."

"There we are again," Susanna said. "That's exactly what I'm talking about. How many years has it been—five almost? And you still get worked up discussing him. He could be doing the exact same thing."

"I am not worked up about him." She might have let him suck her in earlier, but she'd managed to get a grip.

"Could have fooled me. I'm only saying you both could be facing the aftereffects of your divorce. That's all. You used to be in love. Maybe seeing each other again is bringing some unresolved feelings to the surface. It's a thought."

"Fair enough." Which is precisely why people shouldn't let love around marriage. Susanna wouldn't want to hear that, though.

Karan and Charles had loved each other once, in that wild, fearless way of young people. Tonight had proven that love also made things messy and hurtful and let otherwise rational people fall prey to their emotional states, which could be so volatile when chemistry and hormones were involved.

Patrick had been very right about that, which was why Karan had chosen *not* to marry for love the second time around. She'd shopped around until she'd found the perfect husband. Marriage was challenging enough without throwing in uncontrollable variables into the mix.

"Maybe Charles needs a reminder that you did care once," Susanna suggested. "You've got enough on your plate without him making life more difficult. That's selfish. Your involvement at New Hope is a limited engagement."

"Three hundred and thirty-eight hours and counting. I logged every second I spent in that place today including the time it took Charles to exile me. Should have gotten time and a half for that."

Susanna completely missed the attempt at humor. "So, are you coming over? We won't have time to watch a movie unless you get here soon. The kids can sleep in because it's summer, but I've got to work in the morning."

Karan glanced around her stylish bedroom, tried to see the streamlined photographs clustered on the walls from an up-and-coming artist in Soho, the floor-to-ceiling windows where twilight was already shadowing the mountainside, but saw only another long, lonely night.

"Please tell my goddaughter to heist the car and play chauffeur. I'll make it *very* worth her while."

"Trust me. She knows it." Susanna let out an unladylike snort of laughter that managed to change absolutely everything about Karan's mood.

"That's because my goddaughter is a smart girl." Karan hopped off the bed, suddenly ready to tackle the night ahead.

CHAPTER THIRTEEN

CHARLES HAD KNOWN THE INSTANT he sent Karan off property he'd have to deal with Rhonda. His reasoning was solid, but he wasn't convinced she'd want to hear his side of the story.

But after speaking at length with the deputy and getting details about who'd created the malicious program in an attempt to infiltrate New Hope's sensitive data, Charles had all the facts he needed to defend his position.

Rhonda showed up in the office about an hour after he did carrying a plate and silverware. "Hope you don't mind. Margaret was fixing dinner. Total zoo at the crisis center. Haven't had a bite to eat all day, and I'm in session so I'll miss dinner."

Pushing away from the desk, he vacated the chair and motioned for her to sit. "Come on, enjoy your meal. Smells good, whatever it is."

"Thanks. Chicken and dumplings. Comfort food. Perfect for my mood today." She settled herself and dug in.

Folding his arms over his chest, Charles stared at her. "Looks good."

"If you're hungry, you should grab some. Margaret always makes enough for an army, but there won't be anything left after she serves dinner. Have I mentioned lately how happy I am with that particular hire?"

"You and everyone else around here. Did the deputy fill you in on the spyware investigation?"

"I haven't been updated since this morning," she said around a bite.

"The police techs were able to track the program to its source. IP address leads to where Amy's estranged husband works. Apparently, he's involved with computers. Not sure what he does."

Rhonda leaned back in the chair with the fork poised at her lips. "I can't say I'm surprised. But they're sure he didn't get our location?"

"Our security system stopped outgoing data. Another good expense. But what happens now? Do we need to transfer Amy and the boys to another facility as a precaution?"

Rhonda nodded. "I hate to see them leave since they were getting settled, but we don't have a choice. If her husband is already looking our way, we don't take chances. And it's actually a good thing."

"How's that?"

"Her attorney will have something to take to the judge to extend the terms of the injunction for protection."

That would be another protective measure in place, but while there was no public information available about New Hope's address, this emergency shelter was a physical location in the outskirts of town. Victims of domestic violence didn't vanish off the planet when they came here. New Hope had modeled its security after other long-standing, time-tested programs, but there were no guarantees.

"With everyone who comes and goes around here, this location might not be public, but it's not exactly top secret."

Rhonda set down the fork and lifted her gaze. "You know as well as I do that we're nothing without our resources. The people who come and go provide those resources. Amy and the boys will relocate to Albany or

Peekskill. Not optimum, but not that far away from her family. Right now their safety is primary."

Charles nodded. "I think we can be more selective about who comes on site."

"So we're finally getting around to what's really bugging you." Rhonda abandoned dinner and steepled her fingers in front of her. "The alternative sentence program."

"People who are in trouble with the law don't strike me as the best people to trust with our location."

"I won't argue that. But with the proper controls, we're not only filling the holes we have here but assisting other folks who need help in the process."

"And what exactly is Karan offering New Hope?"

Rhonda hopped up, pulled a stack of papers from her in-box on the wall and handed it to him. "I haven't quite nailed it yet, but I'm getting warmer."

He didn't have to glance down to know what he held. "The business correspondence she was printing for you."

"For *New Hope.* Take a look. Not only are those letters professional and articulate but they're worded expertly and delicately to encourage people to continue sponsoring us. Your ex-wife has a master's degree in public relations."

"I was aware of that," he said drily. "For the record, she has zero experience. Never worked a real job in her life."

"Neat trick if you can do it." Rhonda smiled. "*I* couldn't have written these letters nearly as well. I mean, I'm gracious and professional, but these are so far out of my league that I'm almost embarrassed. We're setting up templates so we can use these letters from now on. We don't have the funds to pay someone to produce these. Not yet, anyway. That's something Karan has provided."

"Fair enough, but I'm not willing to concede my point. We've got residents transferring out of this facility because of her error. She was using email on the med data station."

"That was my fault. Karan hasn't been properly trained. You know as well as I do the orientation workshops are filled with all the pertinent basic information. I plunked her down in front of a computer and told her to have at it."

He was not okay with Rhonda's defense, or with the fact that his anger was still simmering beneath the surface, waiting to flare the way it had last night.

He shouldn't be feeling anything.

"You can't take that on yourself," he said. "What do you psychotherapists call it—personal accountability? If Karan had serviceable skills, you wouldn't be trying to outthink the kind of trouble she can get into around here."

"She does have serviceable skills. You're holding the product of one in your hand." Rhonda sank into the chair, thoughtful. "I'll send her through orientation—"

"Absolutely not. It costs money to train these people and she's only going to be here for a short time. It's a total waste of resources. Particularly if we decide the alternative sentencing program isn't working out."

Rhonda didn't respond. Instead, she starting playing with the food on her plate, taking another bite and chewing slowly. Charles knew exactly what she was doing—buying herself time to think up another argument.

He scanned a letter, had no choice but to agree with her assessment. The letter was cordial, professional and written by someone with an obvious skill for getting what she wanted. No surprises there. Karan had a long history of networking. It was what she lived for.

"It's a good letter," he said. "I agree with you about that, but I don't think a stack of these is worth the risk."

"We could also argue that without Karan's mistake, we'd have no clue Amy's husband was looking for her and getting quite clever about it. But we do know now and can take evasive maneuvers to protect her and the boys."

Charles couldn't argue that, either. He set the letters on the desk.

"Listen, Charles. Will it help if I give you my word that if this doesn't pan out for any reason, I'll drop the program? Chief Sloan can find some other place to implement alternative sentencing with his so-called special cases."

He considered that, didn't want to unnecessarily criticize a colleague he'd come to respect a great deal. "I'd say yes, except I'm not entirely comfortable with your partiality. You said you didn't want my opinions coloring your views about Karan, but it seems that you're swinging in the opposite direction and cutting her more slack than she deserves."

"You think I'm overcompensating?" Rhonda eyed him hard. "Are you sure this is really about Karan's mistakes? I'm sensing a lot more going on here, and I'm usually pretty good at sensing that sort of stuff since I make a living at it."

"What does that mean?"

"It means you don't want Karan here. Obviously you two didn't part on the best of terms. I understand that. If I'd had any clue about your history with her, I'd never have agreed to take her on. But Charles, you do realize I have her in session, right? I'm privy to a lot more than you think. I'm asking that you trust me to do my job."

He couldn't argue. He did have more emotion happening here than he should have. So much more. That wasn't Rhonda's fault. But once Karan was gone, he wouldn't be feeling all this anger anymore. Life would return to normal.

"I'm not questioning your ability." He sounded completely calm. "Please be clear about that. But you're handling Karan differently because I have a history with her."

"I could say the very same about you. We've been

working side by side since the inception of New Hope. I've never once seen you act unfairly, even in the face of some big snafus with staff, with contractors, with licensing. I've respected your patience and tact in handling all these situations. Even admired the way you dealt with that woman from the inspector's office." She gave a short laugh. "I'd have wrung that one's neck. Yet you thought the best way to handle Karan was to pack her off to work at the thrift store."

"It's the perfect place for her, trust me on this. It's a store, and she's made a science out of shopping. She's no less skilled than I am in the O.R. Maybe even more because she's been at it longer."

Rhonda narrowed her gaze. "If you're trying to be funny, you're not even coming close."

Silence echoed.

He wasn't getting off so easily. He could tell by the look she leveled at him. "I would think the fact that Karan's trying to identify some difficult issues might mean something to you. If for no reason other than basic human compassion. Forget that she was once your wife."

Here he'd been under the impression that psychotherapists always answered questions with questions. Mistake.

But he had no defense. He had wondered what was going on with Karan, hadn't bothered to find out. He'd let his curiosity die a natural death and kept trying to forget about her until he had no choice but to deal with her.

"I know you care about helping people," he said, "so I'm asking you not to pass judgment on me and the way I feel about Karan. You're right. We didn't part on the best of terms."

"I'm not passing judgment. I'm trying to figure out how to handle the situation effectively. That's my right. Remember, you're not my patient. Karan is."

He knew better than to respond. Smiling, funny, usually professional Rhonda had her back up. Because of him.

"So we have a problem," she continued. "You can't send Karan anywhere because she's *my* patient."

"That sounds so dire. Is there something Karan's dealing with I should know about?"

Rhonda stonewalled him with a glower.

"I'm not asking you to break confidentiality." He shrugged. "It doesn't matter anyway. I just wondered."

"Really? I'm wondering something, too," she said in a tone he'd never heard before as she stood and collected her plate.

"What's that?"

She met his gaze and arched an eyebrow skeptically. "If it doesn't matter, then why are you wondering?"

With that she headed toward the door. He watched her leave. Damned psychotherapists. Whoever said they weren't real doctors? Those leading questions could open veins.

KARAN HAD KNOWN THAT SHOPPING at New Hope Thrift Store would not be in the same league as a trip to Bergdorf Goodman. Or any other store she'd ever had the privilege of shopping in. The sum total of the entire showroom didn't equal what she'd spent on the foyer during her recent remodeling.

Mismatched glassware sold for ten cents apiece.

Paperback books with lots of life left sold for fifty cents while hardcover books went for a whole dollar.

Gently used clothing sold for anywhere from a quarter for a pair of used socks to a pricey five dollars for designer jeans.

Then there were sofas and recliners priced between

ten and twenty-five dollars, depending on condition. All furniture prices were negotiable.

Karan knew because she'd been pricing these treasures, thanks to Charles Steinberg. Curse his black soul. He wanted to make her run screaming from New Hope and the whole alternative sentencing program. And while she wouldn't deny that jail was looking better and better with the way things had been going, to hell with Charles Steinberg.

He thought she couldn't handle pricing some trinkets? True, her secret hope to make him feel bad may have backfired in a big, messy way, but she would not give this man the satisfaction of thinking she couldn't handle whatever he threw her way. He had such a low opinion of her abilities, and she was determined to prove him wrong. So when some random man showed up and asked for her help, a power lifter by the looks of him and apparently well-liked by the other volunteer, she'd agreed without even asking what he needed.

She should have asked.

Now she was sitting in the passenger side of a large truck with no air-conditioning, or any doors that didn't slide for that matter. This vehicle creaked and groaned and bucked so hard over speed bumps and potholes that Karan was convinced she would hit the roof and wind up concussed. *If* she didn't fall out of the open doorway and land on the side of the road with the way Tom, who was indeed a competitive power lifter, whipped around corners.

Knowing her luck, she'd wind up in Charles's operating room, and he'd put an end to her once and for all.

"I did everything humanly possible to save her..."

Yeah, right.

So Karan clung for dear life to the overhead handle as they drove toward a suburb in the valley, where a donation collection had been scheduled. She reminded herself that penance wasn't supposed to be pleasant. Community service was penance for her poor decision to get behind the wheel after a toast.

Exile to New Hope's thrift store was penance for jeopardizing the safety of everyone in the shelter because she'd emailed her letters to the wrong computer.

Driving in this truck was penance for trying to prove herself to Charles Steinberg when she should have kept pricing trinkets and gotten into the spirit of a thrift store.

Raising money for a good cause.

How come she kept forgetting the part about the good cause? Now there was a question for her journal.

Tom chatted nonstop. "You wouldn't believe some of the crazy things people donate."

No, likely Karan wouldn't.

"Usually it's clothes and small appliances. Stuff that people have lying around taking up space. But sometimes we luck out with really good stuff. Few months back, someone put a commercial-grade elliptical machine outside. Couldn't believe it. Was practically brand-new with the instruction manuals and everything." He flashed a charming grin. "That's why I need you. To help me get some of this stuff in the truck."

As if *she* could help *him* lift a commercial-grade elliptical machine.

"I bought that one myself." He paused, waiting for a response.

"Sounds as if you got quite a bargain."

He nodded then was off and running with the conversation again. "We send the notices out in the mail a good two weeks in advance. Gives people time to get their donations ready, but not long enough to forget we're coming. Not a bad deal, actually. They get the stuff to the street and we pick it up. Saves them from making a trip to the collection center. That's convenient. Especially for the bigger stuff."

She nodded.

"It has to have the purple tag on it," he explained. "We schedule the collections for the days there isn't trash service. Sometimes you can hardly tell the difference between the two. That's why the purple tag is so important. We know it's ours."

She wondered what he'd think to arrive at her house on collection day after she put every stick of furniture by the mailbox. Everything. She wouldn't need any of it since she was selling the house and moving far, *far* away. Might as well support a good cause.

There, she'd remembered.

But how much would the volunteers ask for her five-thousand dollar Italian leather platform bed? Would that go for a cool thirty bucks or would they let it go for less?

When they finally arrived in a residential suburb with a secure entry, the guard in the gatehouse apparently expected them and waved them through. The electronic gate ground open and Tom drove into a neighborhood with nicely maintained lawns and roomy houses, six models that were variations of the same design obviously built by a single builder.

She never understood why builders didn't use different architects so developments didn't look so cookie-cutter. If not for the numbers on the identical mailboxes and the street signs on each corner, they could have been driving in circles on the same streets and Karan would have had no clue. Tom seemed to know exactly where he was going, though, and he slowed the truck and ground to the first stop in front of a mailbox.

He left the truck idling and instructed her to climb into the back. "You're the perfect person to collect with. That's why I asked you to help. Small, so you can get around inside."

Wouldn't her personal trainer be thrilled to hear that?

"I'll toss the stuff in to you," he continued. "You don't need to be too fussy about where it goes, just use a little sense to make sure things are where they won't get broken."

He hopped out of the truck, and Karan slid between the seats into the cavernous back, wishing she'd known what she'd signed on for in her haste to get out of the thrift store. At least she could have dressed for grunt labor. As it was, her cropped pants and strappy sandals weren't exactly ideal for mountain climbing over donation bags and boxes.

It was stifling back here, which didn't make much sense to her given the cab of the truck was wide-open. When Tom pulled the large back doors open, some air did get through, thankfully.

He was right about one thing: the donations ran the gamut. Of course there were bags upon bags filled with clothing.

There were microwave ovens that she struggled to push against a wall on one side of the truck. Small furnishings that she made homes for on the other. A crib and toddler bed some child must have outgrown. An ottoman covered in dog fur. A particle-board television stand missing a few screws.

Out of the truck. Back into the truck.

Into gear for a short ride.

Jerking to the next stop.

Back out of the truck to start the process all over again.

"You can stay in the back if you want," Tom finally said on the zillionth trip. "There aren't any seat belts, so you don't have to keep getting back into the seat."

Oh, yes, she did.

He might be getting his daily workout back there, hefting junk her way, but he had to close the doors after each stop, so the junk didn't slide into the street. With the doors closed, the interior felt like a sauna. Otherwise she would stay in the rear. The thought of being recognized in a truck picking up what appeared to be garbage was daunting. Not that she cared what people thought. Helping New Hope was a good cause. But Karan didn't think her mother would feel the same way.

"I'm good," she lied. "Getting my exercise. I don't have a commercial-grade elliptical at home."

He chuckled. "That's the spirit. Hope the volunteers at the store are as good-natured. Lots to sort through today. We don't have to do that part."

Who in their right mind would choose to do *this*?

"This is your job?" Karan couldn't resist asking. It was only June and she'd have sweat off five pounds by the time they finished. She couldn't fathom August or the dead of winter with six feet of snow on the ground.

The thought of spending eight hours a day in this truck, rain or shine, was enough to send a chill up her spine—the only thing chilly on her right now.

"Nope. Today's my day off." Tom shook his head. "Get two days off a week—Sunday and Tuesday. Don't mind sharing one."

"So you're a volunteer?" she asked incredulously. *Not* ordered by the court to help. "You do this for fun?"

He smiled pleasantly. He was a very pleasant man. "It's a good cause. Not everyone is comfortable with driving the truck. Hopefully we'll add a few more drivers. Start adding some shifts if we can drum up more donations."

"I certainly hope so." For his sake. "So what do you do

for a living when you're not driving a truck on your day off?"

He flashed that charming grin. "Drive a route truck for a uniform company."

CHAPTER FOURTEEN

CHARLES STAYED IN THE OFFICE making phone calls to arrange for Amy's transfer while Rhonda spoke with Amy and the boys in between her sessions. He was glad for the opportunity to cool off.

Rhonda had been annoyed, no question. Not such an uncommon occurrence between colleagues. He actually found the fact that they hadn't had any run-ins during all these months of working with nonstop intensity more surprising.

Still, he'd come to respect her opinion. He'd watched her interact with people in so many capacities while getting New Hope up and running—with potential employees during the interview process, volunteers in screenings and training, with residents during group sessions.

Not only had he gained more of an understanding of her field, but a high regard for her personally. Yet she thought he was the one with an issue here. While he wanted to discount her opinion as nonsense, he couldn't.

Not when so much anger had surfaced after Karan had shown up. He'd been surprised by her situation, interested even, but not compassionate.

Rhonda had been right about that.

And even Karan had managed that much for him.

"I'm not talking about the computer," she'd said. *"I'm talking about your patient. Whoever he or she was. I'm sorry you couldn't help."*

That she knew him so well had angered him more.

He'd been at peace with the past. Or thought he'd been. But now he had to ask what his reaction might have been if someone other than Karan had been responsible for burning popcorn. He didn't see anger as part of the equation. Inconvenience aside, the situation hadn't been a big deal. Unfortunate timing, definitely. But accidents happened. He knew that.

The computer situation was a more serious matter.

But Rhonda did have a few points there, as well. An hour ago he hadn't wanted to hear about them. Even now it took a lot of effort to step back and admit her points might be valid. Why?

"So what did you work out for Amy?" Rhonda asked after her return. The air between them was still not quite right.

"Albany. Peekskill is almost at capacity, and I felt better knowing they'd have more eyes watching out for them."

Rhonda inclined her head. "Albany is a good program. I've worked with the head of counseling outreach there before, and they're doing good things. When?"

"Already on the way. Less than an hour, I'd say."

"One of us needs to be on-site when they arrive. A director will have to sign off. I'm due in group soon, but I can start calling the therapists to see if one can cover."

He shook his head. "Not necessary. I'll stay."

She was still eying him in that probing, psychotherapist fashion. Trying to read his mind. Or maybe she didn't really need to. She seemed to see right through him. "You're sure?"

"I've still got plenty to do, and I'm not due in surgery until eight in the morning. I've got it."

"Okay."

He didn't need any mind-reading skills to know she was

waging some internal debate. Probably gauging his mood and considering whether or not confrontation would get results.

"I won't go off all over you," he said. "I promise."

That got a grin, a reassurance that they were heading back down the right track.

"Okay, I'll take you at your word. We've got to come up with some resolution about our alternative sentence."

Not *Karan,* or *ex-wife.* He almost smiled back. Almost. "What do you have in mind?"

"Obviously I'll address the situation with her. Our residents' safety can't be jeopardized for any reason. If she wants to continue being a part of our program, then she needs to understand that. The next step is orientation. Your point about the expense is valid since she is going to be here for only a limited time. The court has already absorbed the cost of the screening process. That leaves covering the training material, and we wrote it. I've got every bit on my laptop. I can put her through a personal version of the class for free."

"When can you possibly find time for that? You're even busier than I am."

She shrugged. "I'll figure it out. Karan's flexible."

What struck Charles the most was Rhonda's commitment to seeing this program through. She believed so much in helping people. He did, too. But his way of helping was diametrically opposed to hers. Diagnosing and repairing a person physically didn't demand he have faith in anything but his own skill and knowledge of the body. He didn't have to put his faith in someone, believe in someone, then help them figure out how to heal on their own time frame. He thought of her story about mentally ill John. Sometimes the healing was never quite completed. Life versus the quality of life. Two sides of the same coin.

Rhonda's work struck him as much more courageous.

"You really think Karan has something to offer New Hope?" he asked.

"I'm sure of it." Her confidence made his lack so glaring. "She hasn't figured it out yet, either, but we're working on it. We'll get there. I'm confident."

She echoed his earlier reassurance, and he was willing to go a step further. To believe. If not in Karan, in Rhonda's assessment of the situation.

"Maybe she should attend an orientation. Like you said, the court has already defrayed some of the cost by screening her, and it's not as if we have guarantees about how long any of our volunteers stays with us."

"True enough," she said graciously. "We'll continue to stick to your schedule if you'll continue to provide it."

Boundaries he'd put in place, complicating all of their lives because he hadn't wanted to see his ex. He might not have a lot of answers right now, but the ones he had he didn't like at all.

"Listen, Rhonda, I know you don't want my opinions about Karan. But just know that I heard what you said before. I've been thinking about it. My past with Karan might not be as in the past as I thought."

In an instant, her usual high-beam smile was in place, brightening her whole face and reassuring him they had moved beyond the trouble. "Thank you for sharing that. And because you're a friend and not a patient, I'd like to share something with you. If you want to hear it."

"Shoot."

"Avoidance. Look it up on the internet." Then she spun on her heels and was gone.

KARAN WALKED THROUGH THE BACK hallway of New Hope and headed straight for the kitchen. She intended to wait there for Rhonda, hoping to avoid Charles entirely. She simply couldn't handle her reaction to the man. Inside her head there was a flood of righteous anger for a litany of valid reasons.

But no matter how angry she was at the way he blamed her for the past and the way he treated her in the present, she couldn't deny that anger wasn't doing a thing to protect her. She felt hurt by his hostility and too eager to arrive at New Hope to find out if he'd stuck to his schedule. Just seeing his Jeep in the parking lot had started her heart thumping.

Anxiety? Or excitement?

She suspected the latter. Anxiety she could have lived with.

Smiling at the night deputy who'd let her in, Karan beat a hasty retreat into the kitchen when she heard Charles.

"Thanks so much for making the trip," he was saying.

Pressing herself against the inner wall, she held her breath and tried to block the dull thud of her racing heart. What had she *ever* seen in this man?

Well, beyond the way he looked, of course.

Another question for her journal?

Charles strolled past the kitchen accompanied by a casually dressed woman and a sheriff wearing a uniform from another county—Albany it seemed from the insignia.

"Come into my office," he said. "I'll sign the paperwork before we get them."

Everything about him bristled with tension. Whatever was going on had his entire attention. Luck seemed to be with her for once. Now if she could avoid him until she caught up with Rhonda. She was too raw tonight to withstand the hostility in his expression, the cool distance in his voice.

Where had they gone so tragically wrong?

That would be a question for her journal.

Susanna had a good point that Charles's perspective about the demise of their marriage likely differed from hers. Karan hadn't thought of that before, but it made sense. Maybe she wouldn't even see things the same way if she looked back now. She was older now, distanced—somewhat—from the hurt.

Glancing at the clock, she went to stand in front of the window over the kitchen sink, gazing at the backyard. It would be dark soon, and the landscape lighting was already on, illuminating the path to the gazebo. There were security lights, too, but the overall effect was a nice compromise between practical and atmospheric. New Hope had done a better job of creating a homey environment outside.

"Excuse me, ma'am," a voice said.

Karan turned to find the night-duty sheriff.

"We've got guests. Gate guard called."

He seemed under the impression she knew what that meant. He didn't hang around long enough for her to tell him otherwise, so she followed him into the reception area where he went straight to the door.

"Good evening," he said.

Karan peered through the open door and saw a woman climbing the steps, a toddler on each hip and a young boy beside her.

That little unsmiling boy reminded her of Susanna's Brandon way before he'd started school. Yet this little guy was dragging a suitcase bigger than he was up those steps, determined, obviously the man of the family.

The young mother was beautiful. Dressed in worn jeans and a T-shirt, she clung to the toddlers, both little girls who, on closer inspection, appeared to be twins. While not identical, they were surely the same age. Both had glossy black curls like their mother and big brother. One sucked her thumb.

At first glance a perfectly beautiful family. Except for the mother's tear-stained cheeks and the absence of a dad.

"Welcome to New Hope," Karan said. She might not have a clue what was supposed to happen, but she certainly knew how to greet guests. "Please come in."

The family was ushered inside and the deputy closed the door behind them.

"Hello, I'm Karan. What a beautiful family you are," she said, easing into the introduction. "And whom do we have here?"

"*Me llama* Marisol," the mother said in an accented voice. She took a deep breath and found her English. "My son, Raphael, and my daughters, Esme and Everleigh."

Definitely twins. "What lovely names. I'm so very pleased to meet you all. Your mom doesn't have any free hands, but you do." Karan extended her hand to Raphael and hoped the child spoke English. "I'm very pleased to meet you, Raphael."

Slipping his small hand into hers, he shook, taking in everything about her with serious dark eyes. *"Hola, senora."*

Another door opened and the triage nurse appeared, a woman with long shiny dark hair—Tammy, according to her name badge. Karan tried not to look relieved that the onus of this meeting was no longer on her. She could exchange pleasantries for only so long and she did not want any more screwups.

"This is Marisol." Karan performed the introductions. That much she could do. "Her handsome son, Raphael, and her beautiful daughters, Esme and Everleigh. Twins, I believe."

Marisol nodded gratefully, eyes glinting suspiciously in the light.

"You are like a family of little angels," Tammy said softly. "No more worrying right now, Marisol. You made the right choice coming here. We'll figure everything out, okay?"

That seemed to be what Marisol needed to hear.

"Come with me, everyone." Tammy motioned to the door she'd come through. "The deputy will take your suitcase."

"You, too," she told Karan, who filed along behind them.

"Marisol, why don't we go talk in here?" Tammy directed the young mother into an examination room. "Are you comfortable leaving the children with Karan?"

Then Tammy caught Karan's gaze with a telling glance, and she suddenly understood what needed to happen. Tammy needed to speak to Marisol alone, possibly even do a physical exam.

"Will your girls come with me?" she asked Marisol. "We can wait for you in the waiting area. We'll do something fun together."

What, she had no clue, but she sounded exactly like Susanna at one of Brooke's Brownie meetings, all capable and fun kindergarten teacher.

Who knew? Susanna would never believe her.

"Go, *mis ninos*." Marisol set the girls down to the floor. "Mama will be right here if you need me. Raphael, help this nice lady with your sisters."

"*Si,* Mama."

He grabbed two little hands with a death grip, and Karan led the children into the other room, where there was nothing to entertain one child let alone three.

Not a ball. Not a book.

Who had designed this place, anyway? New Hope was an emergency shelter for *families,* but someone had obviously overlooked something here.

Raphael helped his sisters get up into a chair, where they sat together, completely adorable with their big dark eyes and curls. They watched her expectantly, almost feral, as if they could sense her fear. Karan was on borrowed time, that much she knew. These children were temporarily out of sorts. A strange place. A vanishing mother. Whatever traumatic situation had brought them here. The lull wouldn't last long.

"So, Raphael, why don't you tell me a little about yourself? How old are you?"

"Five, *senora.*"

"Wow, you're certainly tall for your age. Do you go to school yet?"

"No, *senora.*"

"And how old are your sisters?"

He held up two fingers which, Karan knew, meant the reprieve would be over soon. The twin with the pink barrette in her hair was already starting to fidget.

"Can you help me remember which sister is Esme and which sister is Everleigh?"

Raphael jumped off his own chair and stood before his sisters on sturdy legs, reconciled, as if he'd done this task before. He pointed to one twin. "Esme." Then the other. "Everleigh."

Okay, Esme sucked her thumb. Everleigh had the barrette.

"What do you like to do for fun?" Karan glanced around the room for something, anything, to entertain these children.

"We go to the park with Mama," Raphael told her, "and

play ball. Everleigh runs around. Esme likes to sit with Mama and suck her thumb."

Excellent. Common ground. A place to start. "I've played kickball before. We don't have a ball in here, but there are lots of them outside in the yard. Wouldn't be good for tonight because it's getting dark, but when the sun is out, we can play. Right now we can handle running around, and some thumb-sucking I think. Who likes to suck thumbs? Go on, raise your hands."

Karan raised hers, and Everleigh squealed. Esme smiled around her thumb. Raphael's eyes twinkled and she almost had him smiling. She could tell by the faintest hint of a dimple in his left cheek.

"Well, if we all don't want to suck our thumbs, then we'll leave that to Esme and find something else." Snatching a magazine from the rack, she sat beside the twins and motioned Raphael to sit next to her.

National Geographic. Perfect.

From somewhere in memory, she recalled a game she used to play with her father. They'd played it anytime they'd needed to liven things up.

Flipping through the pages, she found a photographic spread of a market in Taiwan. "Okay, everyone, see this photo?"

She held up the magazine and made eye contact with each child. "I spy with my eye something…red. Who sees what I see? Come on, look really hard!"

"Tomatoes!" Raphael said.

Everleigh pointed to the image of the tomato cart so eagerly she almost knocked the magazine from Karan's hands.

A hit. And the game entertained for nearly ten minutes, which had more to do with her manufactured excitement that kept the twins giggling and won another almost-smile from Raphael.

Until the sound of a raised voice came from behind the exam room door, rapid-fire dialogue. Karan guessed Marisol was coming unglued. The kids certainly seemed to think so because they all spun toward the sound. Raphael hopped up and went to the sisters, slipping an arm around both twins' shoulders and giving a reassuring squeeze. Then they all looked expectantly at her.

I Spy had been fun, but as the door to the exam room still didn't open and produce Marisol, Karan was on her own. So she did what she always did when at a loss—called Susanna. Or texted her in this case.

"Why don't we text Susanna? She's my best friend." She whipped out her trusty BlackBerry and texted furiously. "Do you have a best friend, Raphael?"

Help! I need games to play with preschoolers!

"I play T-ball with Roger," he told her.

"Sounds like a best friend to me."

But Raphael didn't reply. He was too busy eyeing her BlackBerry. She handed it over, considering it a small price to pay for his help.

"I have the bubble game. Have you ever played?"

He shook his head, serious again, and watched as she pulled up the app and showed him how to operate the keypad. Kids today were technologically savvy no matter what their age. Within minutes Raphael's little fingers were flying on the keypad. Those bubbles didn't stand a chance.

Of course the twins wanted what their big brother had and a war was in the making when Raphael, intent on the game, got possessive with the BlackBerry and turned his back.

Karan had no way of knowing if Susanna had responded

to her text yet, so she was on her own. Everleigh was already climbing off the chair and heading for the exam-room door.

Karan spotted a trash can near her. Tearing a page from the magazine, she tossed it across the room and made a basket.

That got the child's attention. She turned big dark eyes onto Karan, who tore out another page. This one she handed to Esme. "Your turn."

National Geographic had been sacrificed on the altar of toddler entertainment by the time the exam room door opened and Marisol and Tammy reappeared.

The twins ran to their mother, wading through the sea of makeshift basketballs that littered the waiting area. Marisol scooped them up in a practiced move and planted one on each hip. From where Karan was standing, the little girls looked as though they were settling into the safest place in their world.

"We're going to stay here," Marisol told Raphael.

He glanced up from the BlackBerry, fingers still moving over the keypad. "Like a hotel?"

She smiled as she watched him. "Just like a hotel."

Karan was still cleaning up when Tammy sidled close and whispered, "I'd like to get them settled before group session lets out. I could use your help."

"Of course," she said. "Lead the way."

Raphael returned her BlackBerry and with his mother's prompting said a polite, "Thank you."

"Thank you for all your help," she said. "You're welcome to play anytime. Just ask."

That hint of dimple flashed. A tiny indentation in his smooth cheek, such a small gesture Karan might have missed it, but hadn't. And she was glad.

Tammy led them toward the back stairs. Karan filed

along behind, checking her messages. Sure enough, Susanna had replied.

Red light green light.

Animal charades.

Hotter/colder

Hide and seek

Can't wait to hear all about this! Hope they help;-)

"You go, Suze," Karan whispered beneath her breath as she climbed the stairs. She'd be armed and ready when they got into this family's new living quarters. Or the next time she had to entertain the little ones.

Once upstairs, it turned out that entertaining the children wasn't on her to-do list.

Karan hadn't been inside any of the suites before, but this one did indeed look much as Marisol had described it: a hotel. Immaculately clean and clearly designed for comfort, the living area was open and spacious with a small dining area attached.

There was a window overlooking the backyard and lots of amenities one would find in a typical family home. A flat-screen television. DVD player. A computer and printer. A gaming station with the same games that Brandon and his friends liked to play.

The decor, at least, was more inviting than downstairs. They'd almost achieved the homey feel. Even the art on the walls was reminiscent of family life with real watercolors and acrylics on canvas.

Definitely not gallery or museum-quality art, but upon closer inspection she discovered a signature plate on one painting that explained that all the paintings in New Hope had been painted by members of Project Return, another not-for-profit organization. This one helped people coping with mental illnesses to return to living productive and rewarding lives.

When Karan took in the effect on the rooms, she agreed with the choice to use real art. The impression was much, *much* more welcoming than generic prints could ever have been.

Well done, New Hope.

She was so taken, in fact, that she had to remind herself she could be standing in what was once Frankie's bedroom. But when she watched Marisol, her children gathered close, touring the place with a look of outright amazement, Karan didn't care. If knocking down a few walls and remodeling Frankie's house could put that look on Marisol's face, then Karan was all for it.

Who would guess she'd find something good to associate with Frankie all these years later. Life was full of surprises.

Tiptoeing behind the group, she peeked into a simple but nicely furnished bedroom with a double bed and more art on the walls—a spray of bright dandelions that looked like mixed media and a forest done in acrylics with shades of green.

The second bedroom had a pitched roof, twin beds and lace curtains on the dormer window. The only painting in this room appeared to have been done by a child. A street scene with stick-figure trees and lots of brightly colored cars zooming in opposite directions. Karan found it charming. Something about the sight seemed to strike Marisol, too, because suddenly she burst into tears and loud heaving sobs.

Raphael was right there, hugging his mom around the legs. Only when she sank to her knees and hugged all her kids in a little pile of bodies did Karan realize that she looked relieved, like she was crying good tears.

CHAPTER FIFTEEN

CHARLES SAT ON THE GALLERY steps, breathing deeply of the breezy night air, glad for the time to decompress before dealing with the situation at hand.

After seeing Amy and her boys off, he'd processed the paperwork for the new arrival, leaving Rhonda free to talk with Karan after wrapping up tonight's group session. He hadn't met the Sanchez family yet, except on paper, but Tammy had gotten them settled.

Tomorrow there would be counseling evaluations and dealing with the practical aspects of leaving an abusive home. Most families arrived here with no more than a desperation to end the violence and an escape bag filled with personal information.

Some families couldn't even bring the bag. Tomorrow the staff counselors would begin the process of helping the Sanchezes replace any important documents that had been left behind. But tonight they would be left to acclimate to their temporary new home, to enjoy the feeling of safety.

When the door opened, Charles knew Karan was behind him. The lighter tread on the wooden floor of the gallery maybe, a sound he suddenly remembered.

Light footsteps skimming over the planked bedroom floor, barely audible in the darkness after she wrapped up her nightly ritual in the bathroom and came to bed.

A sound that ramped up his pulse.

The feel of her sliding between the sheets and slipping

into his arms, her warm, sleek body unfolding against his full length. That first breath he took filled with her.

"You always smell so good," he said.

He could see her smile in the darkness before she snuggled closer. "Must be my moisturizers."

"Oh, Charles." She sounded miserable now to find him sitting exactly where he'd found her last night. "Rhonda asked me to come by. I had no idea you'd still be here."

Rhonda had wanted him to stick around so they could discuss the situation with Amy. Bracing himself, he looked up.

There Karan was, silhouetted by the porch light, the lean, delicate shape of her so familiar, even with her features shadowed by the glare behind her.

No denying that the sight of her jarred him on the inside where it counted. His anger no longer felt so surprising. Charles supposed he shouldn't be surprised by that, either.

He was.

Why? He'd already figured out that part of the problem between them had been him—he wasn't interested in the demands of marriage, or long-term commitments for that matter. Why should he be angry at her because of that? Because she'd figured it out faster than he had?

But had she? Karan had never once called him out for being a bad husband—and he had been, especially toward the end of their marriage. Rhonda was right about one thing—he'd avoided Karan as their relationship had unraveled. He hadn't been able to deal with the amount of emotional energy she demanded on top of what he was expending at the hospital. He couldn't remember if he'd ever told Karan that.

"Did Rhonda talk with you?" he asked.

Karan nodded.

"You're welcome to sit down."

Now it was her turn to brace herself, hesitating as if she suspected him of a trick. He patted the step beside him and left the decision to her.

"If you're feeling the need to make me feel worse, trust me when I say I couldn't possibly. You may not think I feel anything, but you're wrong. Please take my word on this. I'm not entirely sure I can handle your...*input* right now."

His fault. Not only because he'd gone off on her last night, but because he'd been hard on her about stupid things. He hadn't exercised fairness or good judgment, which only undermined his credibility about more important matters. Such as Amy.

Did that have more to do with him than Karan?

"I'm sorry," he said.

"For last night?"

He nodded. "And because I've been making this harder for all of us than it should be."

"Oh."

To his surprise, she did sit then, and he didn't bother to steel himself for the closeness. Nothing he did would minimize his awareness of her beside him, the almost-brush of her bare arm, the hint of that same delicate scent wafting through his senses. Her moisturizers? Or her?

Keeping his gaze steady, he counted the landscaping lights outlining the walkway to the parking lot. Two, four, six...

"Apology accepted. I know I came as a shock. Finding you here was a shock for me, too." She gave a soft laugh. "Finding myself here was a shock."

He wanted to ask what had happened to bring a woman who'd been so meticulous about what she put in her body into community service and therapy on a DWAI charge.

With her sugar issues even a drink or two could get out of control fast, which is why she'd always been so disciplined.

But Charles didn't ask. The right to ask personal questions hadn't been his for a long time, particularly after last night. She didn't offer anything else. Like him, she stared ahead, waiting. Or maybe remembering what it felt like to sit side by side the way they had so long ago.

He was. She shouldn't have the ability to make him feel anything at all. But he did feel.

"You okay?" He wasn't really sure whether he referred to the news about Amy or about whatever had gotten Karan into trouble with the law. Both. Either.

"I had a few stellar moments before Rhonda got a hold of me."

Rhonda wouldn't have been anything but efficient and kind. "Did she mention the orientation?"

Karan nodded, her hair looking pale and luminous in the dim light. "I'm surprised you agreed. I thought I'd been officially banished from the kingdom."

Avoidance, Rhonda had said. Did that explain why sending this woman packing last night had felt like the only solution?

"I reacted in the heat of the moment," he admitted. "Overreacted."

She faced him then. He could see her surprise and he knew she was upset. Enough so she was willing not to blow him off, although after last night he hadn't given her any reason to listen to his apology, not after condemning hers.

"Amy and her sons had to leave because of me."

No argument there. But Charles didn't know what to say or how to respond. She surprised him by how affected she seemed to be, by how much she seemed to care. Why couldn't he remember her ever caring about anyone but herself?

Tammy had told him she'd have had trouble interviewing the new resident earlier without Karan's help with the children. Coverage had proven a problem, but Tammy hadn't needed to pull Rhonda out of session. They'd agreed to address the issue of coverage at the next staff meeting.

Charles wouldn't have thought Karan would be able to handle kids, especially small ones. But when he considered it, he remembered her being very fond of her best friend's kids.

"Rhonda said Amy and the boys would be okay where they're going," Karan said. "Is that true? I know you'll be honest."

He didn't doubt it. He'd been brutally honest ever since she'd reappeared in his life. But without the anger, he didn't feel the need to lash out at her, was relieved he was able to push past it tonight.

He didn't want to make her feel any worse. He didn't like to think of himself as acting like an asshole. Yet that was exactly what Rhonda had thought he was. She might not have said it in so many words. She hadn't had to.

"They're on their way to a safe place. I'm sure Rhonda told you it's a good thing we found out about the threat when we did." That much he could offer.

Karan nodded, but he wasn't convinced she believed him. Not when she remained so stoic.

He couldn't think of anything brilliant to say, nothing that would change the facts, nothing to bridge the distance between them, between the couple they'd once been and the strangers they were now. The only thing he could do was manage his anger. He owed that to both of them.

He'd figure the rest out later.

"Give the orientation a shot," he said. "It will help you navigate this place."

"Do they have a class on making popcorn?"

At face value that statement was intended to be funny. But he heard something so honest in there. *Not* funny. Not in her tone. Not in the smile that seemed to take effort.

"I don't think popcorn's going to be a problem again. That microwave you bought can probably make it without you."

She gave a laugh, a soft sound that whispered through the dark quiet. And somehow he knew he'd made her feel better.

Maybe she wasn't as much a stranger as he thought.

The ensuing silence even felt familiar somehow, broken only by the sounds of the night. A breeze rustling leaves overhead. A branch scratching against the house. A compressor from some delivery truck in the Walmart parking lot. Someone leaning on a car horn in the distance.

"If I'm attending the orientation," she finally said, "does that mean I'm no longer exiled to the thrift store?"

"It's up to you. You can stay there if you want."

She met his gaze, and he got the distinct impression she was trying to gauge whether or not to believe him. "You'll be okay if I'm here?"

He nodded.

"Then I will do my level best not to screw up again because I have to be honest, I wasn't all that crazy about picking up donations. The volunteer is a jewel of a man, just so you know. He deserves a raise or an award or something."

Again, she was using humor to mask how she felt, or keep it manageable, maybe. For her.

"Listen, that schedule I gave Rhonda…I won't make another. You do what you need to do here and don't worry about me."

"We're good?" She didn't bother hiding her surprise.

"We're good." He would not allow his emotions to get out of control again. Period.

"Great." The smile she flashed him was bright enough to light the dark. "Well, I've got to be off the roads by ten or I'll wind up behind bars in an orange jumpsuit."

More humor, but it sounded as if she had a court-ordered curfew to go along with her community service and therapy.

"Drive safely, Karan."

She rose to her feet in one fluid move. "Have a good night, Charles."

Then she headed toward her car with those light steps, a graceful motion so uniquely hers. She didn't look back.

He watched her slide into her car and reverse before flipping on the lights of her sports car. Then she drove toward the security gate. The brake lights flashed. He could see the guard wave at her. Then she was gone.

Charles sat there, going over the night in his head. To his surprise he realized he'd meant what he said. They would be good. For whatever reason Karan was in his life for the present. The situation was temporary. He needed to remember that. Only he could control how much he allowed the past to influence the present. Karan had been the epitome of socially adept when dealing with him, which was no less than he would have expected from her.

Could that be adding to all this anger?

Had he wanted something more personal from her?

His impulse was to dismiss the thought as nonsense, but he didn't need the internet to know what avoidance meant.

Karan had been the first woman he'd fallen in love with. He'd married her, wanting to live life with her. *Before* he'd realized she was too high maintenance and he wasn't marrying material. He enjoyed dating when he met someone who interested him, was content with the lulls in between. He'd married his work, committed heart and soul to his patients. He didn't have much commitment left. Certainly not enough to weather ups and downs or the emotional drain that came with marriage and long-term entanglements.

But Charles hadn't found that out until after marrying Karan. That wasn't her fault. He had a part in the failure of their marriage, too. Was that what Rhonda thought he was avoiding? Then the anger made sense. He still cared for Karan, if only because he'd once loved her. He'd be a heartless bastard if he *didn't* care.

CHAPTER SIXTEEN

Karan's Journal
Just some random thoughts...

I'M SO TIRED BUT NOT AT ALL SLEEPY. Relaxation exercises aren't working. I've tried classical music and a cup of herbal tea. I've tried counting sheep. I'm still awake at 2:00 a.m.

I can't believe that man.

Hot one minute. Cold the next. Is it any wonder I ran screaming from him?

I thought about watching a movie, but somehow watching a movie in my living room all by myself in the wee hours because I can't sleep is too close to the image of Wannabe Jenny eating microwave dinners.

At least she probably hadn't torched anything.

So here I am. I already reviewed the questions Rhonda gave me this week, but, well, I've got to do something with all this stuff floating around in my head, keeping me awake. This journal seems like a good place to put it all.

Most important of the *stuff* is my mood. Or moods, more accurately. Unexpected *and* swinging. I've never thought of myself as a moody person, but I keep reacting to everything. Charles. All the things happening at New Hope. In the span of a week, I've felt utterly dismal about the alternative sentence, shocked by running into my ex, humiliated by the popcorn fiasco, good about my competence because I actually managed to accomplish something of value with my letters. Of course, that feeling got doused by a tsunami-size mistake that wasn't close to being as easily fixed as replacing a microwave.

But as I write, I'm noticing a theme here.

Me, me, *me*.

I seem to be writing that a lot. Why is that? There's so much going on at New Hope, and I'm not really a part of it. Or, only a tiny part at best. Why am I so focused on the effects of everything on *me?*

What about Amy, Cody and Bryce, who are spending their first night in a new emergency shelter, threatened by someone who was supposed to love and care for them? They didn't need another move and more disruption in their lives, did they? Seems to me they've had more than enough.

What about Marisol who only has strangers and her five-year-old son to comfort her when she was so clearly distraught? I don't know much about her situation, but from where I'm standing, she seems to have her hands full.

And LaShanna. She already has two adorable high-energy sons and another on the way. How is she ever going to keep up with those two while caring for a newborn, *trying* to recover from birth *and* hiding from an abusive spouse?

The very thought makes me dizzy…but that's because I'm imagining myself in that situation. I don't get the impression that anyone at New Hope is doing the same. No. They seem to be expending their energy on helping.

Like Tom, who cheerfully gives up one of his two days off to do exactly what he gets paid to do the rest of the week.

And the thrift store volunteers, who sort, clean and

price the never-ending parade of donations Tom brings into the store in trash bags and broken boxes.

The administrative volunteers.

The nurses.

The counselors.

The sheriffs.

Rhonda, who not only cares enough to assist running the place despite a full-time job and a private practice, but who is also willing to take on an alternative sentencing program to see if people who need help can also help.

And Charles, who cares more about his patients than he did me and our marriage, is taking time away from his precious operating room and his spectacularly busy social life to lend his expertise to Rhonda.

From the outside it doesn't appear as if any of them are spending as much time thinking about how things affect them as they are actually helping.

I think about how things affect me a lot. About how humiliated I feel to be court-ordered to help. About how inconvenienced I am not to be able to drive. And about Charles.

I don't know what I feel about him. I only know I seem to think about him an awful lot. About what he thinks of my efforts at New Hope, about his opinion of me every time I screw up. I shouldn't care what he thinks. I told myself I didn't, but after dealing with him again, I realize that's not true. Is there some perverse little part of me that still cares about the man when he's made it loud and clear he doesn't care?

That strikes me as a bit sick, which makes me wonder if there's some divine master plan at work here. Am I at New Hope because I need as much help as the residents?

Or am I just thinking about *me* again?

How do I even tell?

Now here's something to discuss with Rhonda because I don't have a clue. When I look around my living room, I see a lot of effort and expense that doesn't come close to accomplishing what a few paintings on Marisol's walls did. Those paintings took a generic space and made an inviting, albeit temporary, home.

Maybe because the inviting part of a home isn't so much about the furnishings as it is about people.

About real people creating art to grace the walls of temporary housing and people who care enough to hang those paintings.

About a sweet little boy trying to be the man of the family by comforting his mother the best way he knows how.

It reminds me of the differences between the house I grew up in and the home Susanna made for her family. My mother designed a showcase to impress anyone who walked through the door. But when I think about it, I always felt more at home in my dad's boathouse or garage. The places where he spent time.

Susanna's home is the same way now. Her family lives with kid-friendly furniture and sports equipment all over the place. It's filled with her knickknacks and mismatched antiques, of Skip—when he'd been alive—and that stupid fish he'd been so proud of he'd stuffed and hung it on the wall. It was the first thing anyone saw when they walked through front door—a glassy-eyed dead thing with its mouth wide-open.

Just the thought of it makes me smile.

Susanna hated the thing. But she didn't say one word and let him hang it because it had made him so happy. She hadn't been thinking of herself, but him. That fish will grace the wall forever, a treasured memory of the sweet man she'd loved with all her heart.

There aren't memories in my living room.

No, I created a showcase like my mother's house. And I purged these rooms of anything that remotely reminded me of Charles and all those dreams we had for our life together.

Charles had wanted a beach house on the west coast of Florida, so we'd have a place to stay while visiting his family. I wanted an apartment in the city—for the culture as much for the world-class hospitals. But this house would be home base.

We wanted our children to grow up appreciating the beauty of all three places. And we wanted children—three to be exact. Charles wanted two sons because he couldn't imagine life without his brother, and I wanted a daughter.

Idealistic young dreams.

So if I wanted to eliminate all traces of that marriage, why haven't I sold this house?

I have nicer homes. Keeping this place in Bluestone never really mattered.

But I *have* kept it, even though Patrick and I rarely spent time here. He never liked the town and didn't feel comfortable here. Because this was the house I shared with Charles?

I don't know because I never bothered to ask.

But Patrick had known I didn't like staying with my mother when we came to visit, so he'd graciously compromised.

He'd been thinking about my wants, not his own.

Wow. That's a sobering thought.

No wonder the theme of *me* keeps pouring out of this pen. What else do I have to write about except me?

Is that why I've been feeling so restless and bored with life lately—restless and bored enough to get careless with the champagne to make it through Brent's party?

I've been blaming my issues on my divorce from Patrick, on being between husbands, but I suspect the problem runs deeper.

Now here is something juicy to discuss with Rhonda. I hadn't even realized how I've been distancing myself from life until tonight when Charles looked at me and said, "We're okay."

And I felt okay.

Charles, who'd been willing to put aside his unhappiness about seeing me to stop making the situation more difficult than it needs to be. He'd told me to do what I need to do.

And I think I actually know what that is.

I need to help.

CHAPTER SEVENTEEN

"You have no idea what Karan wants?" Charles asked Rhonda after tracking her down inside the triage station.

She shrugged and said to Tammy, "Thanks for getting this report to me. I'm glad they're settling in okay."

Charles acknowledged the nurse then followed Rhonda.

"I know Karan hasn't logged any hours since the night Amy and the boys left. But she did drop by once."

He'd missed that visit. "Is she allowed to do that?"

"She's required to fulfill three hundred and sixty hours. The judge is allowing her to serve them however she chooses. To my knowledge the only requirement is that she fulfill the terms within a year."

As they stepped into the waiting area, he glanced around with surprise. There was no missing the new additions of a brightly colored plastic toy chest, a rack filled with children's books, a child-size picnic table and one of those wooden beaded things to develop toddler motor skills that were standard in any physician's office that dealt with children. "This is new. Did I miss an addendum to the week's expenses?"

Rhonda glanced around with a smile. "You did not."

"A donation?"

"From Karan. She dropped them off the other day. I wasn't here, but Tammy was."

He remembered what Tammy had told him about Karan helping out the night the Sanchez family had arrived.

"That was generous. Guess she must have seen a need."

"Guess so." Rhonda agreed as they made their way to the administrative offices.

"So Karan's sentence is all about how long she wants to be inconvenienced with driving restrictions."

"Wondering again?"

No sense lying to a psychotherapist who obviously thought she could see right through him. "It matters."

"Then I suppose you could say that. Or maybe the judge understands this is a pilot program. Since we're breaking new ground, flexibility is important because each court-appointed volunteer will have to be placed on an individual basis."

"I suppose you could say that, too."

Rhonda settled behind their desk. "I'm curious what Karan has for us."

He glanced at his watch. "You said seven, right?"

She nodded.

"Then you won't have to wonder long. It's three minutes till. Karan's prompt. At least, she used to be."

Sinking onto the office sofa, he was glad to be off his feet after one extremely long day. But he wasn't complaining. He'd made rounds tonight to find every one of his patients progressing satisfactorily. No complaints whatsoever.

Until Rhonda had called about this impromptu meeting.

But Charles was determined to reserve opinion. He didn't have to control himself long, either, because as the minute hand moved to seven, a knock sounded at the door.

"Come in," Rhonda said.

The door opened and Karan slipped inside.

Rhonda smiled. "Well, howdy, stranger."

Trouble was Karan didn't look like a stranger. She waltzed in as graceful as ever, wearing a summery dress made of some clingy fabric that treated him to the sight of every lean curve. The hemline certainly wasn't what he'd call short, but it left an incredible length of shapely legs exposed. She carried a folder tucked under one bare arm… Way too much glowing skin happening in this office for his peace of mind.

"Hi, Rhonda." Karan glanced his way, smiled with such practiced cordiality the past might have never happened between them. "Charles. Thanks for taking the time to meet with me."

"We're wondering," Rhonda said.

That made him smile.

"I want to run something by you two." Karan sat on a chair before the desk, a mere foot away from him. Hooking trim ankles beneath her, she opened the folder in her lap.

"Okay, here goes." She cast another glance between them, excitement radiating off her. Something else, too. He could see it in her shallow breaths, the posture that was a little too erect. Even more, he could sense it. He knew this woman so well. Still. Despite her poker face he sensed nerves.

"We've been struggling to find something useful for me to do around here. I've been giving it a great deal of thought and I think I've come up with something."

"Great," Rhonda said, ever the optimist. "Let's see it."

Karan was instantly on her feet, setting the open folder on the desk. She leaned over enough that the hem of that dress crept up the back of her thighs, treating him to some more skin.

How was it even possible that after all they'd been through she still had the ability to get him to notice her?

"Here we go." She arranged some papers side by side across the desk.

He knew he should join the party, take a look at what

she was presenting. But the view from here seemed to have rendered him stupid. With every motion that clingy hem swayed, molding the curve of her backside until he had the striking memory of exactly what her bottom had felt like when he'd slipped his hands down her back, over her hips, down, *down*.

He stood suddenly. And he had news for Dr. Camden. Not all avoidance was a bad thing. It could be a perfectly legitimate coping skill.

"Oh. My. Goodness." Rhonda stared at what appeared to be promotional materials for various events.

He went to stand beside her and forced his gaze onto the display, grateful for the desk between him and his *ex*-wife.

There was a flyer for a breakfast sponsored by the town council, several blue chip businesses with local plants and Bluestone's *VFW Post*.

There was a brochure detailing a series of presentations that would inform the community about domestic violence and explore ways they could help. Each presentation was to be hosted in a location that targeted a different demographic, such as the drive to collect basic goods at Ashokan High School, which would raise awareness about date violence and the realities of teen pregnancy. Or the sessions at St. Joseph's Hospital, which might recruit skilled volunteers who could expand New Hope's outreach programs.

There was a fashion show to be held at the elite Mill Hill Resort and Spa, featuring the fall collections of several designers, sponsored by local women's organizations.

And a showing at a gallery in Kingston, featuring work from a Manhattan-based photographer and the art of Project Return, the not-for-profit that had supplied paintings for the suites.

Proceeds of each of these events would benefit New

Hope of Bluestone Mountain, Inc. To kick off this ambitious schedule, a Fourth of July picnic in Bluestone Mountain Park was slated.

"Let me get this straight," he said. "You're proposing all these events at these places on these dates?"

Karan nodded. "The schedule is tentative, of course, but everything's in place if I can get an okay from you."

Rhonda was still sorting through the promotional materials, clearly speechless, so no help there.

He frowned. "Karan, how can you get a booth in Bluestone Mountain Park on the Fourth? It's barely three weeks away."

"There's not a venue on this planet that doesn't reserve space for last-minute participants. Our park is no different."

"You've spoken with them? They have this space and are willing to give it to us?"

"Mayor Trant and his wife are friends," she explained, sliding more papers from her folder and placed a spreadsheet onto the desk. "Here are the numbers. The projected costs and the revenue we should generate, taking into account the not-for-profit tax status. With any luck we'll spark some consciences and get some generous people to donate even more. That will be a bonus, though. This is the bottom line."

He wasn't surprised, not by the meticulous research or the top-notch full-color printing or the professional graphic design. Karan never did anything halfway.

She was an intelligent woman, determined when she set her mind to something. A woman who didn't recognize limitations, and never had. Even as an undergrad, she'd been able to accomplish things the deans of an Ivy League University hadn't simply by being creative. That she didn't put her abilities to better use was an absolute waste.

But wasn't that exactly what she was trying to do right now? And if her tentative excitement and almost vulnerable air were any indications, these proposed fundraisers meant something to her.

"I'm amazed." Rhonda shook her head. "I was impressed by your letters, but they're nothing compared to this."

"Writing them is what gave me the idea," Karan said. "I was looking through those event brochures, and Charles keeps talking about budgetary concerns. I can buy all the microwaves and toys I want but that will never cover ongoing expenses. No one person can do that. I want to help, and this is something I can do. I know lots of people so I'll call in favors to get them on board."

Charles couldn't argue her point. Karan had connections and coordinating social events came as naturally to her as breathing. If she said she could pull off these events, he'd be the last person to doubt her. She might not have put her degrees in public relations to conventional use, but she had used her talents.

Charles remembered the photo spread a prominent medical magazine had done on Karan's second husband—more accurately, the remodeling of his offices under Karan's guidance. Patrick Reece was a high-profile oncologist based out of Memorial Sloan-Kettering Cancer Center and Karan had been photographed sitting in the reception area, in an exam room, in front of a computer. In her husband's well-appointed office.

She was as much of a prop in the photo spread as any piece of equipment or stick of furniture. Charles remembered his annoyance that an otherwise reputable magazine had wasted space on such nonsense and capitalized on Karan's appearance.

Now, as much as it galled him to admit it, Karan's

second husband had been a lot smarter in utilizing her talents than Charles ever had. Reece had increased his profile with that little piece that showed how advanced his equipment was and how comfortable patients and family members would be. And, Charles was pretty sure, it was all Karan's doing.

"Wow." Rhonda continued to shuffle through the promotional materials with enthusiasm. There was no missing that she was genuinely pleased. There was also no missing that Karan was pleased Rhonda was pleased.

"You think you can get people to pay money to attend these functions?" Rhonda asked. "Like Charles said, the Fourth of July is barely three weeks away."

"It'll take a concerted effort to get the word out, but I don't see a problem," Karan explained. "I'll just have to be creative. The senator has already promised me an appearance between two and four. Once word gets out, he'll be our draw. I know it's tight, but people will be around for the festivities, so I hated to miss the opportunity."

Rhonda sat back in the chair. "The senator?"

Karan nodded. "He'll sacrifice his family pinochle game if you want to have this event. I know you'll need time to review everything to make a decision, but I'd like to confirm with him as soon as possible."

"Where have you been all my life?" Rhonda let loose laughter that sounded suspiciously like giggling. "You're the dream of anyone in social work."

"I hope that proves to be the case, otherwise I'll be back in your kitchen for another three-hundred plus hours."

"Margaret would quit," he said.

"Charles." Rhonda pointed at the door. "That's where you can go if you plan to start pissing in my cereal."

Karan met his gaze over Rhonda's head, and a soft smile played around her mouth. "I'll leave everything with you.

Any questions before I go? For the record I'll cover the expense of the picnic. If all goes well, we'll have some capital to fund the next events. Hopefully things will snowball and keep us going. Just let me know when you decide."

"That's very generous." Rhonda motioned Karan to sit. "You logged the hours you spent working up this proposal?"

Karan nodded.

"Good girl." Rhonda shot him a what's-there-to-discuss look. "Do you have any questions for Karan? I don't see much to lose here. Minimal risk for the possibility of a lot of gain. Think of the exposure."

Charles's knee-jerk response was to not touch this, to not get in any deeper with Karan. But the simple fact was his emotions were in the way. He might manage to avoid some obvious truths, but he couldn't deny them. He'd been critical of Karan for her self-indulgence, yet here she was trying to accomplish something to benefit others. Didn't he owe it to New Hope to support her attempt? And her, as well?

"Okay." He met Karan's gaze and the expectation he saw in those sparkly depths hit him low in the stomach. "I'm game."

Everything about her beautiful face transformed. She hadn't expected his support. Why should she have? When had he ever been supportive of her? Another revelation that bothered him.

"I'll get busy and keep you up-to-date," she said.

"Sounds great." Rhonda obviously had the utmost confidence in Karan's abilities.

Charles had a great deal of faith in her ability to plan parties. That was a place to start. "Good luck."

Karan exhaled a shallow breath. "Now for the tough part. I'm going to need one of you to check out the venues with me. I assume there are procedures in place since these events will represent New Hope."

"There are." Rhonda frowned. "But nothing out of the ordinary. This might be problematic for me. Sometimes I can sneak away from the crisis center for lunch, but this week is impossible." She glanced at him. "Any chance you can make time between the hospital and your office?"

He nodded, knowing he was involving himself with Karan, yet committing to the course anyway.

"There," Rhonda said. "Tough part all solved."

"Not entirely." Karan gave a sheepish shrug and met his gaze. "I'm going to need a ride. Would you mind picking me up?"

CHAPTER EIGHTEEN

THE SITUATION WAS SO ridiculous Karan might have laughed, *would have* had anyone else been standing in the living room, running back and forth to the window to see if *he'd* arrived.

But she was the one standing here, jumpy and nervous. Why? She refused to speculate, but if that wasn't bad enough, the feeling was distinctly familiar.

Her first date with Charles had involved Karan's entire sorority. He'd been the gorgeous upperclassman—a medical student. The minute everyone had found out he'd invited her to spend the day at a music festival in Woodstock, her sorority sisters had taken over from determining what she should wear to interrogating her afterward for every precious detail.

Of course, Susanna had egged everyone on by telling them how excited Karan was.

That in itself had been singular. She was selective. Once Jack had taken a left turn from law into *law enforcement,* she hadn't been impressed enough by any of the guys who asked her out. She knew what she was looking for and wasn't interested in spending time with anyone who didn't fit the profile.

Charles had been different. She'd known it the instant he'd shown up backstage at a talk she'd arranged for the college. Not only did he fit the profile, but he did something no other male ever had—he made Karan *react.*

She remembered waiting for him to arrive, the way her heart had throbbed every time one of her sorority sisters gasped, *"Is that him?"*

Karan had remained in the common area upstairs, prepared to make her entrance, yet unable to stop herself from constantly running to the window, feeling as ridiculously excited as she did right now.

Pathetic. She tried to manage her nerves. The young man she'd fallen in love with might have resembled the man on his way to pick her up now, but there was a lifetime between them that precluded her feeling anything except grateful for a ride.

She'd had no choice but to ask, since she and Patrick had agreed to joint custody of their personal assistant, an arrangement that was keeping her in the city by default. And Marynia, of course, had run off to Poughkeepsie to care for an elderly aunt who'd taken a fall. A few days or a few weeks, depending on the prognosis. The timing couldn't possibly be worse. For Marynia's aunt, who might have a long recovery ahead, or Karan, who needed transportation until she earned back her driving privileges.

So here she was facing down a ghost from the past. Because for the first time since arriving at New Hope to find him firmly ensconced, she could actually recall a hint of what she'd once seen in this man. Besides the way he looked, of course.

Karan would not speculate about why. There was enough happening in her life without tackling her history with Charles. It was enough he was being civil to her. Period. Her community service stint would be over and she could move on.

But even knowing that didn't stop her heart from racing when his Jeep finally pulled into the drive.

Glancing through the side light, she watched him climb

out with the graceful athleticism of an active man. He wore the years very well as she'd always known he would. Still fit. Still so handsome with his chiseled jaw the closely cropped beard only seemed to accentuate. She could detect a hint of silver in his sandy hair when they were close, but right now the midday sun bleached all of him to shades of platinum and silver.

He was climbing the steps by the time she came out. She locked the door behind her, then turned and their gazes met. A tiny shock wave ran through her.

Honestly. She was pathetic.

"Place looks different," he said.

"It got a face-lift not too long ago."

He glanced at the freshly painted eaves, the window moldings that had replaced the old-fashioned shutters, and she wondered if he approved.

"Looks good." His dark gaze raked over her with the same thoughtful deliberation. "Ready?"

She held up her purse and a folder containing the paperwork. "All set. I appreciate the ride."

"No problem." He opened the car door, and she climbed in, glad she'd dressed casually in long shorts and a tank top. A lightweight sweater around her shoulders and the Valentino thong sandals with a darling bow completed the outfit. She was not going to acknowledge the three outfits she'd discarded in her stupid nervousness about seeing him.

The nerves were to be expected, she decided, when he got into the driver's seat, started the car then wheeled out of the driveway. Here she was sitting beside him in a scene that felt so familiar. Even a simple ride into town wasn't so simple when there was so much water under the bridge.

Made perfect sense. He'd picked her up from the house they'd purchased together. How could she help but remember the first time they'd seen the place only months before the wedding? They'd looked at so many properties and had yet to find their perfect place.

Then luck had struck. Karan's real estate agent friend had known someone who'd known someone who'd heard this house would soon be listed. Taking the initiative on Karan's behalf, he'd called the owners. Karan and Charles had dropped by in the middle of the day, and had fallen in love.

She wondered if he remembered.

"So, how are things at the hospital?" she asked, sounding like a polite stranger.

But she wasn't a stranger. Even though they'd had nothing to do with each other for years, they'd once bought a house together, lived together, dreamed of a future together.

Charles cast her a sidelong glance, and his expression, a mixture of resignation and shrewdness, maybe even amusement, convinced her he knew exactly what she was doing.

"All right," she admitted, "I know this whole situation is awkward, but the silence is killing me."

Actually, the silence was giving her way too much time to notice all the things she'd once noticed about this man.

"The hospital is going well, thanks."

"I was surprised when I heard about your fellowship. I thought you'd be long gone after your residency."

He shrugged. "Thought about it, but Matthew offered me the fellowship and I didn't want to pass up the opportunity. Dr. Chalmers is doing excellent work in mitral valve repair. Matthew was planning to expand the surgical center, and he knows Dr. Chalmers is looking to retire eventually."

"That I hadn't heard. So you're actually thinking about a permanent position?"

Charles gave a short laugh. "Doesn't look like what I want is as important as what Matthew wants."

"I don't understand that. Matthew would be crazy not to want you on staff."

Something about that appeared to amuse him. But it was the truth. Charles was an incredible, dedicated surgeon. That much she knew hadn't changed about him.

"Still working on it," he explained. "Doing what I can to convince him. Just now wrapping up the fellowship so there's still time."

"What does Dr. Chalmers want?"

"To retire. But he won't do that until he's handpicked and trained his replacement. He's possessive. He brought the department to St. Joseph's and wants to make sure he leaves his legacy in good hands."

"And Matthew questions whether or not you're that man? I'm shocked. You've been on staff there for so long. Maybe not as an attending, but you've worked with Dr. Chalmers closely. I'd think you'd be perfect."

"I am."

That made her laugh.

"He's got me jumping through hoops right now. That's what New Hope was all about—me gaining exposure in the community."

Finally some of the pieces were coming together. "I see. I admit I wondered."

"Are you saying I don't strike you as the volunteering type?" His tone was light. His smile was real. And for one split second Karan saw the charming man she'd once known.

"Domestic violence was the only surprise," she said.

"You've always been involved. Now that I think about it you were volunteering when I met you."

The instant the words were out of her mouth she knew they were a mistake. She'd set the past in the front seat between them. One shining moment and the silence returned.

This time Charles broke under the pressure.

"So how's your mother doing?" he asked, taking his turn to keep the conversation going.

Awkward silence. Awkward conversation.

How did two people who once loved each other wind up here?

Karan had lots of answers—all the ones she'd been telling herself for years. And they were valid. Every one.

But right now, those answers didn't explain why he still felt so familiar.

She filled him in on affairs with her family, asked about his and was relieved when he finally pulled into the park.

"Ranger's station?" he asked.

She nodded.

Bluestone Mountain Parks and Recreation operated the public parks in and around the hamlet, including ski slopes, snowmobile and hiking trails, fishing easements and the town common, which was a mini Central Park in the middle of Bluestone proper.

That was where she really wanted to have New Hope's picnic. Right smack-dab in the middle of the Fourth of July festivities at the end of the parade route. Couldn't get any more visible than that.

But the available space was behind the courthouse. Not quite as visible, but still plenty of area to entertain guests. With the insane lack of notice for the event all she could do was put a bug in the mayor's ear, keep her fingers crossed and be grateful with what she got.

Charles parked in front of the station and they made

their way inside. The ranger behind the desk quickly pulled up their reservation on the computer.

"I see there's been a change here." She frowned at the monitor. "Your event has been moved to Shelter One in the city common. Mayor Trant authorized the change himself, but you haven't signed off on it yet. Were you aware?"

The city common. *Thank you, Gary!*

"What about the mayor's event?" she asked.

It was Bluestone Mountain tradition for the mayor to welcome the city council members, town manager, police chief, fire chief and all the hamlet's movers and shakers when they got off their floats after the parade route. Then Hungry Harry's served barbecue to all the families, which is exactly where Karan had gotten the idea for New Hope's picnic.

"The common was reserved for the mayor's parade welcome. But it looks like Mayor Trant intends to combine it with your picnic."

Karan glanced at Charles, who was staring at her with an eyebrow arched skeptically.

"Would you like to see the shelters and make sure the arrangement suits?" She contained her smile.

"Not necessary." He glanced at the ranger. "Where do I sign?"

When they were in the car, he asked, "Did you know Gary was going to let you elbow in on a city event?"

"No."

He eyed her narrowly.

She gave a huff. "All right, I had my fingers crossed. New Hope is a town project, and Gary barely beat Kevin Pierce during the last election. He's running against Kevin again. The senator's support will almost guarantee a victory. I didn't think Gary would want to miss the opportunity so close to the election. Not only will he get to schmooze, but he'll get good press to show his constituents he's in with the senator and that he's doing great work with their tax dollars. He's a very smart man."

Charles shook his head and started the car. "Amazing."

"What?" she asked.

"How you do that."

"What?"

"That." He laughed. "Know exactly how to work people. Here I am thinking no one's going to show up for this event, but we're going to wind up with the whole town."

He looked pleased, and some crazy place inside of her was so pleased, too. Another familiar feeling from the past. Once upon a time, she'd liked pleasing this man. "I'm just glad I found something to do at New Hope that doesn't involve microwaves or computers."

He laughed, a deep whiskey sound that made her stomach swoop straight to her toes. "Me, too, Karan. Me, too."

CHAPTER NINETEEN

CHARLES CROSS-CLAMPED THE aorta. He was the attending in the O.R. today and watched Matthew work for a change. The chief administered cold blood cardioplegic solution into the aortic root to bring about diastolic cardiac arrest.

"So how are you feeling after your surprise this morning?" Matthew asked.

"Besides pleased, you mean?"

Matthew laughed.

The last thing Charles had expected to receive was interest from Mount Sinai Hospital. But he had. Matthew had been copied as a courtesy, so St. Joseph's chief of staff would know that a top-ranked cardiac research hospital was interested in recruiting someone from his team as soon as Charles's fellowship was officially over.

Matthew had had plenty of time to make an offer of his own. Instead, he'd been making Charles prove himself. And he'd been willing. But now the luxury of time was over.

Mount Sinai was first-rate. The school of medicine was a world-class training ground for physicians. Research was groundbreaking with advances like nanotechnology tools to treat various heart and lung diseases, visually guided balloon catheters and cardiac nuclear imaging.

The hospital had once been on top of Charles's dream list, back in the days when Karan had been in the picture.

But in the years since, he'd developed new interests, among them mitral valves and teaching med students at Van Cortlandt. He'd been inviting students in the surgical program to observe in his O.R. ever since completing his own residency program. But was he still hell-bent on building a practice here and working out of St. Joseph's with Karan in town?

He watched his patient's vitals and said, "I'm thinking that since you spent millions on this state-of-the-art cardiac surgical operating room, you'd want a surgeon in the community who specializes in mitral valve repair."

"Matthew, you should have known someone was going to steal Charles if you didn't move fast." Joaquin Castellano chuckled from where he stood monitoring the cardiopulmonary pump. "We're looking good to go here."

"Thank you, Dr. Castellano." Charles glanced at the machine that would take over function of his patient's heart and lungs for the duration of the surgery.

"Your expertise would be a definite asset in the community, and St. Joseph's needs a strong pool of specialists," Matthew said, which didn't explain why he was sitting on an offer. "Mount Sinai knows a good thing when they see it."

"By definition that means you don't," Charles pointed out.

Joaquin laughed. "Last I heard smaller hospitals were having trouble recruiting specialists. Guess now I know why."

"No problems here," Matthew reassured them. "For the record I'm not known for sitting idle while my doctors are *stolen*."

Did that mean he was going to put an offer on the table? Charles didn't know, but there was nothing more he cared to discuss in an O.R. filled with people. Mount Sinai's interest had come out of the blue, and he needed time to think.

Now was not that time.

So, with well-honed skill, he shoved aside all thoughts of anything but the young woman on the table. The routine of physicians and staff working together grounded him as he opened the heart to expose the valve. He inspected the endocardium of the left atrium for jet lesions. "Leaflet prolapse."

"Calcification?" Matthew asked.

Charles tested the pliability of the tissue. "No. Let's look at the others."

The adjacent tissue segments were thin and normal. "We'll re-establish support of the margin of the leaflet without performing a formal resection."

"You called that."

Charles glanced up and found Matthew watching him with amusement in his eyes above the mask. "You're surprised?"

"No, Dr. Steinberg. I'm not surprised."

"Let's get busy, people," Charles said. "This woman is an elementary math resource teacher in her first year. Let's give her a long career."

But while Charles worked, he thought about all he could accomplish at St. Joseph's and the new directions he could explore in the wake of Dr. Chalmer's retirement. He could continue to raise this hospital's ranking with his specialization, particularly in this new surgical environment.

Matthew had maneuvered funding to outfit this O.R. with the latest in high-definition video equipment. Capturing video images of reconstructive procedures of his mitral repair cases would let him educate others with real-time 3-D intraoperative transesophageal echo images.

The possibilities were exciting. Satisfying, too, because in this specialty Charles's patients were often young. He could help them go on to lead active, full lives. A move to Mount Sinai would challenge him, no question, with the research aspects of being a part of a highly funded team.

Being courted was, as Matthew had alluded, an honor.

But nothing was perfect and at this stage of the game, Charles wasn't sure he liked the idea of limiting his involvement of cardiothoracic cases beyond the scope of mitral valve surgery. He needed to decide how specialized a specialist he wanted to be.

He'd thought he had his plan all set, but something was still bugging Matthew. After surgery, Charles had the perfect opportunity to talk privately with Matthew as surgical techs infiltrated the O.R. and they went to scrub down.

Charles plunged his arms beneath the spray. "So you don't plan to let me go?"

"Not if I have my way."

"Then might I ask why you've been making me jump through hoops for a position I know you want to give me?"

Matthew tilted his head to the side and arched a skeptical eyebrow. "I thought I already explained that."

"You want me to reach out and establish myself in the community. I get that part. But something's still bothering you."

"You want me to be totally honest?"

"I've always wanted you to be totally honest. Obviously, I've been asking the wrong questions or I would have answers by now."

"If you've been asking the wrong questions, got a right one by any chance?"

"You mentioned commitment issues. You obviously aren't convinced I'm committed to St. Joseph's even though I've bent over backward proving it. I've done my residency and fellowship here. I'm not sure what's left."

Matthew didn't reply right away, kept up his scrubbing as he seemed to consider his response. "You know I respect your work a great deal and consider you an asset to my staff. You're a strong surgeon. I've always known you would be."

Charles didn't doubt what he said. Matthew had offered him the chance to observe surgeries while he was still in med school. He'd done his internship in Kingston, but the instant Matthew could get him into St. Joseph's residency program, he had.

"I got that part, too," Charles said. "What's the problem?"

"You're not settled. I don't care what you say. I see you. I've been seeing you. And I haven't seen that kid who was on fire for a very long time. It's the only thing that's been holding me back."

Charles couldn't believe what he was hearing. "Because I'm not married with a wife and two-point-five kids?"

"You don't have to be married to be settled. If memory serves you were anything but the year before your divorce."

Memory served. "Then why are you judging me on my personal life, on what you perceive to be my *commitment issues?*"

"There's nothing wrong with working hard and playing hard. But I also know you, and I want the physicians in my practice happy." Matthew shrugged. "It keeps the rest of us happy. I figure if you were, whatever you chose to do with your life, you wouldn't be trying to drown yourself in surgery or blowing through relationships like they were boxes of surgical gloves. You're like a man on the run, Charles. Are you sure you're not ready to move on? I know you were interested in Mount Sinai once."

Once, when he'd also been making life plans with Karan. "Some things don't work out."

"Fair enough." Matthew nodded. "Listen, the last thing I want is for Mount Sinai to get you. But from where I'm standing you don't seem content. You haven't in a long time. The kid I invited into my O.R. was hungry, and the man I brought into the residency program was focused and sharp. He didn't push the boundaries in his personal life, looking for something. I keep thinking you're going to eventually find it, yet you only seem less at peace, less *settled.* I don't know what your deal is, but I don't want that discontent creeping into your work. You're too good a surgeon. As of this minute, my offer is officially on the table, but let me ask you a question before you accept or decline."

"Shoot."

"Have you considered that you're ready to move on? Bluestone Mountain is small fry compared to your Tampa roots. Maybe the novelty of small-town living has finally worn off? Have you considered that?"

"No."

"Maybe you should."

Charles pushed his hand through his hair, surprised. But there was a part of him that wasn't because a lot of what Matthew said rang true. "Been thinking about this awhile?"

He nodded. "Mount Sinai is top-notch and Manhattan isn't Bluestone Mountain. If that's what you want..." He fixed Charles with a level gaze. "As much as I would hate to lose you—and I would, I hope you know that—you need to be at peace. Consider what I've said and take it in the spirit it was meant."

Which was what exactly? "Where did New Hope fit in?"

"Balance, Charles. Balance." Amusement softened that hard gaze and Matthew smiled. "It's a good cause, and I figured you could use something worthwhile to distract you. Something to care about."

"Well, so you know, I do. Good cause. Good people."

"Glad to hear it. You've done great work there. Didn't expect anything less. Now give what I said some thought. Self-reflection isn't a bad thing. Not always easy, but not bad." He clapped Charles on the back. "You heading to CSICU?"

He nodded.

"Good job in there. Always enjoy assisting you."

And Charles didn't question that Matthew meant exactly what he said. More self-reflection.

Discontent? A man on the run?

Karan had accused him of the same thing—running instead of dealing with their marriage.

Suddenly, he could hear Rhonda's voice: *"Avoidance, Charles. Look it up on the internet."*

He hadn't thought he'd needed to, had thought he could figure it out on his own.

Now he wasn't so sure.

BETWEEN CHARLES RUNNING INTO Manhattan to tour the facilities at Mount Sinai and Karan's large-scale promotional efforts on behalf of New Hope, their paths hadn't crossed once in nearly two weeks. Until today.

He'd enjoyed the respite. With so much going on in his

head, he'd needed space and clarity to determine what he wanted for the future.

Clarity was nowhere around when he looked at Karan.

"A Night on the Hudson." Matthew glanced up from the glossy full-color brochure he'd been looking at. "I like it."

Karan leaned a hip against the desk and flashed a bright smile. That was all it took to have St. Joseph's chief of staff eating out of her hand. "I thought you might. That's why I asked Charles to bring me here. He mentioned how you were involved in his work at New Hope."

That was one way to put it. But he didn't say a word. He leaned inside the doorway to Matthew's office, watched Karan work her magic and reflected on how they'd both wound up at New Hope because of others.

Matthew looked amused. "Sounds like Charles isn't the only one."

"It's a great cause." She glided smoothly past details of her court-ordered involvement. "But A Night on the Hudson is actually a joint venture. The cruise line is willing to cut their expenses to cost for the exposure. Admiral Noonan is willing to absorb the rest so your employees can enjoy the boat and its amenities. It's a night cruise, so there will be a buffet, music and dancing. New Hope will make a presentation during the meal." Leaning over, she pointed to the brochure Matthew still held. "Admiral Noonan arranged for this particular vessel himself. I don't know if you know anything about the admiral."

"Just the name," Matthew admitted.

"He's retired navy and a bit of a colorful character. He always has some pet project that involves the Hudson River—environmental concerns, the maritime museum. He's willing to underwrite this cruise to see the cruise line gets positive exposure to help them weather this tough economy."

From Charles's vantage, he could see Karan's hair slide over her shoulder as she straightened. He remembered what it felt like between his fingers.

He had zero business remembering.

Matthew had been right that self-reflection might not be bad, but it wasn't easy. But he'd been coming to some astounding conclusions. The most startling had been reevaluating his perceptions about his commitment to marriage.

When he dissected the problem, Charles found himself asking if avoidance hadn't been the trouble all along.

He'd avoided dealing with Karan when issues had arisen, which had ultimately cost him his marriage. Then he'd chalked up the problem as his unsuitability for the institution and proceeded to avoid the problem ever since by not getting involved.

What wasn't so surprising was his distaste for what that said about him.

He'd run.

Karan had been right about that.

And when he looked at her now, the way she'd walked into New Hope completely unprepared for what she'd found there, he had to admire her persistence. She'd owned up to her mistakes and kept trying until she found some way to contribute.

Charles was witnessing firsthand the way she tackled her issues—legal trouble, ex-husband trouble, whatever other trouble she might be tackling with Rhonda in session. And not once did he see Karan retreat in the face of those challenges.

He admired that a lot.

So Charles stood here, watching her work, reflecting on his revelations, on the courage it was taking her to deal with her situation. And the courage it would take him.

He hadn't expected her to set the example, but when he looked at her, a force of nature that she'd always been, he wasn't so surprised.

"All right, Karan," Matthew was saying. "I like it, and I certainly think my staff deserves a fun night out. But what are you expecting from them in return?"

She leaned back, her blouse stretching taut, and for a tantalizing instant outlining the curve of her breasts in profile and torturing him with reminders he didn't need without anger to shield him.

"Exposure for New Hope. You have a staff of skilled people and we happen to have an emergency shelter that needs those skills. We can look to other areas in the community for financial support, but we need to look to you for volunteers to help us staff the shelter.

"I realize your people work very hard for you, Matthew. They have careers and families and not a lot of spare time. That's why one of our directors—Charles's colleague, in fact—is working on a program to allow volunteer hours at New Hope to fulfill specific continuing education units required by the state. The senator is one hundred percent behind this program, so we should have approval in time for the cruise. Your employees can donate their skills to a good cause and come away not only feeling good but with recompense for their time. Win-win."

Matthew gave a low whistle. "You're not kidding. CEUs will be excellent incentive."

"That's why I came to you instead of the Foundation."

St. Joseph's Foundation organized all the charitable endeavors associated with the hospital such as the fundraisers, the gifts and trusts. The organization did exactly what Karan was doing for New Hope at the moment. He supposed she didn't want to get lost in the shuffle there, didn't want to have to go through endless channels to have her proposal reviewed and accepted or rejected. Karan was working her connection to Matthew to get him on board with her idea. With the chief of staff's endorsement, the Foundation would support her.

She was so skilled at dealing with people. It was an admirable quality that he'd seen in action many times.

Her connections to the manager at the Inn at Laurel Lake had yielded a room block for his entire family so they could afford to stay for all the wedding events.

His internship at Kingston Medical beneath the renowned head of the cardiothoracic program had come as a result of some of her father's friends.

Of course, she didn't always put those skills to good use. There had been dramas involving girlfriend gossip and convoluted interactions with her sorority sisters and wedding crises. The list went on and on.

But Charles had to wonder if Karan simply didn't have enough direction on which to focus her skills, purposes that would challenge her. Because when she was focused and challenged, she accomplished amazing things.

He also had to wonder why he hadn't noticed this before, why instead, he'd remembered her as only petty and theatrical. Was the difference in Karan?

Or was his memory at fault?

Charles only knew that he remembered her in such an unkind light and had painted her that way publicly whenever he'd been forced to think about her. Even Rhonda had shut him down so he wouldn't color her impressions.

That did not make him proud of himself by any stretch. To his knowledge, Charles wasn't usually an ass. Perhaps

Karan had grown up in the years since their divorce, but it didn't sound as if he had at all, not regarding her anyway.

Avoidance is a simple way of coping by not having to cope. As a short-term strategy, avoidance is benign and can even be useful, but as a long-term coping mechanism, it can become a self-protective strategy that is neither balanced nor healthy.

CHARLES HAD FINALLY looked up *avoidance* on the internet. He'd read several definitions, but this one stuck with him. He had to ask himself if criticism was one such way to distance feelings he hadn't wanted to experience about this woman.

CHAPTER TWENTY

KARAN WATCHED CHARLES AS HE drove her home from the hospital. The meeting with Matthew couldn't have gone better, and she was both relieved and pleased he would support an event that would hopefully garner some skilled medical expertise for New Hope.

"Do you think we'll get anyone to sign on?" she asked.

"Don't see why not."

They needed the help. RNs. Occupational therapists. Speech therapists. LPNs. The list went on and on.

"Rhonda said there was really no way to anticipate the needs of the families who come to the shelter, so until New Hope secures a good variety of outreach programs, the needs will have to be attended in house."

"That's right." Charles didn't elaborate, but Karan thought of adorable little Everleigh.

According to Marisol, the pediatrician had recently referred her daughter to a speech therapist. Of course, now the family was at New Hope. Marisol had left home without her insurance cards, and she couldn't exactly bring her daughter to a doctor her abusive husband knew about. Not when he could show up and cause trouble.

Karan wanted to ask how that situation would be handled, but Charles's short answers weren't inviting questions. She appreciated him driving her, so she kept quiet, enjoying the ride after spending so much time cooped up in her house while burning up the phone lines finalizing arrangements for all these events. He had the top down and while the sun wasn't ready to set, the temperature had started to drop.

The breeze lifted her hair and felt so good against her face. The only outdoor time she'd gotten lately was walks around the lake when she could no longer bear looking at the inside of her house.

When Charles took a corner so hard that his oversize tires kicked up gravel, Karan clung to the overhead bar and asked, "Charles, what on earth is wrong?"

"What?" He shot her a sidelong glance, which meant he wasn't looking at the road. Good thing he was a cardiothoracic specialist because her heart stopped right there. He hadn't been paying attention *while* he was looking at the road.

Fixing her gaze ahead, she gave him a visual prompt she hoped he would follow. And she didn't take her eyes off the road again. Hopefully, he wouldn't, either. And if he did…well, she didn't want to know.

"I asked if anything was wrong. You seem out of sorts."

"I got an offer from Mount Sinai."

Karan wasn't sure what she'd expected, but it hadn't been for him to blurt out what was on his mind.

"Wow. Mount Sinai. Congratulations are certainly in order. Are you considering accepting?"

"I'm considering. I've been checking out the facilities and meeting with the team when I can get away from here."

So that's where he'd been lately. Not that she'd been at New Hope a lot these past few weeks with all the event preparations, but she'd heard that he hadn't been, either. She'd wondered if he was dodging her. Now the thought made her roll her eyes. His absence had absolutely nothing

at all to do with her. The world did revolve without Karan
Kowalski Steinberg-Reece at its center. Imagine that.

"What about Matthew? Is he willing to give you up?"

"No. He made me an offer, too. Finally."

The *finally* bothered him. "Difficult decision?"

Charles nodded. "I've been waiting for his offer and
been trying to convince him I'm committed to St. Joseph's.
That's been the plan ever since I finished my residency.
Why I accepted the fellowship here."

Charles could have gone anywhere, including Florida
to be nearer his family, but he chose to stay in Bluestone
Mountain. If nothing else, their marriage hadn't soured
him on the area. She wondered if that meant he'd moved
on emotionally.

She wondered why the thought hurt after so much time.

"This really doesn't sound like Matthew." Of course,
she hadn't seen Matthew more than a handful of times in
the years since the divorce, but he'd always been interested
in getting Charles into St. Joseph's. Even back when he'd
been a medical student. Matthew hadn't been happy when
she'd helped arrange for Charles to do his internship in
Kingston.

"He told me not to make any decisions until I consider
whether or not I'm ready to move on."

"Are you?"

"I honestly don't know."

Well, that was certainly candid. "What's Mount Sinai
promising? Is it significantly better than Matthew?"

"Not really. Different. I'd belong to the mitral valve
repair team. At St. Joseph's I wouldn't be quite as specialized. More exposure at Mount Sinai. More autonomy at
St. Joseph's, especially after Dr. Chalmers retires."

"So, basically you're talking about being a little fish in
a big pond or big fish in a little pond?"

That got a hint of a smile, which was precisely the point. The man loved to fish. Deep sea fishing with his dad in Florida. Devil's Path and the various streams and rivers around. During their marriage he had even sat in a dinghy with a fishing pole in the middle of Mohawk Lake when he only had a few hours off and needed to unwind. His dinghy was still in her garage.

Charles wheeled off the road and pulled into her driveway. The Jeep jerked to a stop. He hopped out and circled to get her door. The sight of him so clearly conflicted bothered her. Every fiber of her being protested letting him leave when he so clearly needed to talk. She wasn't the best choice as his confidante. She didn't even know if he was involved at the moment—but from what she'd heard he wasn't usually *un*involved. But he obviously wasn't talking enough to Ms. Whomever-she-was.

Karan and Charles used to be able to talk about anything. It was one of the things she had liked most about their relationship.

That, and the sex, of course.

Crossing in front of him, she climbed the steps and sat on the top one. Patting the seat beside her, she said, "You're welcome to sit if you'd like."

Then she waited. With the breath lodged in her throat. With her heart thumping so hard it actually hurt.

It shouldn't matter what Charles did.

It did. A lot.

When his dark gaze met hers, almost suspicious, she held it, tried to convey what she was thinking.

She'd listen if he wanted to keep talking.

No more. No less. Simple.

He thrust a hand through his hair, leaving it spiking at odd angles, a sure sign of his tension. She watched, enjoyed the pleasure of looking at him, a privilege that had once been hers. And it had been both a privilege and a pleasure. She didn't think she'd ever realized that before now.

He was such a handsome man with those long legs and straight, broad shoulders. She remembered lying beneath him after making love, looking at the world through the crook of his neck and shoulder and thinking there was nowhere else she would ever want to be.

To her complete surprise he strode up the steps and sat. He looked straight ahead, but she could see a muscle flexing in his jaw beneath the beard.

"Matthew only put the offer on the table because Mount Sinai forced his hand."

Again, that surprised her given that Matthew had been a mentor and friend before Karan had even met Charles. "What's his concern? I really don't understand."

"He doesn't think I'm happy."

"Are you?"

Leaning forward, Charles clasped his hands over his knees, slanted his gaze at her. "Thought so."

"Then Matthew's wrong?"

"I thought so."

"Still think so?"

He shook his head. "Not sure. I haven't been unhappy, but I also used to know what I wanted. Now, I go down to Mount Sinai and like what I see. Then I come back here and think I don't want to leave. Nothing's pushing me in one direction or the other. It's almost like it doesn't matter either way."

Karan understood that feeling all too well. Just ticking along, going through the motions…

"I was interested in Mount Sinai. You know that. A few years ago I would have jumped at this chance. Then I was offered the fellowship here. Matthew started sinking money into the surgical unit, and I could see all kinds of possibilities. Maybe Matthew dragging his heels has turned me off."

"Is there someone here you don't want to leave?"

A smile twitched around his mouth. "That was…delicate. But the answer is no. I'm not seeing anyone."

A miracle from what she'd heard, and one that pleased her, so much more than was smart. "Then what's making you rethink what you want?"

He didn't answer right away. Karan could think of lots of questions to ask, lots of suggestions to make, but she remained silent, so very aware of his closeness. Once upon a time he'd valued her opinions, had appreciated her practicality. But he hadn't asked for her opinion. He wanted to talk, and that meant she should listen.

"I think it's you," he said.

"Me?"

He nodded. "All of a sudden you turned up at New Hope."

"Unexpected, I know, but how on earth does me being at New Hope impact you?" She smiled. "Well, besides the unfortunate inconveniences and the need for an occasional ride?"

"It shouldn't. But for some reason it has."

Now it was Karan's turn to stare. She wasn't sure what to say, didn't know whether or not to brace herself. And she didn't know why she cared so much.

She'd told herself Charles didn't matter. She'd been telling herself that for five years.

She'd lied.

Everything about her was poised on the edge of a breath, waiting for his next word, his next glance, his next smile. Her pulse throbbed so hard that she could barely hear anything else. Karan knew this feeling intimately. And it didn't matter whether or not she should be feeling it.

She did.

"You okay?" he asked.

She wasn't sure what he was referring to. The man wasn't a mind reader. He couldn't know how much he still impacted her. God, she hoped not.

"You know, the community service and stuff with court," he said. "I haven't wanted to ask, but I wondered. Are you okay?"

"Oh, *that*." She exhaled a relieved sigh. What could she say? "A month ago I would have told you I was fine."

"What about now?"

Funny, but her answer sounded a lot like his. "Now I would have to say I'm not entirely sure."

"I know you don't drink. I thought you might have been struggling with your divorce."

She shrugged. "Yes and no. It was a surprise, to be honest, but nothing like ours. I love Patrick but I was never in love with him. We were good friends and great partners."

"Doesn't sound much like a marriage. Were you good with that?"

She considered that. "I thought I was."

"And now?"

"Now I'd have to admit something was missing. I think that's why I started getting careless with the champagne. One stupid glass…"

"Sugar must have been really low."

She nodded.

"First offense?"

She scowled at him, but the grin playing around his mouth told her he was teasing. "*Only* offense. Thank you very much."

He smiled. "No license. A curfew. Community service. Seems steep for an *only* offense."

"Oh, it is." She rolled her eyes and admitted, "Of course, if I hadn't had a history with the judge… Just dumb, bad luck I wound up in front of her."

Now he laughed, a deep, whiskey sound that she once loved to hear. "What did you do to her?"

"What makes you think I did anything?"

He leaned back and gave a snort.

"Fine." She huffed. "She tried out for the cheerleading team in high school."

"No good?"

"No room."

His smile faded. "So the past came back to bite you in the ass."

"That's one way to put it."

"Do you ever remember the good times or do you only remember the end?"

This man was full of surprises today. "If you'd have asked me a month ago, I would have probably said the end."

"Not now?"

She braced herself to face him, found his dark gaze watching her carefully, thoughtfully even. "No, not now. Ever since that night you told me we were okay. I'm not sure why that made any difference, but I've been remembering other times, too. We were friends once."

His gaze was steady. "We were."

"What do you remember, Charles? Anything good?"

The question hung in the air, and for one crazy moment, she was struck by how much his answer mattered. She hated to think all he'd taken away from their marriage was feeling as if nothing he did was ever good enough when she hadn't felt that way at all.

"I remember everything, but it *feels* like the end."

There was something so wistful in that reply, in his expression, that the hurt actually stole her breath. She'd known he felt this way. How could she not when he'd been so openly hostile? So why did it feel like an open wound?

"You said you felt like I didn't care."

He nodded.

"You don't remember things at all the way I do." She remembered talking to the back of his head when he strolled through their home either to or from the hospital. But he'd never stopped long enough to deal with things. How was she supposed to make choices when he wouldn't talk? Why should the responsibility be all hers? What had she been supposed to think?

That he didn't care.

"I felt that same way about you," she admitted.

"I felt like nothing I did was ever good enough. Not in the beginning, but toward the end. I was so busy at the hospital and you wanted more than I had to give. More time to be together, to be with our families and friends. More reassurance. But it was never enough. I didn't think it would ever be."

"*Bottomless pit* was the term you used."

He exhaled hard. "Sorry."

"Not sure why. You obviously felt that way." Why did she even care what he thought? This was the man who'd walked out the door and not looked back. He hadn't cared when she'd finally served him with papers. She'd thought what they'd had was so special and he'd proven her so wrong.

"Karan, for what it's worth, I'm sorry. I'm only now beginning to understand that when I felt pressured—by you, by work, by whatever—I didn't deal with it. I suppose I was keeping things manageable for me at the time.

I haven't figured it all out yet, but I'm not proud of the way I've acted. I hope you'll accept my apology. Especially for being so brutal that night about the computer. I was way out of line."

She could not trust herself to reply. Not when he reached out and took her hand, held it between his, those skilled hands that could save lives, hands that could bring pleasure or reassurance or support.

Could make her remember.

And she did. The warmth of his firm touch, the way she'd once loved this man with all her heart.

His grip tightened imperceptibly. His dark eyes caressed her face. "Are we good?"

"We're good."

He didn't say anything else, just let his hands slide away as he got to his feet. Then he headed to the car. She watched him go, and she remembered this feeling, too.

"Congratulations, Charles." She got the words out on a whisper. "And good luck with the decision."

He opened the door and turned to her. She couldn't miss the stark lines of his expression, the look in his eyes. He seemed as shaken as she was.

"Thanks." He got into the Jeep and took off.

CHAPTER TWENTY-ONE

KARAN DIDN'T KNOW what was wrong with her. She sat on the top step, couldn't bring herself to go inside, even though she was shivering, practically freezing despite her sweater. The cold was coming from inside. And she couldn't bear to be in the house right now. It didn't matter how often she redecorated, didn't matter how hard she tried to purge the memories. It would always be *their* house.

Why hadn't she sold this place?

She had cared. Even if Charles hadn't felt that way. She'd cared so much. Had she even realized how much until watching him leave, driving off to make decisions about his career and his future? And why now? Was she like Charles? Had she been avoiding the difficulties, avoiding feeling?

A tiny voice inside reminded her of the distance she'd only just realized was there, distance that was getting in the way of living. Had that distance kept her from showing Charles how much she really cared?

The questions hammered at her until Karan could no longer sit still. But she couldn't go inside. Not now. Not yet. She was too raw, the pain too fresh, which made no sense whatsoever.

So she circled the house and walked along the lake, needing to keep moving, not caring that her Valentino thong sandals were seriously not meant for walking over slippery grass.

Here she'd been blaming the men she'd been involved with. Jack had derailed their plans with a career change. Charles had flat-out emotionally abandoned her. Too many disappointments, so she'd married Patrick based on brand-new criteria. If they went into a marriage with clearly defined expectations, neither of them would be disappointed. But that wasn't living. That was placing the distance between them on the table.

And she'd been so comfortable.

That relationship had been what she'd wanted.

She'd wanted.

Charles's words struck her. *I was so busy at the hospital and you wanted more than I had to give. More time to be together, to be with our families and friends. More reassurance. But it was never enough. I didn't think it would ever be.*

There was that theme again. *Her. Her. Her.*

What about Charles who'd been trying to keep up with his residency, responsible for people's lives, running days on end with no sleep?

Why couldn't she ever remember thinking about him?

It took two people to make a couple. She thought she'd understood that. Dr. and Mrs. Steinberg. The cardiothoracic surgeon and his supportive wife. But right now all she could see was the damage *she'd* done to her relationship. *Her. Her. Her.*

Maybe Charles had been avoiding things, but she'd given him plenty to avoid.

Karan hadn't realized how far she'd walked until she was approaching a familiar boat dock. She'd walked home. The house she'd grown up in at any rate. The house hadn't really felt like home since her father had died. But where else could she go?

From home to New Hope.

From New Hope to home.

And she might run into Charles at New Hope.

Karan stared at the boat dock, water lapping softly against the pilings, the narrow path that wound up to the house vanishing on the forested slope. She didn't have to close her eyes to see her father, felt so close to him standing here in this place he'd loved.

She missed him.

Another glance at the stone path. It was still early yet. And her mother usually liked visits when she hadn't had to issue an invitation.

Karan felt better the minute the door opened and she was greeted by a smiling Abigail.

"Karan, how nice to see you." She spread those ample arms for a hug. "I was helping your mama get ready."

"She's leaving? Maybe I should come back later."

"Oh, no. Come in. Come in." She ushered Karan in. "The driver won't be here for thirty minutes yet and she's almost ready now. She's in her room."

Karan followed the little housekeeper up the stairs. Abigail knocked on the door and introduced Karan with a singsongy, "Look who's here."

Her mother was seated at her vanity, stunning in a one-shoulder lilac chiffon dress.

"Hi, Mom. You look lovely."

Her mother glanced away from the mirror. "Karan. Which do you think?"

She displayed a diamond drop earring and a platinum hoop.

"Let me see."

Her mother tilted her face and alternately held up each earring.

"The diamonds, I think. Bracelet, right?"

Her mother nodded, scooping up a wide cuff of threaded platinum chains and tiny diamonds. "Vera Wang's new collection."

"It's gorgeous. The diamonds, definitely."

Her mother slipped the bracelet on, such a lovely piece on her slender wrist, a delicate piece for all its width, and then affixed an earring. She caught Karan's gaze in the mirror.

"This is an unexpected surprise," she said. "Is everything all right? You look quite pale."

No, everything wasn't all right. Not even remotely right. Her life was blowing up in her face and she'd thought that had already happened. "I'm fine, thanks. I was taking a walk around the lake and found myself here. Thought I'd pop in to say hi."

Her mother's eyebrow arched in disbelief. "You walked?"

Karan nodded. She wasn't about to go down the lack-of-driving-privileges road with her mother. "It's gorgeous out."

"Just like your father." Her mother turned her attention to the earrings.

Abigail winked before slipping out of the room. Karan sat in a boudoir chair, still feeling shaky now the adrenaline from her walk was wearing off.

"So where are you off to tonight?"

"Engagement party for the Talbots' daughter. Nice man. He's in finance. First wedding for them both."

She let *that* pass. Hardly a fair comparison since the Talbots' daughter was a good five years younger than Karan. "That's nice. Where are they having the party?"

"The Inn at Laurel Lake. Her side of the family. They've got another party scheduled in the Hamptons for his."

"The Inn is always nice. Beautiful this time of year." Her last visit for the senator's fundraiser aside, of course.

"I'm hardly excited, Karan, but short of a death in the family there was simply no polite way to excuse myself. The Talbots have attended all your events."

Karan's events preceding her wedding to Charles, anyway. Her wedding to Patrick had been an intimate destination affair much more suited to a second wedding. "The Talbots are lovely, Mom. Why aren't you excited? You love parties."

The instant the words were out of her mouth, Karan knew they were a mistake. Her mother's beautiful face froze with a look of such deep disapproval that Karan could feel a responding anxiety in the pit of her stomach.

"Tell me. Exactly what should I find exciting about a night where I'm going to have to make excuses for you every time someone asks me what my daughter is up to? Two divorces weren't enough. Now you've had to publicize your disgrace."

"I don't understand. How have I publicized anything?"

Her mother rose from the chair in a fluid motion that sent chiffon swirling around her. "I'm talking about making phone calls to everyone we know soliciting their help for that domestic violence shelter. You might as well have taken out a full-page advertisement announcing your *court-ordered* community service. What's next? Are you going to show up wearing one of those alcohol detection devices around your ankle?"

She could overlook her mother's melodrama. That wasn't anything new. But Karan couldn't overlook the fact that her entire life had boiled down to sitting in her mother's bedroom watching the grand dame put on a rousing display, looking for something she was never going to find here.

She wanted to feel better.

And she'd come *here*.

Because there had been no place else to go.

"Mother." She tried to sound conciliatory, but her voice sounded weak and resigned. "You don't have to share what's going on in my life. Say I'm doing volunteer work for the new shelter. You can tell anyone who's interested I'm hosting events to raise funds for a good cause. It's the truth."

"I can sugarcoat your predicament all I want, but everyone knows why you're involved with New Hope. Marjorie Talbot is so proud of her daughter. She got a law degree and has been recruiting volunteers for the *guardian ad litem* program in the city. That's how she met her fiancé. Let's hope their marriage lasts longer than either of yours. Your father and I were married for forty years. I honestly don't know where you got your penchant for divorce."

Dad had to die to get away. The words almost came out. Almost. It took every ounce of will to keep her mouth shut tight. She could not engage in this. Not right now. The temporary satisfaction of defending herself never outweighed the guilt that came afterward.

Karan stood, clutched the chair when her legs felt rubbery beneath her. "I hope you have a nice time at the engagement party."

"Karan—"

She heard her name but nothing else as she headed through the door into the hall and down the stairs, her thongs slapping gently on each marble step.

She slipped through the front door before Abigail could make it out of the kitchen. Karan didn't want to face anyone right now, not even kind Abigail who would understand better than anyone the effects of her mother's annoyance.

Winding her way around the rear of the house, Karan walked straight out to the boat dock. She sank to her knees, feeling so unsteady. Her chest felt tight and her head light and her stomach queasy. She willed herself to calm down, sat there trying to lose herself in the picturesque surroundings, in the gentle motion of the water rippling with the breeze, the lengthening shadows of the forest in the fading daylight.

Now what? Walk home?

She didn't mind the long trek back, even after the sun went down. This lake might be smack in a crevice of a mountain and forest, but there were houses all around.

But she simply wasn't ready to hang out in the house she'd bought with Charles so she could rehash everything they'd said while sitting on the gallery steps.

Penchant for divorce?

Karan shivered again.

Freezing out here as the temperature dropped to a Catskill Mountain night didn't even bother her. But being a prisoner inside those walls did, as the hours slowly ticked toward midnight and beyond and she'd have nothing to do but obsess over her pathetic life and her broken marriages without the shelter of selfishness to protect her. Obsess over the thousand ways she'd overlooked and lost the man who'd been the love of her life.

Was the love of her life.

No denying that. Not when she felt as if she could step off this dock and slip into the lake, exhale one last time and sink into blessed peace.

So, *so* easy. She would barely make a splash.

She would barely be missed by anyone.

Susanna, maybe.

CHAPTER TWENTY-TWO

THE SIGHT OF THE HOSPITAL ROOM, every spare surface filled with elementary school displays of affection from hand-colored cards to tissue-paper bouquets, made Charles smile.

Even more so the young woman sitting in the bed wearing a hospital gown, IVs and leads sprouting from her in all directions like tentacles. She appeared to be text messaging on her cell phone.

"Good evening, Missy," he said. "I meant to ask you. Are your students in summer school?"

She glanced up, followed his gaze to some of the art that livened up the sterile environment, and she smiled, too. "The after-school program becomes a summer one for the kids with working parents. A few of the teachers sign on to run it. I was planning to work with them myself then...well, you know." She shrugged as if it didn't matter. It did.

"Sign on for next summer. You'll feel up to chasing all those kids around by then. I promise. So how would you like to go home in the morning?"

That got a better response. "I'm a week past ready."

"Did take longer than we anticipated, didn't it?"

"You said I'd go home five to seven days after surgery, Dr. Steinberg. You fibbed."

"I also recall mentioning you shouldn't develop any

complications like an infection." He shook his head in mock disapproval. "What were you thinking?"

"That I needed to drop a few pounds, of course. Hospital food does it every time."

He chuckled and scanned her chart. "Everything looks good here. I'm satisfied. You can have your mom come get you after I make rounds in the morning. I'll sign your discharge papers then and the nurses will have your instructions."

"Anything different because of the infection?"

"Not really. You'll still be tired for a while. I want you to promise me you'll take it easy and listen to your body. And be patient. I mean it, Missy. The more you rest, the faster you'll recover. The more you overdo, the longer you're going to feel cruddy." He met her gaze to drive home his point. She was still young. She'd want to do everything. "There will be no driving for six weeks. You'll probably be ready to work then, too. In time to start the school year."

"Yay! Nothing worse than walking into a classroom after the year has already started."

"Perfect timing then." He made some notations on her chart. "I want to see you in about four weeks, but you'll go in to see Dr. Ebel next week. The discharge nurse will give you appointments. Now let's take a look."

He conducted an exam of the surgical site, pleased. "I do good work. You'll barely see that scar after you heal."

Not that he would have compromised her safety for cosmesis, but he didn't mention that to Missy. With any luck she would never need to repeat the procedure and the scar would eventually fade into a memory.

He reached for the chart again, made another notation. "I'll send Kimberly in to give you a—"

"A shower? Please tell me a shower."

He glanced at her, smiled at the excited longing in her face. "A shower."

Sinking onto the pillows, she beamed. "Finally." She blew him a kiss. "Thanks, Dr. Steinberg."

"You're welcome, Missy. Rest well. I'll see you tomorrow."

"I'll be clean for the first time in forever. I'll sleep like a baby."

Charles headed out the door and was about to leave the floor when he ran into Matthew.

"You're back?"

"Dropped Karan off and came to make rounds."

Matthew's expression warned that he wasn't going to leave it at that. Sure enough…

"She looks good. She's got some great ideas for New Hope."

Charles nodded.

"Listen, I'm on my way out. Want to grab a beer at Gino's? I want an update on what's happening with Mount Sinai."

Charles's knee-jerk reaction was to sidestep the discussion that would likely not only cover the career path that didn't seem to be growing any clearer in his head, but Karan, as well.

However, Charles also realized talking with Matthew was far better than heading home to stew inside his head. And he wasn't about to make an appearance at New Hope tonight, no matter how much work was piling up there. And it was. No question. With all the running back and forth to the city…

"Yeah, a beer sounds good."

Gino's was a welcoming tavern that catered to the various offices and services that surrounded a busy hospital. During the week, staff from the physician's practices around the hospital kept Gino's busy with take-out orders. Patients' families could pop in for a decent meal when they needed a break or wanted something other than the cafeteria fare, which wasn't nearly as tragic as Missy made it sound.

The physicians on call during the weekend could pop in for fast, decent food and to catch up on the scores of whatever games were playing on the flat-screen televisions around the bar.

The owner greeted them cordially when they sat and within minutes produced two dark drafts.

"So, how's it been going?" Matthew asked. "Haven't seen you much, so I figured you've been in the city."

Charles filled Matthew in on the work Mount Sinai was doing, the ways they were breaking ground.

"Their percentages of successful repair are setting national benchmarks," he explained. "Their success rate in avoiding replacement in patients with prolapse is nearing one hundred percent. It's amazing what they're doing there."

"Sounds like it." Matthew raised his glass in salute. "But I'm not hearing whether or not you're excited. Or are you talking around how you feel for my benefit?"

"I wish." Charles took a long cool draught.

"Talk to me then." Matthew smiled. "I have a vested interest. What's holding you up?"

"I've had lots of time to think with all the driving and I think I've figured it out. I never came up with a new plan."

A frown furrowed his brow. "How's that?"

"Karan and I had life all worked out. When things came unglued, I never reevaluated. I kept forging ahead, not really thinking about how I should proceed or where I wanted to go. Consequently, here I am, a man with no plan."

"Makes sense."

Charles nodded, took a swallow of beer and wondered if he might find some answers in the bottom of this glass. If not for Karan's run-in with the law after drinking, he'd probably still be sailing along, in and out of relationships, convinced he simply wasn't cut out for any long-term commitment.

Telling himself he was content with his life, but not really feeling it.

But drinking had gotten Karan into trouble and thrust her front and center into his life again, shining a glaring light on some issues and forcing him to deal with some truths.

Like he wasn't all that content with anything in his life. Least of all himself.

Matthew leaned back and considered him. "You know, I'm not surprised to hear any of this. Divorce is a big deal."

"You know it." And he did. Charles didn't know all the details but from those he did know, Matthew's divorce hadn't been easy.

"You and Karan always seemed so solid," Matthew said. "She fit in anywhere in all this?"

Charles only knew that today when he'd been driving away, he couldn't help glancing in his rearview mirror to see Karan sitting there, on the steps of the house they'd lived in, and wondering where they'd gone so wrong.

He wasn't going to share that with Matthew. "She's trying to help at New Hope. You saw the results today."

"I was impressed, too. I'd definitely like to see more folks giving back around here." Matthew set the glass on the bar and nodded at Gino, who replaced it.

He took another swallow before glancing at Charles. "Is she okay? I was sorry to hear about what happened. Listen, if it's none of my business tell me to buzz off."

"Word does get around."

Matthew snorted. "It's Bluestone. No such thing as a secret around here."

"If I had to guess, I'd say she's doing her fair share of self-reflection. Someone once told me that self-reflection wasn't bad but it wasn't always easy."

Matthew smiled. "Glad to hear it. I heard she'd gotten divorced before she came back and thought it might have something to do with that."

"We haven't discussed that. But what she did say led me to believe she was okay with it."

I wasn't in love with Patrick, she'd told him.

And he'd believed her. He'd also gone one step further by interpreting that to mean that she'd only been in love with *him.*

What a stupid ass he was.

"Looks like she's doing a good thing for New Hope," Matthew said. "Regardless of what got her involved. You know I'll support her efforts however I can."

Charles's turn to tip his glass in honor of the chief. "Guess this round's on me."

"I owe you. Karan's your ex, and I'm the one who sent you to New Hope in the first place."

"This round is on you."

Matthew laughed, but Charles couldn't blame the chief for the way things were working out. Or for voicing his opinion. Rhonda, either.

People who'd understood. People who'd cared.

Charles hadn't. He'd blamed Karan and had been hard on her. Why? Because every time he looked at her, he had to talk himself out of responding, out of noticing how beautiful she was, out of wanting to pull her into his arms and kiss her?

By the time he could even think clearly, he'd expended

so much energy talking himself out of being attracted to her that he'd had no choice but to throw up walls to defend himself.

An emotional last-ditch effort to keep avoiding the truth.

His issue, but he'd made Karan feel bad in the process.

It wasn't her fault that he hadn't moved on with his life, that he still had unresolved feelings for her.

She *had* moved on with hers. She'd come up with a new plan, had implemented it. She'd wanted marriage with a man she hadn't been in love with.

It wasn't her fault that when Charles watched her recede in the rearview mirror, he hadn't wanted to leave. It wasn't her fault that he could only think about her admission that she hadn't been happy, either.

CHAPTER TWENTY-THREE

WITH A SIGH THAT ECHOED through the quiet twilight shadowing Mohawk Lake, Karan slipped the cell phone from her pocket, hit the speed dial and waited.

"Hey, you."

Karan let her eyes flutter shut, let the sound of Susanna's voice filter through her.

"Help." It was a pitiful plea at best. And only a true-blue best friend slash honorary sister could be counted on to drop everything and race to the rescue.

"What's wrong?"

"I'm contemplating suicide. I thought I should give you a heads-up before I do myself in."

A beat of silence. "Where are you?"

"On the dock behind my mother's house."

"What on earth are you doing there?"

"Deciding whether or not to step off the dock."

"Your mother?"

"And Charles." Karan waved a dismissive hand as if she could bat away the swell of emotion accompanying the memory of him driving away. "He took me to the hospital to talk with Matthew. We were doing fine, chatting about New Hope and what he's got going on and then the past came up."

"You're upset." Not a question. "And you went to your mother's house? Don't get me wrong. I love her to pieces, but God, Karan. What were you thinking?"

No one knew better than Susanna—except Abigail maybe—that Karan's mother's ability to be supportive was sketchy at best. Had Karan been thinking clearly, she would have known to at least prepare for what she'd gotten.

Obviously not. She hadn't been prepared one bit.

"I was thinking I couldn't bear to be inside my house with every square inch smothering me with memories, and I couldn't get away because I can't drive anywhere except to New Hope, but I was afraid I'd run into Charles there."

All that on one long breath.

"Got it. Stay right where you are and do not, I repeat, do not step off that dock. Do you swear?"

"You're coming?"

"No, I'm manager on duty tonight and I can't leave until nine. But Brooke has my car and she's ten minutes away. I'll text her this second."

Karan waited, feeling so much better knowing Susanna was on the other end. She didn't even have to say anything. Just keep the line open and be there.

"Perfect timing," Susanna finally said. "See how things work out sometimes? Brooke was just leaving Kaley's house and will be there in a flash. I told her to pull off the road near your mother's driveway but not go up. You'll meet her outside. She'll text you as soon as she's there. Will that work?"

"Perfect."

"Now swear to me you won't off yourself, Karan. I'm not playing. If my daughter is the one to find your corpse, I'm going to be seriously, *seriously* annoyed."

"Cut me a break, Suze. I would never traumatize my goddaughter that way."

"Skip would come after you if you did." There was

relief in her voice. "You wouldn't get out your last breath before he'd be all over you."

"No worries then. I already told you he's not in hell, and that's exactly where I'm headed."

"What happened with you two? Did you fight?"

"No. But he got an offer from Mount Sinai, and now he's not sure if he wants to go because I changed things...." Karan explained everything that had happened in front of her house, everything Charles had said, everything she felt, the very act of talking cathartic.

"What did I tell you?" Susanna said when Karan finished. "I knew things weren't settled between you two. Make a note of this, please. I'm not often right. I'd like to refer back every once and a while."

"You're right a lot more than you give yourself credit for." A smile welled up from inside. She was sorry Susanna wasn't there to see it. "I don't know what I've done to deserve you for a best friend, Suze. Nothing, as far as I can tell. But if I were able to choose a sister, I'd totally choose you."

Another beat of silence. "Now you are freaking me out. Really, Karan. Do I need to call 9-1-1?"

"You do not, my friend. Because I've got a text, and I'm guessing it's your daughter who's here to save me from myself."

"She'll bring you to the lodge, okay? I'll see you soon."

"I'll still be breathing when I get there. I swear."

"You'd better be."

Karan ended the call. Sure enough the text was from Brooke and Karan replied with OMW. *On my way.*

Karan headed around the house, feeling breathless and shaky as she avoided being seen by the driver who was waiting in the circle at the top of the drive.

Susanna's car sat idling with the parking lights on, and

as she drew near, the passenger's door swung wide, and a tall, slender girl stepped out.

"You can have the front seat with Brooke," she said. "I'll get in back."

Karan forced a smile. The girl was lovely despite the nose ring, close in age with Brooke, with wide eyes and creamy skin. "Thanks, but that's okay, sweetie. Stay where you are. Which friend of Brooke's are you?"

The girl opened her mouth to reply, but Brooke's voice squealed from inside, "Aunt Karan! This is Gabby. I was so excited when Mom texted. I've wanted Gabby to meet you forever. This is my aunt Karan. Isn't she everything I said?"

Karan slid into the backseat, appreciating the enthusiastic intro.

Okay, Susanna *and Brooke* might miss her.

Leaning forward, she kissed her goddaughter's cheek. "Hey, Brookie cookie. Thanks for rescuing me. I hope you've been telling your friend only good things."

"What else is there to tell?"

If she only knew.

"So what were you guys doing in this part of town?"

Brooke launched into a tale about hanging out before everyone headed off to their respective colleges. Karan asked a few questions, engaged Gabby, whom she knew all about because Gabby happened to be Frankie's daughter from her first marriage, and Jack's new stepdaughter.

Karan and *Frankie*. Women with a *penchant for divorce*. God, she really should have jumped into the lake and put an end to this misery.

Thankfully, the girls distracted her with their excitement about college plans, and soon Brooke was pulling up at the security gate of the upscale retirement community where Susanna managed the finance department, directly underneath Frankie, who managed the property.

The guard in the gatehouse waved the girls through and Brooke parked in a space in front of the building. Karan opened the door and eased out. Add a pounding head to her jitters. Great. A few deep gulps of air helped.

"I owe you big so call in this favor whenever you want and I'll make good," she told Brooke. "But, for the record, I've been working on the car and dorms. Mom isn't budging. *Yet.*"

"You're the best, Aunt Karan." Brooke gave her a hug that melted away so much of the turmoil.

But not the nausea.

"I'm going upstairs to find my mom," Gabby said. "Nice meeting you, Aunt Karan."

Aunt Karan. Frankie would faint. "You, too, Gabby. If I don't see you before you're off to college, good luck. Remember to have lots of fun and make the most of every opportunity."

"Will do, thanks." She turned to Brooke. "Text you later."

Then she headed for the elevators while Brooke led Karan to the administrative offices, where Susanna took one look at her and said, "You might be breathing, but are you sure you're all right, Karan? You're white as a ghost."

She could only nod. The walk into the office seemed to have sapped all her strength. Motion sickness from riding in the backseat of the car?

Her legs felt like jelly underneath her, so she braced herself against the desk, looked around for a chair. The simple act of turning her head made dizziness swell up like a tide. Her heart thumped sickeningly as she found a chair and staggered like a drunk toward it.

Susanna caught her arm and guided her. "What's wrong?"

Karan couldn't seem stop shaking. "Bet you're sorry you picked up the phone."

Susanna stared at her with a frown. Brooke looked worried and Karan was beyond embarrassed.

"I'm fine," she said.

"Brooke, please do me a favor," Susanna said. "Run into the dining room and grab a carton of orange juice from the fridge. They're in there. Just look around."

"Got it." Brooke vanished.

"I've lost my mind."

"People tend to do that when they're upset," Susanna said drily.

Her teeth were chattering so hard now. "Going to be sick."

"No, you're not. Just put your head between your legs and the feeling will pass."

Susanna stood beside her and tucked Karan's hair behind her ear. "How long since you last ate?"

"Lunch."

She frowned but didn't say anything. There wasn't anything to say. Karan knew better. Susanna knew Karan knew better. One more indicator she'd been out of her mind about Charles.

"I should have jumped in the lake."

"Please. You probably only felt like jumping because your sugar was dropping. Mood swings, remember?"

"Ugh." Karan cradled her head in her hands and tried to stave off the nausea. She would never be able to live with herself if she vomited in Susanna's place of business.

Not even she was *that* selfish.

Brooke returned with the orange juice, which Karan

sipped gingerly. But her goddaughter didn't want to hang around and watch the carnage.

"Mom," she said. "I'm starving. I saw cereal."

Susanna waved her off. "Go on. There's fruit, too. Bring an apple and a banana for Aunt Karan when you're done."

Brooke took off again, and Susanna dragged another chair in front of Karan. "Put your feet up. Any better? Your color's coming back."

"Mmm-hmm. Thanks." She rested her head back and let her eyes drift shut.

She must have dozed because the next thing she knew she was opening her eyes to find Susanna behind her desk, frowning at the computer display.

"Thanks." She tested her voice with a whisper.

Susanna glanced up with a smile. "Feeling better?"

"Much." She rose to her feet, stretched. She saw fruit piled neatly on a napkin on the corner of the desk, grabbed the banana. "I'm such an idiot."

"It happens. Glad you feel better. I've still got half an hour before Jerry gets here for the night shift. You good?"

Karan spread her hands. "I'm at your mercy. Slumber party tonight, do you mind?"

"Of course not. And I even have leftovers from last night. Skip's mom's pot roast with the little onions. We can nibble and get some protein in you." She eyed Karan with an assessing look. "How much better do you feel?"

She swallowed a bite of banana. "Much."

"Then let me give you something to do. You asked me to bring you into work one day so you could talk to Francesca about that event for New Hope. And I'm happy to, but it so happens that she's in her office right now. You can go set up a time."

"*Francesca?* Oh, that's right. I forgot you two were the best of friends nowadays." Karan peeled the banana skin with deliberation and admitted, "Well, I didn't actually forget. I blocked it out."

Susanna scowled. "I would hardly say we're best friends. That would be Brooke and Gabby. But Francesca and I do have a good working relationship. Throw Jack into the mix—"

"Please don't, thank you. So what's she doing here at this time of night? Checking up on her duty manager?"

"Don't be mean. Her grandmother lives here, you know that. She wanted to save Brooke from making an unnecessary trip to drop Gabrielle off at home, so she waited. Of course Gabrielle wanted to run upstairs and visit, too, so Francesca's in her office doing what everyone around here does—work. Go. It's the perfect opportunity to set up an appointment. You'll break the ice and it'll be so much less tense when you do talk business."

Karan sighed. No arguing the logic. Susanna hadn't come out and said she still had work to finish up, but Karan could tell she didn't need any more distractions. Dropping the peel into a trash bin, she wiped her hands on the napkin. "Okay, point me and my banana breath in Frankie's direction."

"More flies with honey, remember?" Susanna cautioned. "Door to the left. I'll give her a heads-up. Good luck."

Frankie the fly. Ugh. More penance, Karan knew without a shred of doubt. What else? She'd been so selfish— the apple obviously hadn't fallen far from the tree—she'd probably spend the rest of her life atoning for all the people she'd offended, all the people she'd hurt by her selfishness.

She had not been kind to Frankie in high school.

Taking a deep breath, Karan was determined to suck it up. She was a Kowalski, after all. She could practically hear her father's voice in memory saying, *"No one's perfect, princess, but at the end of the day, you've got to be able to look yourself in the mirror. That's all any of us have."*

She missed him so much sometimes it hurt.

Another deep breath and she strode through the open doorway into a reception area outside the director's office. She barely got a smile on her face before a door opened.

Karan would have recognized Frankie anywhere, yet she seemed an entirely different person with a lot of years and life between the smart-mouthed teen Karan had despised and this woman dressed professionally in a nicely tailored suit.

"Hello, Frankie." She grabbed the reins. "I'll bet I'm the last person you ever expected to be standing in your office."

Or wanted there.

"I can handle it. For a good cause," Frankie said.

That mouth was still going strong, Karan noted. And the hair, too. Fuzzy as ever. But Susanna had been right about everything else. The years had not played tricks on Frankie, aka Francesca, the way they had with Wannabe Jenny. In fact, Frankie wasn't nearly as unfortunate as she'd been as a teen.

Karan supposed some people were like that. They aged like fine wine. Certainly beat decaying like an overripe banana as Wannabe Jenny would know. Not everyone was fortunate enough to have Karan's good genes.

"I'd like to schedule an appointment with you to discuss sponsoring an event for New Hope."

"Certainly," she said. "But we're here, and I'd be happy to talk now, if you'd like."

Karan couldn't decide if Frankie was trying to be polite or just wanted to get this over with.

Flies with honey. Flies with honey.

"If that's most convenient for you," Karan said.

Frankie invited Karan into the office and motioned to a chair in front of the desk.

Karan didn't miss the twinkling diamond engagement ring and wedding band set. Sizeable enough to be noticed. She approved. Karan launched into her pitch about the golf challenge she hoped to organize with Greywacke Lodge as a sponsor. "I know your facility has supported New Hope in the past—" because it was a pet project of Frankie's husband "—and sponsored the first annual Return to Peace Brunch. We hope that by involving your residents in the golf challenge, we can raise awareness about domestic violence with people who have the resources to contribute through pledges, estate planning or even with titled donations like cars or boats. At this stage of the game everything will help."

Frankie listened attentively, but now she inclined her head and reached for a calendar. "Susanna mentioned some of the things you're doing at New Hope, and we're definitely interested in lending a hand. A golf challenge sounds like a wonderful way to engage our residents. It's important for them to stay connected to the community, to feel valued. Not all of them play golf, of course, but a great many do. Why don't we come up with some tentative dates?"

Karan whipped out her BlackBerry, and they worked out some potential dates and discussed details about the specific needs of targeting this age group. Frankie certainly seemed knowledgeable about the population of the community. Karan jotted notes about specifics to incorporate in her proposal.

"You're willing to provide the transportation?" she asked.

Frankie nodded. "That will be easiest. We're outfitted

to transport our residents. Once I have a solid number, I'll work out the details. Bus, van, cars."

"Great. That will definitely save money that can be put to good use elsewhere."

"While I've got you here, Karan, let me also mention that we have an ongoing activity calendar. If you're interested in scheduling a presentation about New Hope, that might be a good way to make contact with residents who won't participate in the golf challenge. Doesn't have to be anything formal or fancy. We provide refreshments, but we generally have a good turn out."

"Great idea," Karan said, pleased. And she found that she meant it. "Pencil us in. I'll work out the presenter with the directors and get the information to you so you can advertise."

Karan met Frankie's gaze across the desk. Somehow, during the past ten minutes, history had managed to retreat to where it belonged. The present was all about the director of an upscale retirement community trying to actively engage her residents in a cause that would benefit New Hope.

In the present, Frankie seemed to be one more person trying to make a difference, trying to help. Was this good will mentality trending in the new millennium? Or had it been going on all along and Karan hadn't noticed?

Like Frankie. Had the antagonistic girl Karan had once loathed transformed into this professional, not unattractive—despite the fuzzy hair—woman?

Or had Karan's perceptions simply been all wrong?

After gathering up her BlackBerry and notes, she shook Frankie's hand, thanked her for her time and promised to follow up when businesses reopened after the Fourth of July holiday.

Before she left, Karan paused in the doorway. "By the

way, Frankie, I hitched a ride with Brooke and your daughter. She's a lovely girl. You must be very proud."

For the first time since Karan stepped foot inside this office, Frankie smiled. And that smile said absolutely everything. "Thank you. I am."

Karan walked out, knowing that whatever life tossed her way, at least for tonight she'd be able to look herself in the mirror.

CHAPTER TWENTY-FOUR

KARAN SNAPPED THE LEATHER journal she'd been reading aloud from shut and glanced up to find Rhonda watching her with a thoughtful expression.

"Wow," Rhonda said with her gift for understatement. "You've had a lot going on this week. I appreciate you sharing your thoughts. And I agree. There's so much there I would have hated for you to miss anything. I'm so glad the writing is proving a good tool for you."

Karan nodded, all talked out for the moment. She'd taken a leap. *Gone for it* as Brooke would have said. She'd recorded everything that had happened after her visit to Matthew and filled Rhonda in the best way she knew how. She'd written a lot and the reading of it had taken a while. There wasn't much left of this session. She wondered what Rhonda would zero in on.

But Rhonda didn't seem time-conscious as she leaned back in the chair and said again, "Wow."

Karan wouldn't argue. It was funny how she'd first walked into this very office convinced there would be nothing here for her, nothing but whiling away more of her commitment to the alternative sentence. But now she came out of these sessions feeling good. As if she was focused and clear and pulling the pieces together on things she didn't realize needed piecing together. She didn't know how else to explain it. Maybe it was all the talking. Or maybe it was all the listening.

"Well, how do you feel about putting a demon behind you?" Rhonda finally asked.

"Which one?"

"The one you put behind you." She smiled. "Seems to me there are still a few on the table."

"Frankie?"

She nodded.

"I could look myself in the mirror. I felt…good."

Rhonda applauded. "You go, Karan. You should feel good. Moving forward is empowering, liberating even."

She must have looked confused because Rhonda said, "Think about it. When we're willing to let something go, we free ourselves up to move in new directions. That takes the ability to change and the courage to risk the unknown. When we empower ourselves to do that, by definition we're trusting that we can handle whatever comes up, that we'll recognize and enjoy the good stuff and figure out the rest. Can you think of anything more liberating than believing in yourself?"

Karan set the journal on the desk, trying to fit what Rhonda said around what she'd done with Frankie. "I guess not."

"You know, we haven't discussed your mother before," Rhonda pointed out. "And now that you've had a little time to consider the situation with fresh eyes, how do you feel about what happened that night?"

That took some thought. She stretched her legs out before her. "Guilty."

"That's interesting. About what, exactly?"

"For embarrassing her. It's bad enough I'm dealing with it, but by coordinating these events, I'm involving everyone I know and drawing attention to my situation."

"Do you think that's a good reason to be embarrassed of you?"

Even the thought was making Karan uncomfortable. She didn't like remembering her mother's complaints or the way they'd made her feel, so resigned, so *guilty*. "Everything she said is true. I've been married twice and neither of my marriages hit the five-year mark. I can't drive because I'm dealing with a DWAI—"

"That's not what I asked," Rhonda pointed out. "I asked if you feel she has good reason to be embarrassed of you."

"Well, no. Not everything has worked out the way I've planned, but it could be worse."

"You mean you could be a crack addict who gave birth to an addicted baby? Or a high-powered workaholic mom who lets the nanny raise the kids? True, you made a bad choice after a glass of champagne, but you're not someone who sits at a bar after work every night and thinks nothing of getting in the car for the drive home. You're not someone who doesn't care that you have driving restrictions, someone who gets behind the wheel even after her license was suspended."

"None of the above."

"You're not perfect, Karan. Is that what you're saying?"

"Who is?"

Rhonda smiled. "Exactly my point. If you're feeling guilty because you're not the perfect daughter, then guess what?"

"I'm always going to feel guilty."

She nodded. "How is talking about this making you feel?"

"Uncomfortable. Almost mutinous."

"You're feeling disloyal to your mother? Did you feel guilty because you were upset about Charles and you needed your mother to be there for you?"

An easy answer. One of the few tonight. "Yes."

"Do you think you were asking for anything unreasonable?"

"No. I didn't even burden her with the details since she was on her way out. I just didn't want to be alone in the house and I can't drive anywhere but here. I didn't want to run into Charles, either."

"Interesting choice of words. *Burden*."

No denying that she felt that way sometimes. Not always, but definitely some of the time. "My mother's sort of hit or miss with the parenting."

"Fair enough. But you did pick up the phone and call Susanna. Did you feel guilty about needing her?"

"No."

"So you'd reciprocate if she needed you?"

"Of course." And she had. "Susanna's husband Skip was sick for two years before he died."

Two years of doctors' appointments and uncertainty. Through it all Susanna soldiered on to keep her family together when their world was crashing down on top of them.

"Tell me about some of the ways you were there for Susanna during that difficult time," Rhonda said.

Karan explained how she and Patrick had pulled strings with every doctor they'd known to get Skip the best care. She hadn't wanted delays while waiting for tests, time for the non-Hodgkins lymphoma to run rampant and take away his chances to win the fight.

Driving Skip into the city for treatments when Susanna couldn't take time off work and Skip's parents were getting overwhelmed by their only son's struggle.

Slumber parties with the kids when Skip had a bad reaction to the chemotherapy or wound up in the hospital.

Or simply listening when Susanna needed to talk. She hadn't been able to unload on Skip, who was fighting so hard, not when she was bolstering his spirits so he'd keep hope.

Still, knowing what Karan knew now about herself, she'd probably missed a thousand opportunities to help. Of course, Susanna had been so distracted with the way her life had been falling apart she probably hadn't noticed.

Or, knowing Susanna, she'd noticed but had appreciated what Karan had offered.

"Sounds like you were a very good friend." Rhonda smiled. "Do you think you're any less a daughter?"

"That's not such a simple answer."

"Why not?"

"My mother can be…complicated."

"Were you there for her when your father died?"

Karan shrugged. "As much as she'd let me be. Like I said, she's complicated. I go with the flow to see what kind of mood she's in and try to adapt. Doesn't always work. Especially at night. I usually avoid nights."

"What happens?"

Bracing herself, Karan was surprised by how difficult it was to get a few words out, as if sharing the truth was somehow a betrayal of something that should have remained unspoken. "She drinks."

Rhonda steepled her hands in front of her, didn't look at all surprised. "Alcohol can complicate things a lot. But it's not really about your mother, Karan. From what you're saying, it doesn't sound as if she has a lot of strong coping skills in place. She might even be dealing with some narcissism issues."

"Narcissism issues?"

Rhonda nodded. "Follow me here. *You* ran into trouble with the law. *You* were assigned to community service. *You* are here at New Hope, helping out, attending therapy, but your mother hasn't asked how you are, or why you were careless with your drinking or how you're holding up with your ex-husband. This whole situation is about how *she* looks like a bad mother, how *she* can't go to a party without feeling as if she has to make excuses for you. See what I'm saying?"

"It's all about her."

"Bingo. But this isn't about her. I've never evaluated her, so I can only speculate based on what you've said. Please be clear on that. We can't fix her, and that's okay. What we can do is to figure out how her behavior impacts you and give you tools to deal in a more effective way so your interactions aren't so hurtful. We can help you learn to be realistic in your expectations and establish boundaries that can actually benefit both of you. Do you think that might help the situation?"

Karan considered that. "It's always stressful not knowing what to expect whenever I walk in the door or answer the phone."

"Do you think empowering yourself and being responsible for your actions instead of getting bounced around by hers might diminish the need to keep so much distance between yourself and your emotions?"

"Hadn't considered that before."

"Consider it then," Rhonda encouraged her. "You mentioned all the distance you're keeping in your life. The way it has impacted your marriages. I'm thinking not so much with Susanna."

Because Karan trusted her best friend? Because she knew what to expect, knew that she didn't have to protect herself from Susanna?

"No, not so much with Susanna. Because I trust her."

"Or maybe you trust *you* with her? Think about this. You know you can be a good friend because you have been for so long. You never had enough time to develop that confidence in yourself in either of your marriages. And the one relationship you've had longer than any of them constantly leaves you guessing about whether or not you're a good daughter. How do you think that might impact your self-worth?"

Karan was constantly guessing. That much was true. And something struck a deep chord as she tried to imagine what the impact of all that guessing might be.

She remembered her father. He never argued. Never. He stayed in the city working or he entertained himself on the lake or snowmobiling or skiing or attending sports events. He lived life. He enjoyed his relationship with Karan. He included her mother whenever she'd let herself be included and those were the rare times they'd functioned together as a family.

He'd realized he couldn't please his wife, that nothing he did would ever be good enough. He understood that the problem wasn't his, but hers.

You're like a bottomless pit, Charles had said.

Had Karan been looking to Charles to reassure her that she was a good wife? But no matter what he did it never seemed to be enough. "How can anyone make me feel good about me?"

Rhonda pointed a finger at Karan and said, "That's exactly the right question to ask. What's the answer?"

"No one else can. No one but me."

The smile stretched across her face. "Very good."

And it made total sense.

"I should be taking notes," she said. "I've got lightbulbs flashing on, and I don't want to forget anything."

"Don't worry. I'll remind you." There was laughter in Rhonda's voice.

"Okay, answer me this. What's the point? I get that circumstances with my mother have impacted the way

I feel about myself. But I can't blame her for the way I behave."

"I agree entirely."

Karan couldn't help but think about the young girl with the fairy princess mother, who'd taught her to entertain, to socialize, to dress, to groom… "My mother is smart and people savvy. Sometimes she even has great advice about things. That's why I say it's hit or miss with her."

"I don't doubt it." Rhonda considered. "You're a lovely, intelligent and gifted woman. That didn't happen by accident. We all have circumstances we're brought up in. None are perfect. This is simply your situation—the good and the bad. If your mother doesn't possess the ability to step outside herself and perceive another person's perspective, then she can love you all she wants and every situation will still wind up about her.

"It might help to think of her as a lighthouse. When the fog parts, she's there, a shining beacon to lead you through uncharted waters. Then the fog rolls in again and it's all about her. It's not that she doesn't care. It's who she is for whatever the reason. Sounds like she sees everything as a reflection of herself. If that's the case, then it really has nothing to do with you. Personal accountability. That's the key. Who's the only person who can make you feel good about you?"

It was really so simple. "Me."

She nodded. "When we look to others to make us feel good about ourselves, we're at the mercy of a lot of factors we don't have control over, that may or may not have anything to do with us. Our self-worth gets bounced around like a cork in the ocean. Once we accept responsibility and realize we have the control, then we can get to a more solid place, a better place.

"That's exactly what you did with Frankie. You couldn't

change the past, but you could change the present. You had no idea how she would respond to your efforts, but it didn't matter, did it?"

Karan shook her head.

"Why?"

"Because I knew I was doing the right thing."

"Exactly. You assumed control of your actions and made the best choice you could in that moment. Personal accountability. You controlled what you could and trusted yourself to handle the rest. Frankie's response wasn't yours to control. It was hers. But no matter how she responded you could go home and look yourself in the mirror."

The example set everything in place. Karan understood exactly what Rhonda was saying with such clarity it nearly took her breath away. Even better, she saw how it applied to her marriage—to Charles. With Patrick she'd delineated the boundaries so carefully, placed so much distance between them that she'd never had to worry about feeling anything at all.

Except comfortable.

She couldn't help but chuckle.

"What's so funny?" Rhonda asked.

"I have to tell you I only started therapy because I had to. I enjoyed chatting with you, but I really didn't get the point. I wasn't convinced anything was wrong."

"Now?"

"Now everything feels...*right*."

She met Rhonda's gaze and realized that *right* meant empowered, clear, able to handle what came up, in control.

"Thank you," she said.

"You're welcome," Rhonda said. "Your question this week is—*what about you makes you feel good about yourself?*"

"Got it." Karan glanced at her watch. "And we are

seriously over my time. I hope I didn't make you miss anything important."

"You didn't make me do a thing. Personal account-ability, remember? And I wouldn't have missed *this* for the world." Rhonda's smile assured that she meant ex-actly what she said. "This is the very best part of my job. Seriously."

Karan laughed and said goodbye. She waved at Deputy Doug, who was on the phone, as she headed to the back door. Then she hopped in her car, tossed her purse in the passenger seat and turned over the engine. She'd only ar-rived a few hours ago, but the late-day heat had cooked the interior. Lowering the windows, she blasted the air-conditioning, chasing out the stifling heat.

Pausing at the gatehouse, she waited while the elec-tronic gate opened. Then she depressed the accelerator and drove through, still feeling a crazy sense of hope about nothing in particular but everything in general, her head filled with winding thoughts that made sense with such sudden and amazing clarity.

Coasting to the end of the drive, she braked at the stop sign, for the first time noticing a car parked in the grass.

Suddenly, a violence of motion erupted in her periph-ery. She was slow to react, distracted by her thoughts. In an instant the sun vanished as if someone had stepped in front of it, a rough hand thrust through the open window and caught her hair in a fist. Hard fingers dug to the roots of her scalp and snapped her head back painfully.

"Put the car in Park."

She heard only the words, the thick accent, but hadn't made sense of what was happening before feeling the chill, startling pressure of a knife blade against her throat.

CHAPTER TWENTY-FIVE

CHARLES LEFT THE SURGICAL UNIT for the first time all day and arrived on the floor to make rounds. He found a group of people clustered around the open doorway to a break room.

Hospital staff gathered anywhere and *not* doing their duties was never a good sign.

Stopping at the back of the crowd, he asked, "What's going on?"

There was a small TV blaring from within, but he didn't catch what was happening because someone said, "Some crazy took a hostage not too far from here."

"Break it up, people," a voice said. "We'll find out what's going on when the ambulance shows up."

Charles knew his arrival had brought an end to the party. Attending physicians liked to see staff busy taking care of the patients. He was no exception, particularly as he had five patients in this ward.

The crowd thinned, and he had a clear shot of the TV. An orderly was about to turn it off when Charles caught sight of a familiar and unexpected scene.

"Wait," he said.

The orderly shrugged and stepped back.

A breaking news banner was fixed in the upper corner of the television screen. A news anchor spoke into a microphone, emergency vehicles parked haphazardly behind her.

"Hostage negotiators have arrived at the scene..."

There was no mention of New Hope. The reporter kept referring to the event unfolding at a *local business*. But Charles recognized the gatehouse.

And the Jag in front of it.

For one blind moment he stared, every shred of his reason rebelling against what he saw and the facts in his head.

Karan? A hostage?

And suddenly, his very next breath depended on knowing that she was okay.

KARAN COULD HEAR SOUNDS OF activity, couldn't see anything but the security gate directly in front of her windshield. Her whole world had narrowed to the raspy intakes of her captor's breaths in her ear, and the thickly muscled forearm around her neck. The smell of clammy skin and fear almost choked her with every thin breath she managed to take, his grip was so tight her vision grew dark around the edges.

Every time a siren shrieked, he startled and dug the knife blade deeper. Not intentionally. But he would saw through her carotid artery if this kept up.

She had no idea how long they'd been sitting here, although there was a clock on her dash. She would have had to move her head to see it.

Her captor had taken advantage of her surprise and clambered inside the car. If she'd only had her doors locked. She hadn't been driving fast enough to engage the automatic locks, so he'd invited himself in. He'd made her conduct a three-point turn and head back to the gate.

She had no clue what his plan had been. Maybe he'd thought the gate would be opened when he threatened to kill her. Now that the adrenaline was subsiding, Karan was pushing past the fear, trying to understand what was happening. She understood why the guard had refused to comply.

None of this would have been a problem if she had hit the gas and run this man over.

The thought only occurred to her now.

Deputy Doug had tried to negotiate via a bullhorn. He'd only managed to keep her captor talking long enough for police cruisers to crowd into the drive behind them.

Now they were trapped inside her car, and she sincerely hoped the police had a plan. A good one because if this man decided to slit her throat, she'd be dead in her front seat before the police could even react.

They kept trying to talk to him. His cell phone rang and rang and rang, but he wouldn't pick up.

He said he wanted his family. He'd told the security guard he would release Karan in exchange for his wife and kids.

Marisol, Raphael, Esme and Everleigh.

His grip never slackened. Another siren. The blade dug deeper. Karan squeezed her eyes shut tight against the pain, didn't dare breathe, didn't want to wind up bleeding out before someone came up with a plan. Someone would come up with a plan, wouldn't they?

Otherwise, how long would they sit here before someone snapped? Her captor reminded her of Al, the man who owned the landscaping company that cared for her yard and her mother's. A normal man.

But this man, no matter how normal he may have been, had been pushed to the edge, distraught. A man who could stand on a dock and look down at the depths and see peace.

She didn't know what his issues were or what he'd done to send Marisol fleeing with their children, but Karan couldn't get past the thought that at some point Marisol had loved this man enough to reproduce with him. Three beautiful children. This man had had it all.

CHARLES KEPT TRYING EVERY number he had on his speed dial as he drove toward New Hope. The place was on lockdown. Rhonda's line rolled straight to voice mail. The switchboard kept replaying the recorded message. The substation went to the sheriff's main number.

And the damned booties he wore over his sneakers kept catching on the clutch every time he moved to brake. He hadn't changed out of his scrubs, had flown out of the hospital immediately, intent on one thing—finding out whether Karan was alive.

He hadn't tried the crisis line yet. But that line was staffed with counselors who weren't on site and likely would have no more idea about what was going on than he did.

Throwing the phone onto the passenger seat, he slammed a palm against the steering wheel when he caught the light at busy County Road 42 and Millstream. This was downtown Bluestone Mountain, for God's sake. Where did this traffic even come from?

Charles didn't slow until he was about to turn the final corner. The police had the street barricaded. He could see the drive in the distance, blocked by emergency vehicles. BMPD cruisers. Paramedics. He jumped a curb on the opposite side of the street and parked the Jeep on the sidewalk.

"Excuse me. Let me through," he demanded of the onlookers.

Through a gap in the activity, he could see an older-model sedan parked in the grass on the side of the drive. And the taillights of Karan's Jag farther up by the gate.

Was she still inside?

Hostage.

"Away from the perimeter, sir," an officer warned.

"I'm a director of this facility." Charles flashed his hospital ID without thinking, urgency fueling him.

That got a nominally better response. The officer reached for his radio and stepped away from the barricade to converse.

Whomever he spoke with must have confirmed Charles's identity because the officer turned around and warned the onlookers to back away as he moved the wooden barricade so Charles could get through.

"Wait with the paramedics," he said curtly. "The chief will talk with you when he can."

Jack was here. Charles wished that made a difference.

Of course, the media would notice the whole exchange, and the news anchor didn't miss a beat. She rushed along the outside of the barricade until she could reach him, waving her microphone, the cameraman bumping into people to keep up while hauling the bulky equipment.

"Sir, you're affiliated with this business? What is this place? Would you make a statement?"

"No comment." Charles turned his back on the woman and made his way to the front of the ambulance.

The officer stopped him again. "Wait over there."

"The woman inside the car." *Karan.* "Is she alive?"

The officer only leveled a steely gaze.

"I'm a director of this facility," Charles persisted. "I want to know what's going on. There's a hostage being held at knifepoint. I want to know what you're doing to recover her."

"Let the negotiators do their jobs." The officer turned away and resumed glaring at the crowd.

Charles stood there, for a moment so dumbfounded that he didn't have any answers. He had no clue what was happening fifty feet away, no way to help Karan and no idea what the police were doing to protect her. No idea if she'd been hurt. He was separated from the rest of the onlookers by one wooden barricade. But he wasn't just any onlooker, and that hostage wasn't just any woman.

Karan.

"WHAT'S YOUR NAME?" KARAN asked.

The sound of her voice drifted into the confines of the car. There hadn't been a siren in a while. Marisol's husband hadn't made a move in a while. She wondered if the police's plan was to let them asphyxiate from exhaust fumes by sitting in this idling car for so long.

Silence.

But Marisol's husband didn't slit her throat. She tried again.

"You have very beautiful children."

That got more of a response. His breath hitched audibly, a shuddering sound, and Karan slanted her gaze toward him, a barely perceptible move. He was so close his features were distorted. She was struck again by how normal he looked. A normal, nice-looking man.

There were tears streaming down his cheeks.

An angry man?

He looked only broken right now.

How had a man with a beautiful wife and three adorable children fallen so far that he could actually think this was the way to handle his situation?

She remembered Amy, recalled wondering why anyone would marry a man who threatened her.

But Karan thought she understood now.

She'd figured it out tonight in Rhonda's office. Maybe Amy's husband hadn't always been threatening. Maybe Marisol's husband wasn't a bad person, either, but one with horrible coping skills. One who'd gotten kicked around too much in life. If he'd been abused himself, maybe he didn't know any other way. Maybe he felt pressured. Maybe he was an addict. Maybe he'd gotten in over his head with his anger.

She had no way of knowing, but if life kept piling on the problems and they weren't getting resolved in a healthy way, was it really so difficult to understand how someone might wind up very far from where they'd started?

One bad choice at a time.

People went out of their minds every day. Suicides. Murders. Midlife crises. Affairs. Divorces. Bad choice after bad choice. Even her own mother who kept the whole world at bay, wrapped in the cocoon of alcohol and her own perspective.

Was it so hard to believe life could eventually get bigger than a person's ability to deal with it?

"You really do have beautiful children," Karan said again. "They need both their parents."

He shook his head. This man's hope was gone. He was sitting inside a carjacked Jaguar with a hostage, surrounded by police.

She thought of Wannabe Jenny. This relic from a long-ago past hadn't been willing to cut Karan any slack for a first offense. She'd been determined to flex her muscles and exercise her power over Karan the way Karan had once done to her. But in so doing, Wannabe Jenny had sent Karan to New Hope.

Maybe Wannabe Jenny had even been a little sincere when she'd told Karan: *"I want your first offense to be your last."*

Either way, a nightmare of a situation had turned Karan's life around. Wannabe Jenny had sent Karan to New Hope, where she'd met Charles again, and Rhonda, and a lot of people who'd opened Karan's eyes to so many things. And if that much change could happen for her…

"I don't know your circumstances or what happened between you and Marisol, but I do know it's not too late," she said. "Not if you're willing to admit you need help. If you're willing to tackle your issues and do the right thing, then your family will have something to work with, something to respect. If you can look yourself in the mirror, so will the people who love you."

Karan needed to believe that, too.

CHARLES HEARD A voice say, "Positions, men. We have movement."

"Still got him in your site, Naparlo?"

"Yes, sir."

That was all Charles needed to hear to abandon cooperation. Circling the rear of the ambulance, he emerged behind an unmarked cruiser, kept low so the hostage negotiation team wouldn't notice him. He scanned the scene, saw Jack in the thick of things, wearing a headset. Then he saw Karan.

He could barely make out the pale blur of her hair through the tinted window, but she was still upright, not slumped over the steering wheel, lifeless. He exhaled a breath he hadn't realized he'd held, the sight impacting him on so many levels.

"Looks like she's coming out, Captain," the man called Naparlo said, likely able to see inside the car through the site on the sniper rifle.

There was a barrage of activity from the officers. Charles stood riveted as the driver's door swung outward, and Karan emerged piece by piece, feet in strappy sandals, shapely legs bare beneath the hem of her dress. She weaved a bit, took a step to steady herself. There was blood on her neck and she looked pale, but otherwise healthy. Shaken.

Raising her arms above her head, she faced the police in a pose of classic surrender. She held a hunting knife with a curved blade in one hand.

"Excuse me." Her voice was a strained whisper. "Excuse me," she said again, louder this time. "Please, you don't need all those guns. Raphael will come out if you agree not to shoot him. I have his weapon."

She held out the knife.

"Step away from the car, ma'am," a negotiator spoke through the bullhorn.

"You won't shoot him, will you?"

Jack grabbed the bullhorn. "Karan, move away from the car."

"I gave my word, Jack."

Jack had clearly reached his limit because he was already bearing down on her when he said, "If you'll follow a simple direction, we might not have to."

But Charles got to her before Jack could, had his arm around her shoulders and dragged her away. The knife clattered to the ground as she grabbed onto him to keep balanced. The police moved in to form a perimeter, directed her captor to come out with his hands up.

By then Charles had her at the ambulance, but he cut off the paramedics as they approached, pulling her near until he could feel her full-length against him, every curve familiar.

He wrapped his arms around her and held her.

In that moment, as he rested his cheek on the top of her head and held her close, he knew this was right. On some level he'd known, had always known, that if he'd touched her he could never convince himself he was content without her.

He'd known.

"Charles." Her voice filtered through him, the activity around them fading away. For this moment there was only the two of them. The way she fit completely with him, every curve aligned, until he was aware of only her.

So right.

Her slim arms slipped around his waist, her cheek pressed against his chest, her head in the crook of his neck so his every breath was tinged with *her*.

No history. No complications. Just them and a simple, unavoidable truth.

Didn't matter whether they were married or divorced, whether he was avoiding her or she was demanding the impossible of him, their bodies knew each other.

And for this one moment, he didn't want to let go.

But he couldn't ignore how cold she felt. Lowering his face, he pressed his mouth to her neck, felt her pulse beat rapidly. Tasted her moist skin. The minute he loosened his grip, he felt her tremble.

"Okay," he said. "Let's go."

Their moment was over.

She lifted her gaze to his, sparkly gray eyes that had power over him that he couldn't explain. He saw dilated pupils, and regret. He felt hesitation in her arms that didn't seem to want to let him go.

He steered her toward the ambulance, and she didn't say a word. That told Charles everything he needed to know.

"I've got her, gentlemen." He flashed his hospital ID.

"What do you need, Dr. Steinberg?" The paramedic's name badge read *Joe*.

"We'll assess her, Joe, and bandage the lacerations on her neck."

"You got it."

"Come on, Karan, onto the gurney."

"I'm fine," she said weakly.

"Shh." He pressed a finger to her lips. "Indulge me."

She sank onto the gurney boneless, no more argument in her, and Charles helped her swing her legs around. Joe's partner raised the gurney while Joe set a wedge beneath her ankles to raise them then pulled a blanket over her legs.

Charles examined her, leaving Joe to register her vitals, then he checked the lacerations beneath her jaw.

Mere scratches. Nothing that needed more than cleansing to keep the wound site from infection. Nothing that wouldn't heal quickly. Even the scars would eventually fade away. But the idea of that curved blade pressed against her throat, the artery pulsing below her smooth skin, had a grip on his brain.

One stroke between life and death.

The only thing that saved Charles was his training, the need to take familiar action, to minimize the effects of her shock, to deal with an unexpected complication.

"Her sugar's crashing," Charles told Joe. "Hypoglycemic."

"Glucagon?" Joe asked.

"One milligram." To cause a rapid release of glucose stores from her liver and get her on track again.

Charles ran his fingers along her cheek while waiting for Joe to prepare the dosage. "Come on, Karan. Stay with me."

"Here you go, Dr. Steinberg."

Joe pulled aside the blanket and brushed up her hem, revealing an expanse of smooth hip. Charles checked the syringe then swabbed the site for an intramuscular injection.

"You'll feel better in a minute," he told her, gave her the injection then stroked the hair from her face and waited.

Jack showed up, scowling when he saw her, obviously

not expecting to find her stretched out on the gurney nearly unconscious. "Is she okay?"

"Sugar bottomed out."

Jack's scowl deepened, but he didn't drag his eyes away. "She's not hurt?"

"Only the lacerations on her throat. Shock's to be expected."

Jack nodded. Whatever their past history, he still cared. It was all over him.

Karan had that effect on the men in her life.

"I need a statement," he said. "But I'll come back when she's feeling better. Don't let her leave until I do."

"You got it. Everything working out over there?"

"Got him in custody. I don't like that he found this place. We'll question him, and I'll let you know."

"We'll relocate his family. They'll be all right."

Jack nodded then headed toward the officer at the barricade. "Let's keep the media away from the triage site."

Karan would definitely appreciate that.

She was rousing by the time her visitors showed up.

Rhonda headed toward them. "Oh, please tell me she's okay."

"She'll be fine."

"We couldn't get out until they got Marisol's husband in custody. We followed safety protocol, and it worked to a T."

"That's good to know. Marisol and the kids okay?"

"Perfect. They knew there was commotion, but they didn't have a clue what it was about. I already placed a call to Albany. I'll address everything with her when I get inside."

Charles nodded, glanced at Karan. "You have visitors." He helped her sit up. Her color had started to return.

"Ever think of a career as a hostage negotiator?" Deputy Doug asked. "You talked that guy down like a pro."

Rhonda placed her fingers in her ears and warned Karan, "Do not listen. You're New Hope's promotional director."

Karan smiled, still visibly weak. "Rhonda, he wants his family back. He knows he needs help. Will you make sure he gets it? *Good* help."

"I'll follow up personally."

Charles knew Rhonda well enough to know she'd grown fond of Karan. He had no idea how that had happened, hadn't expected it, but there it was. Rhonda had a unique ability to cut through pretenses and see the real person within. He knew it was a skill honed by her profession, but the faith she had in people was a gift unique to her.

He was glad she'd shared it with him. And Karan.

The huddle of emergency vehicles began breaking up in the wake of the officers' departure with Marisol's husband. Jack returned to take Karan's statement and Deputy Doug returned the house from lockdown to normal. Rhonda was gearing up to have a difficult conversation with Marisol.

But Charles remained with Karan, listened to her recount events inside the car, convincing Jack to get Marisol's husband help with some sort of program to help him address his problems.

Charles was unclear about so many things in his life, but he had absolute clarity about one thing.

He would do what he hadn't done five years ago. He was going to stand beside Karan right now because she needed him.

CHAPTER TWENTY-SIX

CHARLES EASED THE JEEP TO A stop in front of the dark house. Karan had fallen asleep on the ride, wedged between the seat and the door. She looked perfectly content with a blanket covering her, her hair a pale cloud around her face in the darkness. The only reminder of today's events was the bandage on her neck.

Not for him, though.

The past and present collided when he looked at her. He'd almost lost her today. It shouldn't have felt this way. He'd given up on them long ago.

Grabbing her purse from the floor by her feet, he whispered, "Karan, we're here."

She burrowed into the seat, and he debated attempting to carry her in.

He'd carried her over this threshold before.

Taking advantage of the moment, he reached out to stroke the hair from her cheek, a reflexive action that came so easily.

"Karan."

Her lashes fluttered. When she finally opened her eyes, she looked disoriented, surprised to see him.

"We're here."

We're home.

The words popped into his head, surreal, shades of another lifetime.

"Okay." She nodded, shook off sleep.

"I'll come around and get the door."

The Jeep's headlights lit their way to the steps. The house was dark. Not even a porch light. Karan clearly hadn't expected to be out past sunset, had no one awaiting her return.

She dug through her purse to find keys, unlocked the door. She reached inside to flip on the foyer light, and backlit from the interior he could see her expression, recognized when it occurred to her that he needed to be dealt with. It must have been a remnant from the day's events, but he could see the debate in her expression, vulnerability leaving her unusually transparent.

Did she say goodbye or invite him in?

"Mind if I come in?" He made his wishes known.

That surprised her. He could see it all over a face that was usually so skilled at concealing her thoughts.

Or had he not looked closely enough?

"You don't have to, Charles. I appreciate all you've done already."

A few things struck him about that.

She was thinking of his feelings when he'd been so convinced she thought only of herself.

And he didn't want her to be alone.

"Not a problem. I'd like to see you settled."

She held his gaze for a second, clearly not sure what to make of his interest. Then she motioned him in.

Since the headlights would time out in a few minutes, he followed her inside, still carrying the blanket.

Lightning didn't strike.

This was nothing more than a house, and they were only two people who'd once lived together. Nothing momentous here.

Except inside him. It felt momentous in there.

She set her purse and keys on a small table in the foyer,

flipped another switch, throwing the living room into low light. The Tuscan villa of his memory, the endless shopping expeditions to find *lighter finishes, earthy tones and terra cotta that would bring to mind sun-washed vineyards* had vanished beneath a sleek contemporary look.

Had her second husband been as accommodating? Karan knew every furniture store between Bluestone and the city.

"It's different," he commented unnecessarily.

"I created a new environment."

"For your husband?" The second one.

She accepted the blanket from him. "No, we didn't really spend much time here. He wasn't comfortable."

Charles didn't have to ask why. He wouldn't have been, either. Why hadn't she sold the place? He didn't ask that, either, wasn't prepared to hear the answer. Not when he'd realized how much he could still feel for Karan.

"May I get you something, Charles?"

The perfect hostess. She had no clue how conflicted he was right now. Once, she might have known.

"No, thanks." Slipping an arm around her shoulder, he steered her toward the living room.

He told himself he wasn't taking advantage because he wanted to touch her.

"That's my job. I'll get you whatever you need. I want you settled and resting. You call it—couch or bed."

She let him lead, still looked undecided as she dropped the blanket onto an ottoman. "Bed, I guess. It's been an eventful day. I should probably call it a night and cut my losses."

"Who's going to stay with you?"

That took her off guard. She tipped her face to his, and he met her gaze, sensed she was about to rebel.

"I'm fine by myself. I'll sleep." A soft laugh burst from her lips. "Trust me, I'll sleep."

But she wasn't fine. She'd been abducted and held at knifepoint. She was still suffering the effects of shock, her sugar bottoming out.

And he wasn't fine, either. Because every time he looked at her, he wanted to touch her, to reassure himself that she was here, okay, *alive.*

He shook his head, unprepared to yield. "What about your mother, or Susanna?"

"Not a good time for my mother, and I can't call Susanna. Rescuing me has become a full-time job for her lately, and she has an important presentation to give to her management company in the morning. She's stressed enough without losing sleep because of me. I texted her and told her I was fine. If she thinks I lied, she'll kill me."

"I'm the attending physician, so I call the shots. Produce someone to spend the night or you'll have me sleeping on your couch. It's not a problem. I've got my spare bag in the car."

The spare bag had been her idea. She used to pack it for him so he could swap out the clothes in his hospital locker. He still kept the bag in the car, always prepared, so he'd never get stuck without something clean and decent to wear. He wondered if she remembered.

He did. She'd always left notes stuffed in odd places so he'd come across them unexpectedly. A pocket. A shoe. Cut-out hearts with their names. Notes that read: *"Miss you."* Personalized stationary handwritten in her elegant script detailing what she wanted to do with him in bed—so bold that Charles remembered thinking it would be safer to chew and swallow them rather than risk a colleague coming across one.

She called them love notes, so he wouldn't forget how much she loved him no matter where he was.

He'd forgotten.

"What's it going to be?" he asked.

Her expression melted. Wistful, maybe. Not displeasure. That was something. Leaving her alone wasn't an option.

"I really appreciate you being here for me today, Charles. It was very nice of you, but you don't have to worry—"

"It wasn't nice. It was selfish. I almost lost you. I didn't know it would matter. It did."

There, he'd admitted it aloud, put the truth between them. There was nothing noble about it. He was simply being honest. *Not* avoiding how he felt. He was unclear about so many things, but not about being here. That much felt right.

She stared at him in the soft light, that melting expression on her face, looking so beautiful, so damned beautiful, that he wanted to pull her close again, erase the past five years.

He should never have given up on them.

Why had he ever given up on them?

"Charles, I..." Her words trailed off.

He waited.

"Charles." She exhaled his name on a sigh, turned toward him and slipped her arms around his waist.

For one blind second, he froze, the memory of the way she'd felt in his arms today assaulting him.

Right.

Resting her cheek against his chest, she gave another breathy sigh and eased against him. And he knew then that standing in his arms today had felt right to her, too.

He knew.

Then there was no more conflict, no more debate, no more confusion, nothing mattered now except that she'd come to him willingly, nothing mattered but the way she felt.

So right.

His arms came around her, anchored her. He inhaled the scent of her hair and remembered this feeling. The way he felt much stronger than he was. Human. Complex. Frail. One blade stroke to wipe out a life. But when he held her, he felt as if he could protect her against anything, the fears of the day, the hurts of the past. He held her and felt complete.

Loved.

He'd forgotten.

Avoided.

Because he remembered this feeling, had known he would never be whole without her. Not consciously, maybe, but inside where it counted. He knew the body, the physical intricacies and functions. But he did not know the heart, hadn't comprehended his own capacity for self-preservation or self-deception.

He sought and found her mouth with his, no longer able to resist. He wanted her, was through avoiding that truth.

Her lips parted against his, so willing, the motion natural. Their breaths ebbed and flowed, the rhythm familiar. Their tongues met and he tasted her desire, knew that she wanted as much as he did.

He swung her into his arms then. Her gasp of surprise broke against his mouth as she brought her arms around his neck to hang on. But she didn't stop kissing him.

Their tongues tangled and their breaths collided in a kiss with no beginning and no end. Awkward sometimes. Sensual always.

He might avoid, but he could never forget.

They crossed the threshold into the bedroom that had once been theirs, now a stranger in the moonlit darkness.

But Karan wasn't a stranger.

And she was the only thing that mattered right now.

The way she kissed him with such enthusiasm as if she'd waited forever for the chance. With gentle laughter when her mouth slid over his jaw as he turned to get through the door.

With no inhibitions.

No, he could never forget.

Tomorrow would be there when they got to it. They could make sense of things then. Right now was a gift. And the only thing he cared about was the way she slid against him when he lowered her to her feet. The way she half turned and lifted her hair, presenting her back to him in a task he'd once performed by right.

With unsteady fingers he dragged down her zipper, brushed aside the soft fabric so she could disengage her arms. The dress slipped to the floor with a whisper of silk. Her lingerie right behind it. She stepped lightly out of the puddle of fabric.

And the only thing that mattered was the way she looked naked in the moonlight.

He sank to the edge of the bed, muscles drained by the reality of her, unable to support him any longer.

His hands, surgeon's hands capable of such precision, traced her body, outlined each lustrous curve, remembered the supple feel of her skin.

Her fingers grazed through his hair, a light touch, as tentative and awed as his own. He knew this woman, knew everything about her.

His touch grew bolder. Trailing his hands up her thighs, he rounded her smooth bottom, pulled her close enough that he could drag his mouth across a nipple.

A shiver coursed through her, and her fingers that had grazed now hung on for support. He pressed his face in that valley between her breasts, felt her heartbeat, her shallow breaths, her excitement.

"Charles." Another sigh.

That sigh undid him. In a burst of motion, he ripped the shirt over his head, grateful for the scrubs that found their way onto the floor with speed.

Then he caught her against him and pulled her down on the bed, stretched out in his arms, their legs gliding together, their mouths seeking, until he could feel her everywhere, remembered that only she had ever felt this way.

Five years may have passed, but their bodies remembered, responded, because he knew her by heart.

SOME BARELY SANE PART OF KARAN warned that the reality of tomorrow wouldn't outweigh the excitement of tonight.

But she had no will to resist when Charles pressed her onto the bed, didn't care about anything except the chance to hold him again, to make the most of this moment together.

She'd never expected to hold him again.

Had never even dared to hope.

But after these past weeks, after today…she would not miss this moment. She was through with distance, through with wasting any more time. She'd already wasted so much.

And she knew exactly how to make this man burn. With hot kisses and bold caresses, until his arousal fueled her own.

And when he finally coaxed his way between her thighs and sank deep, she could only gasp aloud, press her mouth to the base of his throat, feel his pulse throbbing hard. Her eyes fluttered open for an instant. She remembered this place, this sweet heat inside, this view of the world through the crook of his shoulders and neck, and how much she loved being here.

And his every stroke bridged the distance between them until there was nothing in the world but him and her and the pleasure they made together. She could only meet him stroke for desperate stroke, his name tumbling from her lips as the pleasure welled up inside.

But from someplace deep within, emotion rose alongside the pleasure with the same intensity, the same urgency, and when she heard Charles growl her name as his climax broke, she went over the edge with him. Those waves broke, one after another, not giving her a chance to catch her breath. Against her will, sighs of pleasure transformed into gut-wrenching sobs. She had no idea where they came from, no ability to resist, no strength to fight. She could only let them carry her away, the way the pleasure had.

And poor Charles…some barely functioning part of her brain told her that he was wasted, too. But he knew she couldn't stop, he knew. Rolling over, he took her with him, pulling the covers over them, sheltering her in his embrace, shielding her with his body, his strong arms her only anchor.

She was being pulled inside out, but those sobs kept coming from someplace she didn't even know she had, someplace she'd lost touch with long ago, washing her with tears, leaving her drained and so very weak.

And through it all, Charles smoothed her hair and pressed his lips to her face and weathered the storm, skillfully handling all the emotion coming at him. He whispered throaty reassurances against her ear, words meant to comfort, although she couldn't make out anything over her sobs. He held her until she finally stopped and all that was left was weakness.

Darkness.

Silence.

And the man who held her.

As Karan recovered, she felt nothing but overwhelming relief. As if everything that had been closed off had burst open wide. She was so weak, she could only press a kiss to Charles's throat for his kindness, taste her tears on his skin. She wondered what he thought of that display, felt so bad to burden him during their only time together in so long.

"I have no idea what happened," she finally admitted, her voice the barest whisper.

"Don't you?" His voice was strong between them, such a welcome sound.

There was no hiding from his question, from the truth of the way she felt in his arms, not now, not after that spectacular display.

He shifted so she could snuggle closer, rested his chin on the top of her head in a position from long ago. "You asked me if there was someone I didn't want to leave. I don't think I wanted to leave my memories. All the plans we made. They were all I had left of us. It kept me from moving on."

"I gave up on us."

He rubbed his cheek against her head, his silky-rough beard tousling her hair. "Did you?"

Karan considered the distance she'd placed between herself and Patrick, between herself and her emotions, between herself and life. No, she hadn't given up on them, had just reconciled herself to a life without him. She may have moved on, but she hadn't given up, had never allowed herself to replace him.

She'd kept their house, had run away from it, had tried to scour it clean, but she'd always needed to know it was there.

"No," she admitted. "I didn't."

"I know."

And those sweet words brought tears to her eyes again, but he kissed them away and held her close, his voice so certain. "I don't want to lose you again. I love you. I don't think I ever stopped." He smoothed her hair from her face, such a tender touch. "I don't know where we go from here, but it's not over. *We're* not over. I want to figure it out with you. Together."

She had no words in that moment. She didn't have to tell him she loved him, because he already knew, so she tipped her face to his, and met his gaze, those liquid-dark eyes that had always sent a thrill through her.

She kissed his mouth, showed him that she wanted nothing more than to figure things out with him. A promise.

CHAPTER TWENTY-SEVEN

CHARLES APPLAUDED AFTER KARAN announced the senator, who kissed her cheek and took his place behind the podium of the makeshift stage the mayor had generously vacated. The American flag hung majestically and the entire park dripped red, white and blue in a patriotic display for the holiday celebration.

The crowds quieted. All eyes riveted on the senator as he greeted the guests of the Fourth of July parade and began his speech that would—hopefully—plug his support for New Hope of Bluestone Mountain, Inc.

Charles had eyes only for Karan. She'd retreated to the rear of the stage and appeared to listen intently as she stood beside the mayor, city manager and Jack. She looked beautiful in a simple tailored dress with a nautical theme with her hair pulled back from her face, her long legs bare. Charles was reminded of a similar scene from the first time he'd ever set eyes on her.

"Well, would you look at that?" Rhonda whispered. "She does do something other than shop."

"And tan." He remembered the comment he'd made the day Karan had arrived at New Hope.

"Oh, she definitely tans. That sun-kissed glow takes work."

Charles couldn't argue. He happened to know that sun-kissed glow covered every inch of smooth skin, every delicious inch.

To their surprise, the senator did a lot more than plug New Hope. He announced a grant he intended to author that would aid children who had witnessed domestic violence. With both hands he seized the opportunity to campaign for a cause that would make him look good among both right and left.

As Karan had no doubt known he would.

The media would be all over his speech, and Charles, Rhonda and everyone else affiliated with New Hope could not have asked for better exposure. People applauded whenever the senator drove home an important point about expanding the Violence Against Women Act. Rhonda was so thrilled that she pumped a fist in the air and whistled *loudly* when he concluded.

"Privilege is a very good thing when it's put it to good use, don't you think, Dr. Steinberg?" she asked.

"I do indeed, Dr. Camden."

"I'm happy to see you two getting along, by the way."

Rhonda didn't know the half of it—yet. No doubt she'd get the unabridged version the next time Karan went in for a session.

"I'd give you more details, but I know you don't like me to color your opinions."

She laughed, loud enough to be heard over the avalanche of applause as the senator left the stage. "I don't think I need details. The sight of you two together... You beam, and I'm glad. That's why I'm going to go out on a limb here and introduce you to someone you need to know. A colleague of mine who specializes in marital issues."

Charles inclined his head, more than willing to accept any recommendation from Rhonda. She accompanied him to collect Karan, and Charles's pulse ramped up at the sight of her as she made her way off the stage to join them. Her eyes sparkled when she spotted him, and he marveled at how in the span of a few days, his entire life could change. From blurry to sharp focus. That fast. Because all the pieces were suddenly in place.

He and Karan were committed.

The rest they would figure out. Together.

"The senator was amazing," she said, slipping her hand into his, a subtle gesture of greeting, but one that gave him so much hope for their future together. "What did you think?"

"He was generous," Charles agreed.

"I'll vote for him," Rhonda said, barely able to contain herself. She hugged Karan, then dragged them through the crowd to meet the *someone* they needed to know.

His name was Joel. He was a friendly, unassuming man in private practice at Rhonda's office. "We've worked together for years," she explained. "I wanted to introduce you."

They met his wife and son, chatted about a recent trip to Alaska and the future of New Hope's outreach programs before moving on to join the mayor and his wife at the shelter where they were guests. Rhonda obviously didn't need details. She'd already assessed the need and addressed it.

Karan didn't miss a beat, either. "Can't get anything past you, can we, Rhonda?"

"It was the hand-holding. Dead giveaway. Even for someone without my special gifts." She rolled her eyes.

"So you're saying there's no need to pull my provider list for marriage counselors," Charles said. "I should call and book an appointment with Joel."

"You should. He's brilliant. *Brilliant.* Just take my word for it. I want to see you two keep beaming. I'm quite fond of you both."

"Beaming?" Karan lifted that sparkly gaze to him, surprised.

He leaned close so only she could hear. "I love you. It shows."

KARAN FOUND HERSELF WITH A quiet moment in the non-stop excitement when Jack appeared at the shelter with the president of a regional civic organization to meet Charles and Rhonda about supporting New Hope.

She took their plates and stepped away to find a trash can, so they could discuss business without hanging on to the remnants of their meals.

Then she hung back and waited for the right opportunity to insert herself into the conversation, enjoying a chance to catch her breath now the senator had left to salvage what he could of the family pinochle game.

She couldn't be more pleased with the way the picnic was turning out. The weather was temperate with a clear sky and mountain breeze. The town square was jam-packed. The event had garnered an amazing turnout.

The senator was happy. The mayor was happy. Charles and Rhonda were happy.

Karan was happy, too, almost giddy over all the changes happening in her life. She cautioned herself to take one step at a time, not to get too far ahead. But every time she looked at Charles… She couldn't ever remember feeling this way, so hopeful about the future, so happy in the here and now.

She was still standing there, caught up in her thoughts

and her warm and fuzzy feelings when she saw a familiar figure approaching… "Mother."

Her mother smiled, looking entirely summer chic in a sleeveless pantsuit and wide-brimmed hat. "Karan, darling. How wonderful you look. I was hoping you'd stand still long enough for me to find you, otherwise I was going to send out a runner."

She tipped her cheek for a kiss and Karan obliged.

"You're here."

"Of course, the Ladies' Guild always reserves a shelter. We sponsor Bluestone's garden club, and they have a float in the parade. I'm sure you saw it—a large wooden cart with every blooming flower imaginable, and the garden club members, of course."

Not one word about disapproval. Not one word about disappointment. Not one word about broadcasting Karan's entire sordid situation and embarrassing their family in front of all their friends and acquaintances.

Her mother hadn't been drinking before the Talbots' party, so Karan was sure she must remember the exchange. For a moment she felt uncertain, then she remembered something Rhonda had said.

Seems to me when we look to others to make us feel good about ourselves, we're at the mercy of a lot of factors we don't have any control over, that may or may not have anything to do with us.

Karan could choose to hang on to how she felt about that night, hurt and criticized when she'd needed her mother. She could make this moment about herself, but it didn't have to be. She could go on enjoying her day if she chose.

Her mother wasn't going to change unless she perceived a need. But Karan certainly could.

"I hope you're enjoying the day," she said simply.

Her mother nodded. "The senator was quite a hit with all his campaigning about domestic violence. New Hope sounds like a good cause. I'm sure it will reap a good deal of support now."

"He was very generous. Everyone is ecstatic."

"I imagine so." She fixed Karan with an assessing gaze. "You and Charles seem awfully close. I know he's a director at New Hope but…is there anything you want to tell me?"

There was a large part of Karan that wanted to keep her shiny new excitement about Charles all to herself, not expose it to her mother's potentially negative response.

But she reminded herself about personal accountability.

Only she could allow anyone to tarnish her mood.

So she decided to keep things simple and honest. "We've been talking, Mom, about putting the past behind us."

Her mother didn't reply for a moment. Then she said as simply, "Well, keep me posted. I always thought Charles could be a suitable husband. Maybe he simply needed some time to figure out what he wanted. And, Karan, thank you for calling to let me know you were all right the other night. I would have hated to find out about that situation on the ten o'clock news."

"Of course, Mom."

Today the fogs seemed to have receded, leaving the lighthouse smiling her beautiful smile. "I'll head back now. You should bring Charles by our shelter so he can say hello."

She kissed her mother's cheek. "I'll bring him by."

CHARLES FOLDED HIS ARMS OVER his chest and faced Matthew across the desk. "I'd like to accept your offer to join the Catskill Center."

Matthew sank into his cushy leather wing chair. "So you finally made a decision. You're sure?"

"Not a doubt in my mind. In fact, I'm so sure that I drove to the city yesterday to thank the Mount Sinai board in person for their interest and offer my regrets."

He nodded, looked content. "What made you decide?"

"Missy."

"Missy?"

"One of my patients. The first-year elementary teacher."

"I remember. What did Missy do to convince you?"

"As exciting as it would be to be a part of a world-class research team, I don't want to lose contact with my patients. I like caring for them from start to finish. I want to specialize, but I don't want to shift my focus off that personal level of care to put all my emphasis on research."

"Got you. Now I've got a question for you. I've been seeing Karan around here for the past week. Does she have anything to do with your decision?"

Charles nodded. "We made the decision together, in fact. We've decided to work things out. We're listing both our places and looking for something north, closer to Devil's Path."

"A commute?"

"Not really. Add another thirty minutes maybe." Just enough to get them out of town. Close to Bluestone, but not too close.

"I see. I'm guessing Mount Sinai wasn't happy."

Charles shrugged. There would be another up-and-coming surgeon to take his place, one with a little more ambition than Charles had at the moment. He needed to have time for his marriage and maybe even a family one day. What was the point of having one if he wasn't around to parent, to take family vacations to the beach, to visit the grandparents, to attend school functions, to fish?

"The point is that I'm happy, Matthew. I fully expect you to give me run of the place when Dr. Chalmers retires so I can work my magic and put St. Joseph's on the map."

"Now that I'm glad to hear." Matthew reached over the desk, extended his hand. "Welcome aboard. You made a good decision about your career, and about Karan. She's a sharp woman."

Charles knew. He'd made good decisions about his career, about facing his issues, about reclaiming the woman he loved. All the right decisions for him. He *knew* it, deep inside where it counted.

"OMG, MOM! WAIT UNTIL YOU SEE it." Brooke hopped out of the car, gathering her garment bag as if the contents were precious. Then she leaned in and asked as an obvious afterthought, "Aunt Karan, you don't mind if I put it on to show Mom, do you?"

"Of course not," Karan said. "You've got to model for us. Let's go." Pushing open the passenger door, she got out of Susanna's car and dug her house keys from her purse.

It was a fall formal gown. Brooke had called in her favor when she discovered the fall formal would take place within a few weeks of the start of the semester. So she and Karan had taken the train into the city for a shopping excursion. Susanna picked them up at the train station.

Once inside, Brooke took off to change and Karan dropped her purchases on the couch, one of the few remaining pieces of furniture in the room. Most of her personal items had already been packed in preparation of the move.

"Thanks for the lift," she told Susanna. "I'll be so glad

when I get my driving privileges back. Lugging all these bags around was not my idea of fun."

"Not a problem," Susanna said. "Thank you for taking her. She was so looking forward to shopping."

"Me, too."

She glanced around the living room. "Looks like you're making progress around here. I still can't believe you're under contract already. It's barely been a month since you listed."

"You know what they say—location, location, location."

"Any interest in Charles's place yet?"

Karan sank onto the couch with a sigh and toed off her shoes. "Not yet, but then he's not on a lake."

"Lots of memories here. You're ready to move on?"

"I am." And she was. No regrets. Bittersweet didn't fit her mood, not with so much excitement about the future. "You might take one more peek while you're here to make sure you don't want anything. Last chance to call dibs. Movers are coming Friday."

"They're taking the furniture?"

"I really wanted to drag all of it out to the mailbox and call Tom for a delivery. But I didn't think New Hope Thrift Store would get the best prices."

Susanna laughed. "I'm guessing not."

Karan had called a friend instead, the owner of a furniture chain, and arranged for a private sale, the proceeds of which would defray costs for the gallery showing in Kingston that would feature work from a Manhattan-based photographer and the art of Project Return. They'd get three-for-one in that deal—raising funds for New Hope while gaining exposure for a talented new photographer and a not-for-profit organization that was helping in an unusual way.

All her furniture went except for the Bowflex training machine, which she'd never actually used. Marynia had long ago turned the thing into an expensive clothesline as the laundry room was part of the home gym.

That would get put out at the mailbox with a purple tag because she knew a truck-driving power lifter who could pick it up for a song.

She couldn't resist.

"Okay, I'm coming," Brooke called out. "Close your eyes."

They exchanged a glance and did as directed.

"Ready? Now look!"

Brooke twirled in her cocktail-length dress, kicking up a heel to reveal the accompanying strappy sandals. The dress was lovely, but as far as Karan was concerned, the beaming smile was her goddaughter's best accessory. She was so beautiful, so excited about life.

Karan took one look at Susanna's misty expression and knew she was coming unglued, which likely had more to do with the reality of Brooke's impending departure than the dress.

Motioning Brooke to twirl slowly again, Karan spoke into an imaginary microphone. "Today our gorgeous college freshman is modeling a signature cocktail dress with floral lace embroidery, a strapless sweetheart neckline and fit-and-flare silhouette. This divine creation was made in the good old U.S. of A. of the finest French silk, of course."

"It's lovely." Susanna's voice broke as she went to hug her daughter. "You're lovely."

Brooke beamed. Susanna blinked back tears.

Karan had accomplished a good day's work. Of course, contentment only lasted until Susanna got past her tears, then she ran her fingers over the fabric.

"This is *really* lovely. Where did you shop?"

From behind Susanna's back, Karan motioned Brooke to take off. Too late, Susanna spotted Karan's bags and narrowed her gaze. "Tell me you didn't buy this at Berg-dorf Goodman?"

"It came off the rack, Mom."

"Karan, you swore you wouldn't go crazy."

Brooke launched into a rational defense. "Aunt Karan said it was a very good price."

"Aunt Karan's yardstick is different than mine."

Karan stretched, propping her feet on the coffee table and settling in to enjoy the show. "Lighten up, Suze. It was a steal. I promise."

"How much?"

"Thirty-four ninety-five."

Susanna blanched, looked like she might actually swoon. "Please tell me you mean $34.95."

Karan exchanged a glance with Brooke. The price of the dress was worth the look on her mother's face. No question. "It's my goddaughter's first fall formal in col-lege. She has to make an impression so she gets to choose from all the right sororities. You know that. Just look at her. She's gorgeous."

Susanna collapsed onto the couch and fell forward, head between her legs as if she was staving off a faint.

"Never fear, Suze." Karan patted her back. "We'll get our money's worth. Brooke's promised to lend it to me for New Hope's fashion show at Christmas."

"And I'm wearing it for Aunt Karan's wedding." Brooke twirled again and announced, "She asked me to be a bridesmaid."

That got Susanna's attention. She sat up. "You did?"

Karan nodded. "And I'd like you to be my matron of honor."

"Again?"

"Of course." Karan nudged against Susanna, rested her head on her best friend's shoulder. "Third time's a charm."

KARAN STOOD BESIDE HER LAWYER, hands clasped behind her back, expression stoic as they waited for Wannabe Jenny to review the documents before her. Both Charles and Susanna had insisted on accompanying her to court today, and though they sat behind her, silent, she could feel their presence, felt their love and support as she faced the bench.

Wannabe Jenny finally glanced up and met Karan's gaze.

"Welcome back, Ms. Kowalski Steinberg-Reece," she said in exactly the tone Karan had prepared herself for. "I see community service didn't have any adverse effects."

A compliment? Not likely.

"As I'm sure you guessed I've been reviewing your progress with interest. To be quite honest, I'm surprised at all you've accomplished."

Was there a compliment in there?

"From what I hear, you've lent your skills to a good cause and been an asset to a worthy program. I've gotten more than a few glowing reports. Not to mention what I've read in the paper. Your alternative sentence appears to have been a good fit, and I commend your efforts."

Definitely a compliment.

Karan inclined her head to acknowledge Wannabe Jenny and received the same gesture in return.

"I hope you've learned a lesson, Karan, because I don't want to see you back in my courtroom again."

"You won't, Your Honor."

Wannabe Jenny forced what might have been a smile. "Then good luck in your future. The State of New York recognizes you've fulfilled the terms of your sentence. Case dismissed."

The gavel crashed.

Susanna exhaled a relieved sigh, and Charles brushed his fingers over the hands Karan still held clasped behind her back, a reassuring touch.

"Thank you for this opportunity, Your Honor," Karan said. And meant it.

* * * * *

COMING NEXT MONTH

Available August 9, 2011

REQUEST YOUR FREE BOOKS!
2 FREE NOVELS PLUS 2 FREE GIFTS!

Harlequin®

Super Romance®

Exciting, emotional, unexpected!

YES! Please send me 2 FREE Harlequin® Superromance® novels and my 2 FREE gifts (gifts are worth about $10). After receiving them, if I don't wish to receive any more books, I can return the shipping statement marked "cancel." If I don't cancel, I will receive 6 brand-new novels every month and be billed just $4.69 per book in the U.S. or $5.24 per book in Canada. That's a saving of at least 15% off the cover price! It's quite a bargain! Shipping and handling is just 50¢ per book in the U.S. and 75¢ per book in Canada.* I understand that accepting the 2 free books and gifts places me under no obligation to buy anything. I can always return a shipment and cancel at any time. Even if I never buy another book, the two free books and gifts are mine to keep forever.

135/336 HDN FC6T

Name	(PLEASE PRINT)

Address	Apt. #

City	State/Prov.	Zip/Postal Code

Signature (if under 18, a parent or guardian must sign)

Mail to the **Reader Service:**
IN U.S.A.: P.O. Box 1867, Buffalo, NY 14240-1867
IN CANADA: P.O. Box 609, Fort Erie, Ontario L2A 5X3

Not valid for current subscribers to Harlequin Superromance books.

**Are you a current subscriber to Harlequin Superromance books and want to receive the larger-print edition?
Call 1-800-873-8635 or visit www.ReaderService.com.**

* Terms and prices subject to change without notice. Prices do not include applicable taxes. Sales tax applicable in N.Y. Canadian residents will be charged applicable taxes. Offer not valid in Quebec. This offer is limited to one order per household. All orders subject to credit approval. Credit or debit balances in a customer's account(s) may be offset by any other outstanding balance owed by or to the customer. Please allow 4 to 6 weeks for delivery. Offer available while quantities last.

Your Privacy—The Reader Service is committed to protecting your privacy. Our Privacy Policy is available online at www.ReaderService.com or upon request from the Reader Service.

We make a portion of our mailing list available to reputable third parties that offer products we believe may interest you. If you prefer that we not exchange your name with third parties, or if you wish to clarify or modify your communication preferences, please visit us at www.ReaderService.com/consumerschoice or write to us at Reader Service Preference Service, P.O. Box 9062, Buffalo, NY 14269. Include your complete name and address.

*Once bitten, twice shy. That's Gabby Wade's motto—
especially when it comes to Adamson men.
And the moment she meets Jon Adamson her theory
is confirmed. But with each encounter a little something
sparks between them, making her wonder if she's been
too hasty to dismiss this one!*

*Enjoy this sneak peek from ONE GOOD REASON
by Sarah Mayberry, available August 2011
from Harlequin® Superromance®.*

Gabby Wade's heartbeat thumped in her ears as she marched to her office. She wanted to pretend it was because of her brisk pace returning from the file room, but she wasn't that good a liar.

Her heart was beating like a tom-tom because Jon Adamson had touched her. In a very male, very possessive way. She could still feel the heat of his big hand burning through the seat of her khakis as he'd steadied her on the ladder.

It had taken every ounce of self-control to tell him to unhand her. What she'd really wanted was to grab him by his shirt and, well, explore all those urges his touch had instantly brought to life.

While she might not like him, she was wise enough to understand that it wasn't always about liking the other person. Sometimes it was about pure animal attraction.

Refusing to think about it, she turned to work. When she'd typed in the wrong figures three times, Gabby admitted she was too tired and too distracted. Time to call it a day.

As she was leaving, she spied Jon at his workbench in the shop. His head was propped on his hand as he studied blueprints. It wasn't until she got closer that she saw his eyes were shut.

He looked oddly boyish. There was something innocent and unguarded in his expression. She felt a weakening in her resistance to him.

"Jon." She put her hand on his shoulder, intending to shake him awake. Instead, it rested there like a caress.

His eyes snapped open.

"You were asleep."

"No, I was, uh, visualizing something on this design." He gestured to the blueprint in front of him then rubbed his eyes.

That gesture dealt a bigger blow to her resistance. She realized it wasn't only animal attraction pulling them together. She took a step backward as if to get away from the knowledge.

She cleared her throat. "I'm heading off now."

He gave her a smile, and she could see his exhaustion.

"Yeah, I should, too." He stood and stretched. The hem of his T-shirt rose as he arched his back and she caught a flash of hard male belly. She looked away, but it was too late. Her mind had committed the image to permanent memory.

And suddenly she knew, for good or bad, she'd never look at Jon the same way again.

Find out what happens next in ONE GOOD REASON, available August 2011 from Harlequin® Superromance®!

SPECIAL EDITION

Life, Love, Family and Top Authors!

IN AUGUST, HARLEQUIN SPECIAL EDITION FEATURES
USA TODAY BESTSELLING AUTHORS
MARIE FERRARELLA AND *ALLISON LEIGH*.

THE BABY WORE A BADGE
BY *MARIE FERRARELLA*

The second title in the **Montana Mavericks:
The Texans Are Coming!** miniseries....

Suddenly single father Jake Castro has his hands full with
the baby he never expected—and with a beautiful young
woman too wise for her years.

COURTNEY'S BABY PLAN
BY *ALLISON LEIGH*

The third title in the **Return to the Double C** miniseries....

Tired of waiting for Mr. Right, nurse Courtney Clay takes
matters into her own hands to create the family she's
always wanted— but her surly patient may just be
the Mr. Right she's been searching for all along.

**Look for these titles and others in August 2011
from Harlequin Special Edition wherever books are sold.**

BIG SKY BRIDE, BE MINE! *(Northridge Nuptials)* by *VICTORIA PADE*
THE MOMMY MIRACLE by *LILIAN DARCY*
THE MOGUL'S MAYBE MARRIAGE by *MINDY KLASKY*
LIAM'S PERFECT WOMAN by *BETH KERY*

---

www.Harlequin.com

SEUSA0811

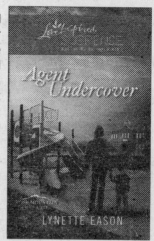